SUPERDREADNOUGHT 2

SUPERDREADNOUGHT 2

SUPERDREADNOUGHT™ BOOK TWO

CH GIDEON   CRAIG MARTELLE   MICHAEL ANDERLE

We can't write without those who support us
On the home front, we thank you for being there for us

We wouldn't be able to do this for a living if it weren't for our readers
We thank you for reading our books

CONNECT WITH THE AUTHORS

Craig Martelle Social

Website & Newsletter:
http://www.craigmartelle.com

Facebook:
https://www.facebook.com/AuthorCraigMartelle/

Michael Anderle Social

Website: http://www.lmbpn.com

Email List: https://lmbpn.com/email/
Facebook:
https://www.facebook.com/TheKurtherianGambitBooks/

Superdreadnought 2 (this book) is a work of fiction.

All of the characters, organizations, and events portrayed in this novel are either products of the author's imagination or are used fictitiously. Sometimes both.

Cover by Luca Oleastri, Typography by Jeff Brown

A Michael Anderle Production

LMBPN Publishing
PMB 196, 2540 South Maryland Pkwy
Las Vegas, NV 89109

First US edition, November 2018
Version 1.01, November 2018

SUPERDREADNOUGHT 2 TEAM

Thanks to our Beta Readers

James Caplan
Kelly O'Donnell
Micky Cocker

Thanks to the JIT Readers

Danika Fedeli
James Caplan
J-M Rodier
Chrisa Changala
Kelly O'Donnell
Nicole Emens
Mary Morris
John Ashmore
Diane L. Smith
Daniel Weigert

If I've missed anyone, please let me know!

Editor
Lynne Stiegler

CHAPTER ONE

A vortex opened and the Superdreadnought *Reynolds* emerged, slipping from the Loranian System and settling into open space. The wormhole stitched back together and faded in the wake of the massive ship.

"We're here," the new helm operator—whose name, Reynolds had learned during the transit, was Tanirika 'Ria' Alcott—announced unnecessarily.

"Where is 'here,' exactly?" Reynolds asked, having decided as they jumped that he would allow the humanoid crew to do their jobs. He thought he would try to not interfere with the basic operations of the ship.

Unless he had to, of course.

Perks of being the captain, right?

"Is that a philosophical question or a geographical one?" Navigation asked from his post. Well, from the speaker *above* his post seeing as how no one was actually there.

Still in his chrome body, which had replaced the Jonny-taxi android but wasn't that much of an upgrade, Reynolds rolled his eyes at the question. He thought he heard the orbs squeak in their sockets. Takal would need to get better at creating a long-term home for his intelligence before he burned this one out.

Reynolds had decided that he liked being mobile.

Jiya Lemaire chuckled at Navigation's question from somewhere behind Reynolds. "We've landed in the Grindlevik System." She answered quickly to keep the AI's banter among himself to a minimum.

She was getting good at playing mediator.

"Say that three times quickly," Tactical muttered.

"Better yet, don't," Reynolds replied.

Jiya sauntered over casually to stand alongside the android body that contained the AI that was Reynolds.

"Jiya, report," the captain requested.

"Four planets in an elliptical orbit around a pair of suns. The smaller of the suns circles the greater of the two. There's a gas giant on the other side of the system that's kicking the scanners off something fierce. The atmosphere is toxic to everyone aboard..."

"Only you meatbags," Tactical cut in.

"Who need air to live," Jiya clarified, sliding a hairy eyeball in Tactical's direction, "and the planet is approximately seventy-five percent liquid," she reported, then made a sour face. "That liquid happens to be methane, should you want to know."

"I suggest we skip that one," Maddox offered from his post.

"I agree," Reynolds replied. "I'm starting to like having you people around. Would be a shame to lose you so soon."

"Uh...thanks?" Maddox muttered, watching the screen scroll reams of data.

"There's another mid-sized planet nearer to us," Jiya continued, choosing to ignore Reynolds' comment. "It's got a pretty harsh atmosphere, too. It has oxygen, but the levels are so low as to be negligible." She shook of her head. "That one's out, looks like. There are two planets that scanners report as capable of supporting life. I'm not sure, though. Maybe only one."

Reynolds had known everything that Jiya reported before she said her first word, but if he were going to make her his first officer, she needed to not only deliver the report but understand what aspects from it were important.

The captain acknowledged her report with a nod. "That makes it easy. Set course for the obvious planet, Ensign Alcott."

"Setting a course, sir," Ria replied.

"This planet have a name?" Reynolds asked, glancing at Jiya.

"It is listed under the incredibly original Grindlevik 3," she answered. "Nothing in the way of intel on it, seeing as how the system is barely a blip in the databases. It appears to be densely populated, though, which is a good sign regarding interaction.

"We're also picking up a lot of electronic warbles in and around their atmosphere. Place looks to be fairly high-tech, but we're not able to get a clear picture of their capabilities."

"You mean they're purposely blocking the scans?" Reynolds wondered.

"Either that or their tech is sufficiently advanced to prevent intrusion. Hard to tell if it's intentional or just business as usual. We're getting lots of feedback against the scanners. I suspect we'll know more as we get closer." Jiya wound her hands together as she studied the main screen.

One of Reynolds' chrome eyebrows rose. "Are you picking up Kurtherian energy signatures in any of that noise?" he asked.

"Yes and no," Jiya answered.

"I'm impressed by your clarity," Tactical muttered. "Which is it?"

"There's nothing definitive." Jiya walked to the front of the bridge and examined the readings. "There are trace signatures that make me suspicious about their source."

Reynolds joined her. "Suspicious how? Explain." All part of the training process. The AI didn't have a definitive answer either. Jiya pointed at General Maddox, who was working at his console, and together they trooped to his station.

Maddox shrugged, tapping on his console and showing the captain his findings. "I'm not exactly sure how to describe it," he said. "It's like their technology has been *influenced* by Kurtherian tech, but it's *not* Kurtherian tech."

"Tomato, orange," Tactical called. "It is, or it isn't."

Maddox shrugged. "Then I'd say it's not, but there's no way to rule out the obvious influence that's there. Either the Grindlovian society has had interactions with Kurtherians at some point in their evolution, or you have inexplicable coincidences in the similarity of technological advancement. Not sure what else to tell you."

"Maybe there are Kurtherians in hiding on the planet,

secretly guiding their evolution," Reynolds said, rubbing his metallic hands together.

"Entirely possible," Maddox answered. "We could always take a look."

"Good thing we're going there already, huh?" Jiya asked with a grin. "You can snoop to your metal heart's content once we arrive, Reynolds. How about that?"

Reynolds returned to standing in front of the main viewscreen as the planet grew closer and he could pick out more detail. His eyes narrowed as he spied what was clearly not a natural formation around the planet.

A great ring encircled the planet, visible even from a distance, but it was difficult to see just what it was.

"Zoom in on the planet, Jiya."

She did, and Reynolds could finally make out what he was seeing.

"There's a man-made defensive perimeter around the planet," he noted. "It looks like a space station has been built around the entire planet. If I were a betting AI, I'd say it's heavy with weapons emplacements. We may not want to get too close without their approval."

"It is in synchronized orbit with Grindlevik 3. That's impressive," XO said.

"Are those...ships around it?" Jiya asked as they drew closer.

"They are indeed," Reynolds answered, knowing that the ring station served as a docking platform for the mass of destroyers that filled the space around the planet.

"Whoa!" Ria muttered. "There sure are a lot of them."

The new kid was right.

Reynolds made a quick count and was surprised to find

a fleet of over fifty ships holding a defensive posture above Grindlevik 3.

"We should probably reach out before we get too close," Maddox reiterated.

"Already on it," Comm replied. "Hailing all frequencies, but that perimeter squall is going to make it difficult to get a signal through."

"It'll have ears, guaranteed," Reynolds replied. "It might not reach planet-side, but it'll get through to the people it needs to."

"How can you be sure?" Jiya asked.

"You mean besides the ten destroyers that just peeled out of formation from the fleet and are now headed our way?" he asked.

Jiya stiffened. "I'd say that's a pretty good indication they heard us."

"Just a matter of whether they understood us," Comm mentioned. "If not, we might be in for a fight."

"I wonder what they're packing?" Tactical asked.

"Scanners show solid firepower," Jiya answered, "but we've got them beat in pure muscle. They don't have rail-guns or the absolute beast of the ESD system."

"'Eat Shit and Die.'" Tactical chuckled, emphasizing each word. "I love that thing."

Klaxons sounded on the bridge, bathing it in a flashing red glow and forcing the crew to hunker down under the unexpected sonic onslaught. The sound faded a moment later.

"Was that absolutely necessary?" Jiya asked, rubbing her ears.

"Just making sure everyone's awake and on their toes," Reynolds answered.

"A cup of coffee would have sufficed, or a simple word."

"Where's the fun in that?" Reynolds asked her.

Jiya grunted.

"We getting anything back from our greeting?" Reynolds asked.

"Nope," Comm told him. "Their ships are moving into formation and powering shields. I'm still knocking at their door, but they aren't letting me in."

"I'm sure that happens more often than you'll admit," Tactical joked.

"Let's follow their example and raise the gravitic shields in case someone on one of the ships gets trigger-happy," Reynolds ordered.

"There'd have to actually *be* someone on the ships for that to happen," Jiya replied.

Reynolds spun and glared at the first officer. "The ships are automated?"

Jiya nodded. "As is the defensive ring. We're having a hard time getting specs on their tech, but it's damn clear there are no lifeforms up here in space with us. Everyone with a heartbeat is on the planet."

"Interesting," Reynolds muttered, turning back to the viewscreen to examine the approaching ships more closely. "They bringing up weapons yet?"

"No, sir," Jiya answered, "but they are moving into attack formation. Their ships are edging out to flank us on both sides, so either way we turn we're going to get hit."

"What do you think, Jiya? Are they going to attack or

escort us in?" Reynolds asked with a wry smile on his metal face.

"I think they are going to escort us in. I think they would have already fired if they were hostile, as well as launched more ships. They have to know what we are and that their ten destroyers aren't a match. We'll be fine."

"Unless they're assholes," Tactical countered.

"There is that." Reynolds nodded. "Bring us to a halt, but stay ready just in case these guys want to tangle. I'm not in the mood to get holes shot through me."

"I concur," Maddox said. "Looks like they're responding to the adjustment and have slowed their advance." He looked at the big screen. "They're being defensive—staying at range and keeping us in their sights, Captain."

"They're scanning us," XO warned. "How much do you want me to give them?"

"Name, rank, and serial number, but not much else," Reynolds answered. "I'm okay with them knowing who and what we are since that will probably help us here, but I don't want them getting a clear picture of what we're capable of. That needs to be a surprise in case we need to do something besides wave at them."

"Roger that," XO replied, fortifying the firewall and applying extra security measures to the system to keep even the most insistent snoopers at bay.

"The probes have pulled back," Jiya reported. "That was fast."

"They hit a wall and knew they weren't getting any farther," XO told her. "That means they're cautious. Good sign."

"Incoming message," Comm announced.

"On screen," Reynolds told him.

A few seconds later, the screen wavered and changed focus. However, where Reynolds had expected to see a face of some kind, he was surprised to see nothing more than a placard with what appeared to be a Grindlevik 3 Space Defense logo, which was two arms crossed in an X, one clearly flesh and bone, the other quite obviously mechanoid in origin. A red circle enclosed both.

"Is there no other visual?" Reynolds asked.

"That's all they're sending," Comm answered.

"Oh, great, it's an infomercial," Tactical complained. "Wonder what they're selling?"

"Voice transmission coming in now," Comm reported.

Almost immediately, a mechanical voice that sounded similar to Reynolds' ship voice came over the speakers.

"Greetings, Superdreadnought *Reynolds*," the voice announced. "I am Gorad, the Grindlevik 3 Orbital Space Defense Command. State your intentions or face the consequences of trespassing in Grindlovian space."

"I feel so welcome," Tactical mumbled, making sure only the crew could hear him. "Why do we always run into the gruff bastards?"

"Greetings, Gorad," Reynolds answered, ignoring Tactical's commentary—although he had to admit he might be on to something with his assessment. "We are on an exploratory mission to seek out allies and...others throughout the universe. Our intentions are peaceful." He didn't think it was wise to mention his quest for Kurtherian heads, given the trace signals coming from the planet.

"Unless you fuck with us," Tactical said with a grin in

his voice, again making sure Gorad couldn't actually hear him. "Then we'll get all up in your shit."

Reynolds flipped a cyber switch and cut off Tactical's communication interface.

"That is good news," Gorad replied. "Still, you have to understand our position and why it warrants caution on our behalf."

"Exactly whose behalf might that be?"

"That of my Grindlovian creators, of course, and those in their service, the Telluride.

"Are you…sentient?" Reynolds asked, surprised to realize the person they were talking to might be an AI similar to him and not just some automated security system with a cadre of rote responses prepared to counter any situation thrown its way.

"That's an interesting question with an interesting answer," Gorad answered, though Reynolds noted he had avoided the question. "I could ask the same of you."

"I guess that depends on your definition of sentient, then," Reynolds shot back. "I most certainly feel as though I am."

"Then we are much the same, Superdreadnought *Reynolds*," Gorad told him.

"You can simply call me 'Reynolds.'"

"As you wish, Reynolds," Gorad replied. "Now, as to the meat of your intentions…"

Jiya raised an eyebrow, waiting for Tactical to jump in at Gorad's pause. Everyone was surprised when he didn't. Little did they know, he was raging within his muted console.

"What is it specifically that you want with the people of Grindlevik 3?"

"Our primary mission is largely to create positive relationships with the various worlds we come across, and to trade technological advances for safe harbor and for supplies as needed."

"Largely?"

Reynolds bit back a sigh, realizing he was going to have to be very careful how he worded his statements. As a fellow AI, Gorad would parse and analyze their substance, intended or otherwise, much deeper than most beings would. The captain had spent too much time among humans and others whose grasp of the subtleties of language was nowhere near as comprehensive as an artificial intelligence's would be.

"We, of course, have our *masters'* best interests in mind," he answered, amused by how weird the word sounded, "but we have no desire to instigate a conflict where one can be avoided. There is much we can offer one another, should you deign to allow us to visit Grindlevik 3."

The possibility of smashing Kurtherian skulls not least, Reynolds thought.

"What assurances do I have that you will not harm the people of Grindlevik 3, Reynolds?"

"You have my word as one AI to another," he answered.

"Yeah, because that's worth the scrap metal your tongue's made out of," Tactical called, having wrestled himself free of the captain's block. Reynolds was glad once more that Tactical had at least had the good sense to mute the system.

"I see you have a flesh-and-blood crew behind you,"

Gorad continued pondering whether to let the *SD Reynolds* pass without a fight. “Do you find their presence better conditions you to be kind to those who are less than you?”

Jiya grunted. “We’re right here, you know.” She had little patience for any being that considered itself superior, having been conditioned to despise such attitudes by her father.

Reynolds waved a hand behind his back to rein her in.

“I have found that creating relationships with all manner of beings has been both rewarding *and* challenging,” Reynolds answered honestly. “Still, the people of my crew prove daily that they are honorable *and* worthy of my respect. I would not trade them for any automated system.”

Jiya pumped a fist and whispered, “Take that, Robo-dick!”

Comm wisely muted the system so her comments wouldn’t make it to Gorad. Reynolds held up a metal hand. “Please give me a moment.” He blanked the main screen and turned to the crew. “Everyone needs to shut their mouths! Although we can defeat ten destroyers, we cannot survive if their forty brothers join them. This is a delicate negotiation, and you people and my alternate selves are playing goat-fuck games. Everyone shut the fuck up and let me concentrate or get your dumbasses off my bridge!”

Ria looked shocked, her lips white from clenching her jaw. Jiya hung her head and nodded. Her transition from hovercab driver to first officer on the *Reynolds’* space exploration mission had not been easy. She was a well-educated brawler, ready to fight at the drop of a slight, intentional or otherwise.

Maddox remained stoic. He brought up the tactical display on his terminal and studied it, looking for a weakness in the planet's position should a fight begin. He calculated ranges and closing times for the remaining forty destroyers. They could escape if need be, but if there was a chance that there were Kurtherians on the planet, they needed access. Leaving an enemy to one's rear was bad strategy.

Reynolds stormed over to Tactical's position and punched his metal hand into the speaker, crushed it, and ripped it free. He threw it to the deck before restoring the main screen.

"And you believe what you have to offer will better the lives of those on Grindlevik 3?" Gorad immediately questioned.

"I believe it's worth the effort of trying," Reynolds answered without pause. "All lessons are worth learning, and no matter who you are, you can learn something from every other being you encounter. From the lowest to the highest, we are better as compatriots rather than competitors."

There was a pause. Gorad didn't deliver a verbal answer, letting his actions speak for him. The array of destroyers began to ease back, using their positional thrusters to clear a path through their ranks.

"I find myself obliged to trust you, Reynolds," Gorad told him. "To a degree, of course."

"Of course," Reynolds replied, understanding where the other AI was coming from. He sure as hell didn't trust Gorad yet—and he wasn't sure he ever would—but being allowed past the blockade was a good start.

He could build on that, or nuke Gorad, turning him into space debris.

Whatever needed doing.

Especially if Kurtherians were hiding somewhere on the planet.

"Please follow the course we have sent you and do not deviate," Gorad explained. "It would ease my mind to know that you respect our sovereign space and will abide by our rules while you are here."

"We are your guests, and we will act accordingly," Reynolds assured. Jiya nodded from behind the captain, where she stood with her hands behind her back.

"Welcome to Grindlevik 3, Superdreadnought *Reynolds* and crew," Gorad told them. "I will guide you in, and a shuttle will arrive shortly to ferry you and your select crew to the planet. A representative of the Grindlovian people will meet you there."

"Thank you for your generosity," Reynolds answered, offering the other AI a shallow nod.

The screen went blank, then returned to the outside view showing the still-lurking destroyers. Reynolds heard Jiya and Maddox shuffle uncomfortably behind him. He turned, wondering which of the two would confront him first.

I'll bet on Jiya, he thought.

"You believe him?" she asked.

Reynolds chuckled. "Belief isn't necessary. We're here on a mission. If the Grindlovians and Telluride are good people, there won't be a problem. If they're not—"

"Eat shit and die, motherfuckers!" Tactical shouted

from Helm's position, rocking Ria back in her seat. "It's clobberin' time!"

Reynolds gestured to the speaker on the deck by Tactical's position and shrugged. "There you go."

Asya came onto the bridge then, side-eyeing Tactical's damaged position. "What did I miss?"

"An alien AI and Reynolds waving mechanical dicks and deciding to get a closer look so they can measure to see whose is bigger," Jiya answered. "That's pretty much it."

Asya nodded. "Good to know." She assumed her station and stared up at the viewscreen. "That's one hell of a greeting party."

"We inspire confidence wherever we go," Maddox told her. She snorted a half-laugh.

"I get that. It's your thing. A gift or a curse? I'm not sure, but let's see what we can make of this...*opportunity*."

"Well, what are we waiting for?" Reynolds asked Ria. "Let's go make some new friends, Ensign Alcott."

"Yes, sir," Ria replied, eyes focused on her console and the three-dimensional display of the course the ship was to follow. She eased the *Reynolds* into the gap between the mass of destroyers. "Setting course based on the coordinates provided."

"No, that's not ominous at all," Asya muttered, staring at the ships surrounding them. Their weapons followed the *Reynolds* the entire way. She hunched over her console, preparing herself in case something happened.

Jiya leaned close and whispered, "Next time, Asya, please get to the bridge sooner. We need you manning your position before we go into battle."

Asya readied a retort but let it die on her lips. Jiya

wasn't wrong. The standoff had happened and been resolved while her combat station remained empty. The ship could fight. It didn't need her.

But she wanted it to. "I am sorry, Jiya. I won't let it happen again." Asya nodded once and started running through tactical scenarios, coordinating with Maddox and his strategic combat projections.

"Ready the landing crew, Jiya," Reynolds ordered. "Don't want to keep our host waiting."

Jiya saluted and left the bridge to find the others.

Reynolds watched as they closed on the floating defensive perimeter, smiling appreciatively at its complexity. He had a feeling the trip to Grindlevik 3 would be productive.

"All right, folks," he called. "We're off to see the wizard."

CHAPTER TWO

As the *Reynolds* drew closer to the space station, Asya felt a shiver dance down her spine.

"That is a hell of a lot of firepower stationed in orbit around a planet," she noted. "I wonder what their military budget runs them?"

"It does seem a bit excessive," XO agreed. "Scans aren't picking up anything planetside that would warrant such a posture. It makes me nervous."

"Me too," Asya replied. She drew a deep breath, unable to pull her eyes from the viewscreen. "Tactically, it makes me think we're being invited into a spider's web."

"You think it's a trap?" Reynolds asked.

"Think? No," she replied. "It feels suspicious, though." She pointed out the destroyers that had turned and matched pace with the *Reynolds,* each ship at a precise distance to maximize the effectiveness of the weapons they carried. "This other AI—"

"Gorad," Reynolds filled in.

"This *Gorad* appears to have had a lot of experience with outsiders, or there wouldn't be a need for such excessive systems. I wonder how often people come to this out-of-the-way planet, and how often Gorad is forced to rise to its defense."

"That's a good question," XO said.

Reynolds nodded, letting everything sink in for a good nanosecond or so, which was a long time for an AI.

"I've seen systems similar to this," Asya told them. "Not exactly, of course, but close. There's more going on here than simple space defense. No planet needs this much firepower above it unless they're in the middle of a war or looking to start one."

"Maybe that is the case," Reynolds concurred. "They're engaged with another species, or have been recently, and they're still on a war footing. That would explain it."

Maddox rubbed his chin in thought. He wasn't sure. "In moments, we'll be past the point of no return. If we have to fight our way out, it'll get real ugly real fast."

"Then why let our Trojan Horse through the gate?" XO asked. "It didn't take a whole lot of smooching ass to get Gorad to open up and let us in. He sure as hell didn't get anything from our systems when he scanned us."

"Meaning he can't know if we're a friend or enemy," Asya added. "Given the number of ships he has available to blast us into oblivion, I suspect he's still making up his mind as to which."

Reynolds adjusted the viewscreen to see where Gorad was leading them—directly into the middle of the massive ring floating in orbit over Grindlevik 3. That would put them well within range of twenty destroyers by the time they settled, not to mention the ring itself.

"A number of the destroyers have tightened their posture around the ring," XO warned. "He could hit us with half his fleet if he wanted to."

"He's not taking any chances," Maddox said. "And here we are, now within range of enough firepower that our odds of escape are fifty-fifty."

Asya cut in. "I don't like this, but we are now committed."

"Worst case scenario," Reynolds questioned, "what are we looking at if things go south?"

"We talking a Slayer song here?" Tactical wondered. "*South of Heaven*, maybe?"

"I have no idea who that is, but if by south of Heaven you mean Hell, then yeah, that sounds about right," Asya replied. "I'm betting that defensive ring is equipped with a planetary shield as well as all those guns it's packing. Add the fifty destroyers, and we're looking at ending up as floating space dust unless the *Reynolds* has some last-resort defensive system I don't know about."

"We have *you*," Tactical told her.

Asya chuckled. "You're going to need more than that if this Gorad guy decides he wants to take a bite out of our ass."

"What do you suggest?" Reynolds asked, having already assessed that Gorad would not attack the super-dreadnought.

"You have a favorite god?" she proffered with a shrug. "Divine intervention is always a good option to have on call."

"*Deus ex Machina*," XO chimed in. "The choice of sub-par scribes the universe around."

"If that means what I think it does, then yes, exactly," Asya returned. "I'd normally say kick-ass railguns are better than an act of God any day, but we'll need both if Gorad gets it in his AI head that we're a threat to him," she said. "I'm not seeing a lot of ways out of this that don't end up with us splatted like a bug."

"So much for optimism," Reynolds complained. "My assessment is that we are dealing with a cautious entity like me. We will be fine, and if not, my bad."

"Believe me, I hope I'm wrong," Asya replied. "Maybe Gorad's an AI with a heart of gold and he doesn't have any ulterior motives for letting us visit his planet, but I'm not sure any AI can be entirely guileless. No offense, of course."

"Some taken," Tactical muttered from the Helm speaker, "meatbag."

Asya gestured to Tactical's position. "See what I mean?"

Reynolds let out a mechanical sigh while watching the ship maneuver toward the docking mechanism.

"Get maintenance up here to fix my speaker," Tactical ordered.

"Belay that, and bugger all. Furl the sails and let her drift to dock." Chrome Reynolds stood tall, one foot on the pedestal surrounding the captain's chair, his hands on what passed for his metal hips.

"I suspect Gorad has something in mind, and he's got the firepower to back up any demands he might choose to make," she advised, examining the weaponry splayed around the Superdreadnought *Reynolds*. "Based on my experience, we can't win a fair fight against these odds."

"You suggesting we bail already?" Reynolds turned his head one hundred and eighty degrees to assess her claim.

She shook her head. "We're here for a reason, right?"

Reynolds nodded.

"Then I'd say we follow through and complete the mission." She stood ramrod-straight in a position of calm confidence. "Still, I'd make sure the ship is on standby at all times, ready to do something drastic if need be." She pointed to the defensive ring now filling the whole of the viewscreen. "If anything happens, get as close to that thing as possible after taking out the guns directly in front of us. That'd give us some relief from the ring's weaponry, and maybe buy us a pause from the destroyers. They might not be so willing to engage if there's a chance they'll damage their own space station."

"You don't know us AIs very well then," Reynolds clarified.

"I said 'maybe,'" she countered. "Gorad could have a better-defined sense of self-preservation than you do."

"No one is more self-important than Reynolds," Tactical made sure to point out.

Asya shrugged. "If that were true, we wouldn't be here now, willfully putting ourselves into range of enough weapons to blow the gravitic shields in a single salvo. I think what would happen after that is self-explanatory."

"You're like Rod Serling," Reynolds mentioned to her blank expression. He shook his head when she missed the reference. "All we need is a creepy soundtrack to go along with your fearmongering."

The *Twilight Zone* theme song played over the speakers.

Asya ignored it, returning her attention to the tactical display.

Reynolds waved it to silence. "Helm, prepare to dock." Reynolds switched to ship-wide broadcast. "Jiya, what's the status of the landing crew?"

"Assembled in the hangar bay and standing by."

"Very well," Reynolds replied. "Asya, XO—don't scratch my ship. I'll be back when I get back."

He crooked a metal finger at the general, and together, they prepared to leave the bridge.

Reynolds took one last look at the viewscreen. He *needed* to check the planet to be sure. If there were Kurtherians there, he had to root them out and destroy them. He couldn't leave the bastards behind to plot against the Federation and its people.

"Shuttle incoming," XO announced as Ensign Ria settled the *Reynolds* into the indicated extended berth jutting from the ring. "No lifeforms detected. No sign of weapons or explosive compounds."

"Good to know Gorad's not sending us a bomb," Reynolds snarked.

"I'm sure Jiya and the others appreciate it," Asya replied.

"I'm thinking Ka'nak might not mind too much." Maddox chuckled. "He'd love the chance to beat up a bomb."

"Which says so very much about his mindset." XO sighed. "Perhaps it might be in our best interests to administer psychological testing before we commit to taking on more crew?"

"What's the point of that? You and Reynolds wouldn't

pass it even if you had Comm administer it," Tactical told XO.

"He has a point," Maddox agreed. "Ria here would likely be the only person left aboard if we tested everyone. Maybe Asya as well, though I have my doubts."

"I've been questioning my sanity ever since I left Loran, Maddox, so you're probably right," she told him.

The general grinned and let out a hoarse laugh. "What did Jiya call Reynolds' issues? Oh yeah, 'quirks.'"

"Master of the understatement, that one," Tactical announced.

"Good thing I'm going dirtside with the crew rather than sitting up here with you chosen few—the insane, the inane, and the urbane," Reynolds told them. "An AI could get his feelings hurt up here."

"Wouldn't that make you an EI?" Maddox asked.

The AI sighed. "I don't think you understand me at all," he said, feigning a pout. "Asya and XO, you're in charge while we're gone."

"I see how it is," Tactical muttered darkly.

"Keep me—"

"The ship," she clarified.

"Keep *the ship* safe," he adjusted. "Stay in touch on the comm, and try to keep us on scanners. I don't want to give in to your pessimism, but you're right about AIs. You can only trust them about as far as you can throw them."

"Given that you're a superdreadnought, that's saying a lot," she said.

"Exactly my point," Reynolds replied, marching off the bridge with Maddox close behind. "Keep us in one piece," he called before the bridge doors sealed behind them.

They headed toward the hangar bay, but Asya's warnings had taken root in Reynolds' head. He wasn't sufficiently certain about Gorad's intentions, and that bothered him.

Of course, that wasn't going to stop his search for Kurtherians or negotiating to establish a safe haven on Grindlevik 3. He had always planned a calculated approach to the alien AI. He was a significant unknown.

His only experience with AIs were those he'd known in the Federation, and they, of course, were motivated and inspired by Bethany Anne and Michael and the others, their loyalty unquestionably to the Federation and its people.

Gorad, however, was a completely different type of entity.

He hadn't been created by humans, and Reynolds had no idea what his base motivations were. He figured he'd have a better idea once he went dirtside and got a good look at the locals, but that didn't satisfy his curiosity right then.

But with no risk taken, there would be no gain.

Or some such quaint expression.

Reynolds had to trust that he—the ship—would be up to whatever Gorad might try to test it/him with, and that Asya and the rest of the crew would perform as admirably as he expected them to.

Actually, he admitted to himself, that was more like what he was worried about.

"You big baby," he muttered to himself.

"What was that?" Maddox asked.

"Oh, nothing," Reynolds replied, having forgotten the general was with him.

And that was the point of his concern.

It wasn't just Reynolds any longer. He'd dragged a crew into his madness, and they would suffer were anything to happen along the way.

But wasn't that what Bethany Anne had told him?

She'd wanted him to have a crew, but he'd never given it much thought until he'd been damaged and needed people to help repair the hull because the bots weren't capable.

Then he had realized she hadn't wanted him to get a crew simply because they were useful. They were more than that, which was why Bethany Anne had insisted. That was the wisdom of the Queen.

She didn't want him to be alone, knowing what isolation had already done to him: split his personality and made him question his own sanity. The more he was around the crew, the more he could feel himself coming back together as one again—as long as that bastard Tactical played along and gave up his independence. That was a battle for a different time.

Reynolds grumbled as he entered the hangar bay's foyer and saw the crew lined up at the window waiting for the shuttle to arrive.

Jiya stared at him with that stupid grin of hers as if she knew Reynolds had been moping since he'd left the bridge.

He ignored her, not wanting to admit that he had been.

He appraised the rest of the crew at a glance.

Takal Durba was distracted, as he often was. He was

making last-minute adjustments to the armored suits the crew were wearing, as he always did.

The guy couldn't stop tinkering, which was probably a good thing, Reynolds thought. He would be the one to help Reynolds get into a better body, one he didn't have to worry about wearing down or falling apart during normal, everyday use.

That was what Reynolds wanted.

He'd gotten a taste of freedom in the android forms—even the Jonny-Taxi one, crappy as it had been—and Reynolds had enjoyed it.

As much as he loved being plugged into the super-dreadnought, there was something special about being mobile in a vehicle that wasn't the size of a skyscraper.

Geroux Durba, Takal's niece and the ship's resident computer genius, hung out by Jiya, which was also expected.

The two had been friends since long before Reynolds had arrived in their galaxy, and he didn't expect them to part company just because they were now flying blindly through space in search of Kurtherians to kill.

The last of the crew bounced around in an open area of the hangar bay a short distance from the others. He shadow-boxed relentlessly, although the term simplified the motions the warrior was going through considerably. He used all eight points of contact—fists, elbows, knees, and feet—in his routine.

The male was a master of combat. Built like a tank, and although Reynolds hated to say this, about as thick as one, too. Ka'nak had honed his skills in the fighting pits of his world and come out the other side of it scarred and brutal but alive.

Given the uncertainty of their mission, Reynolds was glad to have him along.

He was glad to have all of them. They made a good team.

Together, they'd handle whatever Gorad threw their way.

He went over and stood beside Jiya, looking out the massive window that separated them from where the smaller ships docked around them. Maddox stood at their backs.

The shuttle slipped into the hangar bay with a casual grace that made it clear to Reynolds that Gorad was piloting it. He hadn't subbed the task to any old automated system.

That was both flattering and disconcerting, but Reynolds could see the reasoning behind it.

Gorad would get firsthand knowledge of the crew and Reynolds as they traveled dirtside, giving the alien AI an advantage in treating with them. He would see their interactions, however unintentional or subconscious, and he'd be able to manipulate circumstances based on those findings.

But in doing so, Gorad had made it clear to Reynolds that, regardless who the crew were going to meet down on the planet, Gorad was in charge. This was *his* domain, and Reynolds realized he'd better tread lightly around the alien AI to keep from offending him.

Easier said than done, he thought, grinning. At least

Tactical wasn't able to come down to the planet with them. That bastard! He would wreak havoc.

Reynolds would miss his snark.

The shuttle settled in, and the hangar bay pressurized shortly after. The shuttle door eased open. Facing their way, it almost looked like a hand waving for its passengers to come aboard.

Showoff.

"Let's go, people," Reynolds said. "Our host is waiting for his first look at the Etheric Federation's representatives. He wants to see us up close and personal."

"Hopefully not *too* personally," Jiya mumbled. "I didn't shower today."

"That's all?" Ka'nak asked. "I haven't showered all week."

"That explains the smell," Geroux said, covering her nose and giggling.

Reynolds triggered the panel by the door and waved the crew into the hangar. He thought about warning them about not saying too much during the flight but decided against it.

He'd let the situation serve as a teaching moment for the crew to see how they acted and how aware they were in strange and possibly hostile situations.

They climbed into the shuttle and took their seats, Reynolds bringing up the rear. He quickly and methodically examined the ship's interior as he entered. He noted that the shuttle's seats were designed for humanoids the shape and size of the Larians.

Nothing stood out as sinister or odd, which made him happy.

Whatever Gorad's plans were, it didn't seem to involve harming them.

As for anything else, Reynolds would have to wait until they were on the ground to see if the alien AI had anything else planned.

That was okay. Reynolds was patient.

Sort of.

CHAPTER THREE

The shuttle hurtled toward Grindlevik 3's surface, and Reynolds was rather surprised by what he saw as they drew closer.

Not necessarily surprised, since he hadn't known what to expect to begin with, but he had thought the planet would be less…sterile looking.

"That's, interesting," Jiya remarked beside him, peering out the shuttle's windows as he was.

"What's that?" Maddox asked, leaning over to follow her gaze.

The gray and antiseptic atmosphere looked back at them.

And that was exactly how to describe it. There was very little in the way of color in the city they were flying over, not to mention very little in the way of variety. Everything was so similar it was a blur.

"It's like a black and white image," Takal noted. "Only…starker."

"I like it," Geroux said. "It's symmetrical and neat. It's like computer code stretched out and made into houses."

Jiya chuckled. "You're right, it does look like code on a screen."

Reynolds nodded at hearing that, realizing he shouldn't have expected much else from Gorad. It was obvious that the AI had a hand in everything they had seen, from the orbiting space station to the planet's surface.

Whatever part of Gorad piloted the shuttle remained quiet. While he had to know that Reynolds knew he was there, listening, he was keeping a low profile, not interrupting the crew or involving himself in their conversation. As Reynolds was doing, Gorad was collecting data.

The shuttle came in smoothly and landed gently, the door opening as soon as the ship touched down.

The crew chattered curiously among themselves as they slipped free of the restraining gear and clambered to their feet. Once up, they gathered their equipment and made their way off the transport shuttle.

Ka'nak went first, filling his role as team security.

Maddox followed on the warrior's heels, likely imagining the same scenario as Reynolds.

Reynolds appreciated the general's cognizance in situations like this. He could count on the male to keep a level head at times of stress. Since the treatments following his lengthy incarceration, the general had greatly improved, becoming affable and keen.

Unless there was gambling and a neuromanipulator was involved—then all bets with the general were off.

Reynolds chuckled at that, but he realized the male's captivity had made him more susceptible to the device back on Loran. He couldn't be blamed for his loss of control.

Once the crew was outside, the inhuman nature of the planet became even more apparent. Automated vehicles and devices flitted back and forth in a rigid fashion, following an obvious grid, none deviating from their course or making a sound beyond a mechanical whir.

Bots filled the space between, overseeing everything that was happening. They were imperious in their presence, and Reynolds was amazed to see just how many there were. They were everywhere; way more than he suspected were necessary for the tasks. It was overkill. The living creatures of Grindlevik 3 were nowhere to be seen.

Reynolds figured there might be more to the excessive bot population than just oversight.

As he took in the environment, he spied a vehicle coming their way in defiance of the meticulous order of everything else around them. It was also the only thing that had even a remote splash of color to it.

That turned out to be its occupants, not the vehicle itself.

Reynolds turned his focus on the beings. Pasty blue, almost sickly-looking, and rail-thin, the two locals pulled up alongside the shuttle and parked in front of the crew.

There were no instruments on either side of the vehicle where the greeters sat. Like the rest of the machines around the landing area, this vehicle was automated.

Which would explain the complete lack of muscle tone the two males—although Reynolds couldn't be sure of their gender, he assumed they were male—had going on.

"Greetings, Reynolds and crew," the alien on the far side

of them said. He barely turned his head to look their direction as he spoke, side-eyeing them as if his head were incapable of movement. The other didn't turn at all.

"Hello," Jiya said with a smile, offering them a half-hearted wave despite their obvious lack of excitement at seeing the crew. She lowered her hand when they didn't react.

Maddox pulled a face that clearly said he didn't appreciate the aliens' disinterest.

"I am Vor Gna," the other said, sparing a glance at the one in the seat beside him, though it looked as if the movement was almost too much for him. There was the barest hint of a smile on his lips. "This is Vor Ilm. It is our pleasure to make your acquaintance on behalf of the Grindlovian people and our overseer, the great and generous Gorad."

"Pleasure to meet you both," Reynold replied, modifying his tone to match theirs. He wasn't sure if the monotone was a cultural thing, but he didn't want to appear as if he were yelling at the aliens. He suspected that might be considered rude.

"Please join us in the vehicle, and we will transport you to the meeting chambers where you can speak to our leaders."

Vor Gna waved at the crew to join them, but to Reynolds, it looked more like his hand had suffered an involuntary spasm.

Jiya glanced at Reynolds, and the AI offered a subtle shrug and mouthed, "Go along with it," unsure how to approach the Grindlovians.

Never before had he seen such indifference in a

greeting party. They normally put on a big happy face and were all smiles, or they pointed guns and threatened. This behavior was strange.

The crew did as they were asked and clambered into the vehicle, making a conscious effort to do so casually and calmly. All but Ka'nak.

The Melowi warrior jumped in last, landing heavily next to Maddox and setting the vehicle to shuddering before its antigrav systems recalibrated.

Reynolds glanced at the aliens, expecting a reaction of some sort, but if they *had* responded, the movement had been too subtle for him to notice. They sat there, slumped in their seats and stared straight ahead.

He wasn't sure the two even blinked.

Once the crew was aboard, the vehicle shot forward of its own accord. Reynolds had the feeling that, once again, Gorad was in complete control.

He wondered why the other AI had even bothered to send the two alien beings. They'd hardly done anything to soften the image of a mechanical overlord controlling every aspect of their lives.

The rest of the trip did nothing to disabuse him of that idea.

The vehicle shot across perfectly ordered tarmac to slip into perfectly ordered traffic and proceeded through a perfectly ordered neighborhood. Absolutely nothing was out of place.

Except, of course, the few Grindlovians they saw as they passed.

Splotches of pale blue stuck out here and there on the sidewalks, but it seemed as if, despite the scanners showing

Grindlevik 3 having a large population, there were maybe only a dozen or so Grindlovians out and about.

And those who were seemed almost incapable of independent movement.

The Grindlovians scooted about in automated chairs. Well, chairs might be a stretch. They were close to being beds.

They reclined deeply, and the passengers barely sat upright, letting the cart drive them wherever they were going without any obvious direction from the rider. What little traffic there was on the sidewalks was also perfectly organized, no two chairs getting close to colliding despite the inability of their passengers to see anything around them clearly.

The chairs went about their business, whatever that might be, as if that was how things had always been.

Reynolds suspected that might well be true, and wondered how Gorad had taken such complete control of the humanoids.

As they continued on, Reynolds caught sight of a lift device deploying out of the back of one of the chairs. It reached around and clutched the Grindlovian in a padded harness, which lifted the being up and out of the chair.

The arm maneuvered him in front of a small outdoor shop—more a simple counter with a board with alien writing behind it and not much else—where another Grindlovian sat in a chair similar to the first. The two carried on a slow, quiet conversation, and Reynolds noted that additional limbs sprouted out of the lift's arm and did the pointing for the Grindlovian, jabbing mechanical fingers at various parts of the board.

"He's...shopping," Takal murmured, eyes wide. "Interesting."

"Yes," Vor Gna said, catching all of them off-guard with his soft incantation. They'd almost forgotten the silent beings were in the front of the vehicle. "It is a Csma shop. Best in town. You should try some before you leave." Before the vehicle moved on, the crew spotted a dull gray drink being handed over by a mechanical arm. A second one stuffed a straw into the cup, and a third moved the end of that straw into the Grindlovian's mouth.

Jiya tapped Reynolds' leg and stared at him from under raised eyebrows.

The ride lasted several minutes longer, during which the crew were treated to similar views of Grindlovian society.

No one did anything for themselves. The superdreadnought's crew found that disconcerting. They were an active bunch, unable to contemplate being bedridden as a matter of course.

It wasn't until the vehicle passed through a walled section of town—the two Vors announcing this to be the inner sanctum of Gorad—that the crew saw another race of beings scurrying about.

Jiya sighed, and Reynolds found himself nodding. *These must be the Telluride,* he thought.

The polar opposite of the Grindlovians, the Telluride were full of life.

They strolled behind the mass of chaired Grindlovians. The Telluride, while perhaps a bit short and stocky, were in fantastic physical shape. Their golden skin gleamed under the sunlight in sharp contrast to the overwhelming palette of gray that surrounded them.

Their hair was a deep red, almost fiery in the way it reflected the light, and many wore an array of colorful bands to keep the wild strands at bay.

These people had none of the restraint of the Grindlovians, though neither group seemed to balk at the huge difference between the species.

Where the area outside of the wall had been maintained by bots and automated services, it appeared that much of what went on inside the wall was handled by the Telluride.

Where mechanical arms had lifted things and helped the pale Grindlovians around, the strong Telluride were hands-on inside the compound.

Reynolds spied one of the golden beings pointing and discussing something with the shopkeeper at what looked to be a clothing store, apparently on behalf of the Grindlovian in the chair beside him.

Another Telluride came up to the first and the two had a raucous debate, albeit a friendly one, before the Telluride worker handed a pale gray scarf to the first. Reynolds didn't notice an exchange of money of any kind, but the Telluride wrapped the ugly scarf around the neck of the Grindlovian in the chair.

The two Telluride said their goodbyes, and the pair moved on at a slow and leisurely pace down the street.

"We're here," Vor Ilm announced quietly, and the vehicle came to a gentle stop in front of a huge building.

A moving walkway ran from the curb, which the vehicle had parked within a centimeter of, all the way to the front door of the building.

"Please disembark and take the walkway to the door," Vor Gna told them. Again, a flicker of his hand appeared to be what passed for a wave or a point on Grindlevik 3. "Servants will meet you there to take you the rest of the way to the meeting hall."

"Once more, we are honored by your presence," Vor Ilm said, then both the Grindlovians went silent, clearly waiting for the crew to climb out of the vehicle.

"That sounds like our cue," Maddox muttered, hopping over the side of the vehicle and landing next to the walk to wait for the others.

Ka'nak grunted and scrambled out, followed by Jiya, Takal, Geroux, and Reynolds last. The AI glanced back to say goodbye to the two Grindlovians, but the vehicle shot off before he could. Neither of the aliens had said a word.

He watched their blue heads disappear around a corner, leaving the crew on a nearly empty street. Only a few Grindlovians traveled nearby, each having at least one of the Telluride nearby.

"This is quite…interesting," Takal said, nodding as he looked about, clearly unable to think of a better word for what he saw.

"'Disturbing' is the word I'd use for it," Geroux countered, helping him. "These Grindlovians look ill," she suggested. "I wonder what's happened to them to make them so frail?"

"I'm afraid to ask," Jiya muttered, her expression sharper than it normally was

The first officer was taking in all she could see before making an assessment.

Reynolds grinned at that.

"It looks like they're waiting for us," Ka'nak said, gesturing toward the distant door.

Two of the colorful Telluride stood at attention just inside the glass, staring out at the crew.

"Let's not keep our hosts waiting," Reynold announced. "Weird as they might be," he added more quietly.

Jiya, the only one close enough to hear him, chuckled.

The crew stepped onto the moving walkway, and it carried them at a comfortable speed toward the doors.

There were a number of humanoid bots spread around the open courtyard in odd postures and positions. It took Reynolds a moment to realize that they were intended to be statues.

They were held in the air by steel rods, displayed almost as if they were victims of a battle, staked in public as a warning.

Their eyes were dim and lifeless, and their arms hung limply at their sides. Their feet dangled about a foot off the ground, and their heads drooped to their chests.

"That's…kinda creepy," Geroux noted, her eyes scanning the multitude of bot statues.

"I'd be nervous if I were you," Ka'nak told Reynolds.

Reynolds nodded. "I'd be nervous if I were me, too."

The walkway quickly took them past the odd robot museum *cum* cemetery, and the doors hissed open in front of them. Two Telluride grinned and offered the crew a deep bow.

"Welcome to Goranton," the first said. "I am San Paget, and this is L'Eliana. We work for the Grindlovian Council and are to see you to them for an audience.

The pair positively beamed as they welcomed the crew,

stepping out of the way with a grace that belied their sturdy builds.

Like those Telluride the crew had seen on the street, these two were dressed far more gaudily than the Grindlovians. Red hair and colorful ties were present, and there was little to distinguish the male from the female outside of a slight softening of the features that made L'Eliana look cheerier than her counterpart, if only by a little.

"This way, please," L'Eliana told them, not waiting for a reply. She started off immediately with a light step.

After the meeting with the Grindlovians, it was almost as if the crew were forced into fast-forward.

The Telluride pair led them through Goranton, as they'd called it. Reynolds suspected that it had been named after the reigning AI.

The walls and floor were gray and featureless, not a hint of art or style anywhere.

Jiya leaned in close so only Reynolds could hear her. "This feels like a prison," she said, sneering. "With very vibrant and happy guards."

Reynolds nodded. It did feel as if it were some form of institution. Like the view from the city above, it was cold and plain; functional but nothing more.

There was no hint that anyone lived in the place, let alone worked there.

The hallway they traveled seemed to last forever, going on and on and on until L'Eliana and San Paget came to a halt outside a pair of plain doors without handles. San Paget waved his hand in front of a sensor plate, which was so simplistic that Reynolds hadn't even noticed it before then, and the doors swung inward, clearing the way for the crew.

"Please enter and have a seat before the council," L'Eliana told them.

The room was fairly large, but like everything else they'd passed, it had no character. Automated chairs that looked more like mobile podiums stood at attention near the back of the room, and several rows of plain chairs were arrayed before them.

Each of the five podium chairs had a Grindlovian in it, although they were hard to see, hunkered down in their seats as they were and hidden by the mechanical apparatus of the chairs.

The crew marched in, offered a greeting to the council, and sat when L'Eliana encouraged them to. The council members simply stared.

Reynolds was sure he saw one of them blink, though.

He thought he might die from all the excitement, but by dint of great effort, he contained himself.

The Telluride came over and flanked the crew after they'd settled in, apparently waiting on some clue or another.

"Greetings, off-worlders," a Grindlovian said from the middle of the group. A light flickered on the floor below her, spotlighting the female. "I am Fulla Sol. To my left is Fulla Vae, then Vor Stygn." The light jumped to each as she introduced him. "To my right are Vor Hiln and Fulla Lofn."

As the light flickered in front of the last person indicated, Reynolds realized that was the extent of the introductions they'd receive.

None of the council waved or did anything more than

make the most basic eye contact, and even that seemed as if it might have been too much for them.

"Gorad has told us that you wish to observe our society and make allies among our shared people, Grindlovians and the Telluride, perhaps even trading with us should we find a suitable matching of goods or intelligence," Fulla Sol went on. Her monotone voice was more mechanical than Gorad's, Reynolds mused. There wasn't a hint of inflection in the words, and he realized that the crew was probably cursing their translators for spewing the translation out in the exact same manner.

"Those are indeed our hopes," Jiya answered for him. She almost huffed as she spoke, possibly in subconscious defiance of the Grindlovian's placid tone of voice.

"Then it shall be," Fulla Sol answered. "San Paget and L'Eliana will see you to your quarters. From there, Gorad will arrange for you to visit our world and its wonders. Our servants will come for you."

Reynolds bit back a chuckle as he wondered what kind of wonders they might see.

"Until we meet again," Fulla Sol said, letting San Paget wave goodbye to the crew for her.

A moment later the meeting unexpectedly ended. The chair-bearing podium sank into the ground and disappeared, smooth steel hatches closing behind it.

"The council thanks you for a productive meeting," L'Eliana told the crew, smiling happily as if reveling in secret joy before waving them to their feet. "We will now escort you to your quarters. Gorad will reach out to you soon for your tour of the town and to speak with you."

The Telluride trotted off, and the crew followed.

They were led through more plain halls until they came to another set of double doors.

"This will be your quarters as long as you are here on Grindlevik 3," San Paget announced. "Make yourselves comfortable, and have a pleasant stay."

The doors opened and the crew entered a room that was barely more functional than the council chamber, its gray color almost overwhelming in its negative sheen.

The doors shut behind the crew, leaving them alone.

"You know what this place needs to brighten it up a bit?" Ka'nak started. He stuck his tongue out in a playful manner as he looked from face to face. "A nice splash of blood across the wall."

CHAPTER FOUR

Reynolds circled the room one way as Geroux went the other. They met at the middle and nodded at each other.

"The room's clear of listening devices, far as I can tell," Geroux announced.

"Perhaps our host is not as much a dictator as he could be," Ka'nak said, looking around the place. "He sure could use an interior decorator, though. I spend all my time in dirty, sandy pits fighting for my life, and even *I* think this place is bland."

Ka'nak dropped onto one of the two couches in the main chamber and leaned back with a dissatisfied grunt.

"About as comfy as squatting on the floor," he grumbled, doing his best to find a sustainable position.

"How many times did you guys need to bite your tongues to keep from asking the Grindlovians if there was something wrong with them?" Jiya asked. "They look sickly."

Takal grunted as he glanced about, wishing he had

something to drink to take the mundane edge off the place and make it more interesting. Something with the sting that indicated a high percentage of alcohol.

"I was examining the people as we passed, but I'm no more certain they are afflicted by anything than when we first arrived," Takal explained. "I think that perhaps they are simply so pampered that they have devolved physically."

"Is that possible?" Jiya wondered.

Takal shrugged and pointed to the doors. "I'm not sure how else to explain it. From what I've seen, that is the only conclusion I can arrive at."

Reynolds agreed. "Yeah, they look like balls of dough with twigs for arms and legs. I hope Gorad controls the weather here, too, or one stiff wind will send them tumbling from their automated thrones."

"And the meeting?" Geroux commented. "What was up with that? We didn't say anything, and they were ready to boot us out and send us on our way."

"I suspect that's Gorad's doing," Jiya told them, motioning to the room around them. "These people aren't in charge of their existence. It reminds me of home," she said, letting out a sad chuckle, "but on a much larger scale."

Geroux sighed. "That's depressing."

"It most definitely is," Ka'nak mumbled from his seat, where he was still squirming to get comfortable. "Can you imagine what the food will taste like? Cardboard and water, I'm picturing. Yummy."

"I'll slip out and find a Telluride home to eat at if that's the case," Maddox announced. "Those folks look like they eat fairly well."

"Yeah," Geroux started. "Why would they choose to serve these…" She raised her hands in surrender. "I'm not even sure what word to use for them."

"Lazy bastards?" Ka'nak offered.

"I'm not sure that's it," Reynolds countered, "although I'm shitting presumptions out my ass."

"That's a beautiful visual," Geroux noted, her upper lip peeling back into a disgusted sneer.

"Regardless, we need to determine if there is a back door to find what we seek without going directly at Gorad," Reynolds went on. "It's clear he's in control of everything and has been directing our every move since we climbed aboard the shuttle, but how much say do the Grindlovians and Telluride have in their daily lives?"

"You sure we can't just chit-chat with Gorad and get out of here without having to quiz the locals?" Ka'nak asked. "I'm not seeing much potential for this trip to be fun by any definition of the word."

"We're here for more than just fun, Ka'nak," Maddox advised, waggling a finger at him. "We're here—"

A knock at the door interrupted the general.

"That was quick," Geroux muttered. "You think they're here to get us already?"

"Probably," Reynolds answered. "Gorad didn't strike me as one to sit around waiting."

"You AIs aren't exactly patient," Jiya added.

Another knock sounded, and the crew stared at each other for a moment as if waiting to see who'd volunteer to get it.

"I just got comfortable," Ka'nak called, shaking his head and taking himself out of the running.

Takal finally shrugged and acknowledged that he'd get the door when it came open on its own.

L'Eliana stood outside, smiling. "Are you ready for your tour?"

"Absolutely," Reynolds answered, attempting to be cheery despite the mundane start. "Shall we?" he asked the others.

Geroux took Jiya's hand in hers and they started forward, Takal right behind them. Maddox followed them out. Ka'nak stayed seated, staring at the rest of the crew.

"I'm not much for taking in the sights," he said, "so I'll stick around and hold down the fort. If you need me for something—you know, something that requires my particular talents—let me know."

Reynolds sighed, but Jiya didn't want to argue with the pit fighter. It'd be easier to leave him behind and reach out via comm if they needed him.

Jiya didn't think they would, given what they'd seen of the people so far.

The Grindlovians couldn't be bothered to harm them, and the Telluride seemed far too friendly.

"Don't get into any trouble while we're gone," Jiya ordered Ka'nak.

The warrior nodded. "Yes, sir."

"He can take care of himself," Reynolds whispered to Jiya. "He'll probably nap the whole time we're gone anyway."

"We can take care of ourselves, too," she shot back, clenching a fist and causing Reynolds to grin.

"Indeed."

L'Eliana led them outside to the mobile walk, where

another hovercraft awaited. This time, there were no Grindlovians in the seats. L'Eliana clambered in front and let the crew pick their own seats. Once they had gotten comfortable, the craft took off on its own.

Jiya was amazed by the smooth operation of the transport and everything else in it, but as Reynolds had said, Gorad's hands were pulling the strings for everything. She could picture the AI as a twisted version of Reynolds, sitting in a fortress lair in a tin-can body, rubbing his hands together maniacally.

It was exactly how she pictured Reynolds.

Occasionally.

She bit back a chuckle and ignored the AI's sideways glance at her sudden amusement.

L'Eliana spoke about the town as they traveled, pointing out various aspects. The route this time took the crew deeper into the populated areas of Grindlevik 3, or Goranton, which Jiya wasn't really sure was the city as a whole or just the part inside the walls.

"Where are we headed?" Reynolds asked.

"Our first stop is the droid factory, where all of the planet's machines are created and maintained," L'Eliana replied. "That's the huge chrome area you can see over that way." She motioned toward a building that gleamed as if it might be radioactive, given the lights illuminating it. "After that, we'll visit the agro sector and go wherever you like from there."

"Accommodating," Takal replied, smiling.

The crew stayed silent, listening to L'Eliana chatter about landmarks that looked the same as all the others she described while Jiya took in the whole of the gray nothingness that sprawled before her.

Jiya stifled a yawn more than once.

They passed additional Grindlovians, and like those inside the walls, each had a Telluride with them, appearing in a sudden splash of color and assisting them in whatever they were doing. Jiya watched one of the golden-skinned servants leverage a Grindlovian female out of her chair and carry her to another at a street-side café, adjusting her so she leaned awkwardly against the table.

The Telluride moved the female's elbows into what looked like stirrups to hold her in place.

She spotted several more instances of similar activity as they traveled, and after a while, she couldn't stop herself from asking about it.

"Are the Grindlovians…crippled?" she wondered, unsure if she was asking the right question.

L'Eliana laughed, a musical burst of a sound. "No, of course, they aren't," she replied. "They are simply comfortable with their circumstances. They have both Gorad and us, the Telluride, to cater to their every whim or wish. They want for nothing."

"So, you guys just go around lifting and cleaning and caring for them all the time?" Geroux followed up.

L'Eliana's smile faltered a little at that. "It's nothing like that," she answered, but there was the vaguest quaver in her voice. Jiya wondered if it was because L'Eliana knew Gorad was listening to their conversation. "We are happy serving the Grindlovians and maintaining all of Grindlevik 3."

Reynolds shot Jiya a warning glance and the first officer returned a furtive nod that said she'd understood him.

"Of course." Jiya smiled and dipped her head. "Didn't mean to imply otherwise. I was simply curious as to the nature of your society."

"It's quite effective," L'Eliana told her, clearly grateful to be on familiar ground.

Effective, Jiya repeated in her head. *That was definitely a word an AI would use, not a normal person explaining the nature of their life.*

The thought struck a nerve in her, but Jiya took a deep breath and let it go as best she could. She knew Reynolds hadn't brought them there to muck around in the lives of the locals, but she was also starting to think she knew him well enough to realize that he wasn't as hard around the edges as he acted.

He cared for other beings—she'd seen evidence of that on Lariest—and she suspected he had more in mind for this trip than simply safe harbor and trade.

Jiya definitely wanted more than that. Otherwise, she'd have stayed on Lariest and wasted the rest of her life driving a hovercab and dodging her father and his demands as she had been for years.

Before she could dwell on that disturbing thought, the hovercraft pulled up to a chrome doorway, which led into the droid compound L'Eliana had been describing.

"Here we are at the droid factory," she announced as the doors whooshed open and their craft drifted inside. A sudden burst of chilly air struck them full-on, and Jiya shivered at the abrupt change in temperature. "It's a marvel of technological glory," L'Eliana said, and Jiya noted the rote nature of the exclamation.

The poor female had been made to pitch it like a used hovercraft salesperson.

The craft dropped them off, and as L'Eliana led them into the factory, Jiya realized the apparently overzealous description might well be spot-on.

"Wow!" Geroux muttered when he saw the factory splayed out before them.

Maddox enthusiastically agreed.

The place was humongous, and every meter of space was devoted to the creation or maintenance of a wide variety of droids and robots.

There were copies of models they'd passed on the way there, both at the landing field and in town, as well as a multitude more that they hadn't noticed before.

What struck her the most was that there was not a single living, breathing being in the whole building except for the crew and L'Eliana.

Everything was automated.

Everything.

Machines hummed and whined in the background, mechanical limbs lifting and tugging and twisting, working with delicate electronics and hardened chassis frames all at the same time in a spellbinding dance of mechanized acrobatics.

Jiya looked at the assembly area and could see no room for error in the delicate operations going on at high speed right in front of her.

"The timing of the system is exquisite," Takal said. He was staring over Jiya's shoulder, his wide eyes gleaming.

"This is...quite impressive," Reynolds was forced to admit, although Jiya heard the pause in his declaration and knew he was contemplating much more than the precision of the operation.

L'Eliana had begun to explain the process when Reynolds' voice came over the comm, reverberating within her head.

There are no servants here. No workers. Nothing, he told her, glancing around.

Realizing he'd sent the message only to her, she nodded without replying.

He was right.

Gorad was in complete control of the operation, and there was no one looking over the overseer's shoulder. Reminded her of one of her father's favorite sayings: Who watches the watchers?

That is rather ominous, Jiya thought.

"Does Gorad control all this?" Reynolds asked their guide. "The production of the droids?"

L'Eliana nodded. "He does indeed. Gorad builds and maintains all of our electronics and technology, and keeps us safe from invasion by maintaining the Space Defense Initiative."

"And...you're okay with that?" Geroux asked, eyes narrowed.

"Why wouldn't we be?" L'Eliana answered, no hint of subterfuge in her reply. She truly believed allowing that the AI absolute and total control over their world was a positive thing.

Jiya shuddered, wondering where that mentality could lead these beings if everyone believed the same way.

She pictured Grindlevik 3 and figured she was already seeing its effects, or at least the beginning stages.

Jiya wanted to question the young Telluride further, but she knew better than to put the female in a tough position. Jiya *really* wanted to interrogate her and take all the information from her mind since Gorad was obviously everywhere, but Jiya didn't want to do anything that might put L'Eliana in danger.

Still, thinking about it made a knot grow in her stomach. L'Eliana appeared safe and healthy and didn't look mistreated, but Jiya couldn't help but feel that she and her people, as well as the Grindlovians, were missing out on something Jiya took for granted: freedom of choice.

L'Eliana led them through the building, letting the crew marvel at the setup and watch as legions of droids were crafted and assembled in a blur of motion.

It was breathtaking.

And then they were being ushered back into the hovercraft.

It shot off at a fast clip, and Jiya stared over her shoulder at the droid factory until it receded.

She'd felt the unspoken tension in Reynolds and wondered what he was thinking while taking the whole of Gorad's operation in.

She could only imagine he was probing and surveying everything to find something he could take advantage of in all the order and conformity; something that would benefit the crew and their mission. He also was hesitant to talk in case Gorad had a way to intercept their internal comms. Paranoia seized her.

Other than the possibility of a new android body for

Reynolds—or at least some good parts for one—there wasn't much at the factory that she could see him being interested in.

Swing and a miss, Jiya thought as they rode off, picturing the growing contest of wills between the two AIs like a game of chess. It had laser blasters and energy blades, though, the two hacking and shooting at each other in their quest for an advantage.

The grin still on her face from that image, Jiya held on tight as the hovercraft came to a stop outside an even more remote location than the last.

"What's here?" Geroux asked, always inquisitive.

L'Eliana hopped out of the hovercraft, smiling. "This is our agro-sector, where all of our food products are created and modified for each of our peoples. This is Grindlevik 3's greenhouse, or as we call it, "the Greenhouse."

Jiya looked for the expected fields, but there were none. There was nothing more than a long warehouse-looking building that seemed to stretch for miles and miles away from them. There was nothing but barren earth on either side of the building.

L'Eliana went up to the building and, as had happened everywhere else, the doors opened of their own accord.

The scent of fresh foliage struck them almost like a physical blow as they stepped inside. Jiya groaned.

"That smells delicious," she said, unable to wipe the silly grin from her face.

"Ka'nak will be upset that he missed this," Takal mentioned, following L'Eliana into The Greenhouse, marveling at its magnificence.

"It definitely puts to rest his idea of the food around here," Maddox said.

Once the crew were inside, the impressiveness of the system overwhelmed them like a cascading waterfall.

The Greenhouse held five levels separated into subsections, each controlling a different type of food production.

Fantastically mutated versions of 3-D printers covered the whole of each row. A quiet murmur filled the air as the food printers ran, quickly and effectively producing everything from bushels of wheat to corn to fruits and other vegetables, as well as slabs of fresh-looking meat that appeared as if they had been freshly harvested from prized livestock.

Each food-type dropped from the printer and landed on the conveyor belt, the product traveling down the line to disappear into the distance, along with tons and tons of other food products.

Amazed and awed, they watched as the printers shifted to a new product line, printing and delivering the finished products to the material-handling system. The new foodstuffs joined the previous batch somewhere at the far end of the belts.

In the few minutes the crew stood watching, enough food was produced to feed the entire *Reynolds* crew for weeks.

"Unbelievable," Takal muttered, stumbling forward, desperate to take a closer look.

L'Eliana stopped him with a hand on his arm. "I'm sorry, but you must stay behind the line here," she said, pointing to a yellow line on the floor that none of the crew had noticed, their sole focus on the wizardry of creation before them.

Takal spun to face Reynolds. "This would be a boon to the SD *Reynolds* like no other," he called.

Reynolds bit back a groan at the male's enthusiasm.

"We'll discuss this with Gorad," Reynolds answered, clearly hoping Takal would leave it at that.

Of course, he didn't.

Too excited to see Reynolds' subtle attempt at quieting him, Takal went on, "This would change everything, Reynolds. We would no longer need to barter for foodstuffs. We could create our own and truly be independent of external—"

Jiya leaned in and pinched Takal's side. He grunted and spun around, wondering what had happened, and Jiya gave him a stern look, putting one finger to her lips.

Takal glared for a moment, appearing ready to say something, then suddenly looked guilty when he realized what he'd divulged. He groaned at his indiscretion.

"Oh, dear."

"This is most certainly impressive, although I've seen similar systems," Reynolds told L'Eliana, but Jiya knew the damage had been done.

Gorad understood the value the inventor placed on the food production devices and he'd undoubtedly seen his excitement. That would play a role in the negotiations moving forward.

Jiya took Takal by the arm on one side, and Geroux hooked his other arm with hers.

"Let's go to the hovercraft, Uncle," Geroux told him.

"I suppose that's for the best," he moaned, skulking toward it like a punished child.

Jiya glanced at Reynolds, who had already turned back to face L'Eliana.

"I suppose now is as good a time as any to speak with Gorad."

"Most certainly." L'Eliana smiled, accommodating as always. "He's looking forward to it."

Now more than ever, Jiya thought, leading Takal away. Maddox shuffled after them trying to capture any secrets that might be in the open, but he was denied. The systems particulars didn't reveal themselves.

"I wonder how things are going down there." Asya paced in front of the viewscreens, wishing she'd gone with the rest of the crew.

She hated waiting.

"Things are fine, or they would have notified us," Comm assured her.

"Or they could all be dead," Tactical countered. "We could be cut off from the rest of the crew, and they could be down there getting tortured and murdered as we speak. Torn to bits by robotic spiders or rabid, mutant orangutans."

"We've got them on the scanner," Comm confirmed, confidence in his voice. "Biostats are stable and well within range. No sign of spiders or monkeys, or even spider-monkeys."

"Or they could be fine," Tactical went on after Comm's declaration. "You never know."

Ria gasped, bolting upright at her station with her cheeks paling.

"See what you did, Tactical?" Asya grunted his way. "You've scared the probie with all your talk of torture."

"That's not what I'm..." Ria started to explain, her eyes growing wider and wider. "Oh...shit."

Klaxons sounded overhead as XO discovered what had spooked the young helmsman.

"A ship has appeared on the screens," Comm clarified, putting the image on the screen. At this distance, it was little more than a tiny dot despite magnification.

Asya stared at the viewscreen, examining the data. "That's impressive, Ensign," she commented. "That ship is at the very edge of the system. I'm surprised you managed to pick it up."

Ria sucked in a deep breath to calm her nerves. "I was... playing with the scanner settings, just kind of sweeping randomly as far out as I could to see what was out there to keep from being bored," she admitted.

"Well, looks like you landed a big fish on your first trip out," XO told her. "We're looking at a cruiser, based on its relative size. It appears to have Gated in at damn near the exact location where we did earlier."

"That's not suspicious at all," Tactical said. "There's no way their positioning was coincidental. They must have trailed our Etheric signature somehow and plotted a course based on it."

"Can they do that? Even if they did, her crew doesn't seem to realize we know she's there," XO announced. "I'm not getting any scans pinging us or the Grindlovian fleet or the defensive ring."

"I wasn't sending active signals while I was scanning," Ria explained, her cheeks flushing with color now that the initial scare had passed. "I was taking readings of the various gravity wells in the system and watching for anomalies. The ship triggered a wave as it Gated in and I caught sight of the motion, allowing me to zero in on it without alerting it to our presence."

"That's why they're running dark still," XO explained. "They came in stealthy and haven't realized the ensign here has spotted them. They're orienting to our position before they do anything else."

"However she managed it, it worked out perfectly," Asya replied, slipping into Reynolds' captain's chair to more closely examine the intel the *Reynolds* was feeding across the screen. "It gives us a few minutes to sneak a peek and see who and what we're looking at without letting them know we've got our eyes on them."

"Should we notify Reynolds?" Ria asked.

Asya cracked her knuckles and leaned over the console to work. "Not yet. Let's see what we've got first, then we can worry the captain with the details." She motioned to Comm. "Eyes on that ship. Cross-reference the shape and design in the databases and let's see who the hell is following us. I want to know who we're dealing with."

CHAPTER FIVE

Jiya and the crew found themselves in a domed meeting chamber, a different one than where they'd earlier met the Council.

A round table occupied the center of the room and several Telluride servants brought in chairs for the crew. Maddox found a spot, and Jiya sat alongside Reynolds, with Geroux to her right. Takal sat beside his niece, eyes gleaming and distant. Jiya realized he was still contemplating the agroprinters they'd seen a short while ago.

Drinks were prepared for the crew, and L'Eliana hovered nearby to refill them after the rest of the servants vacated the room. San Paget returned to join her, standing nearby and offering the crew various snacks. Takal took one of each, examining them as if they might spill the secret of their creation right then and there.

A massive viewscreen filled the far wall, and Jiya watched it carefully, wondering if Gorad was watching them through its dark surface.

As she narrowed her eyes and tried to see through the screen, she heard the hiss of the door at her back. She glanced over her shoulder to see an android form step into the room.

She understood almost intuitively that this was Gorad himself.

The android moved fluidly but with a hitch about every third step. It was subtle, but it gave her the impression that the android was limping.

The android had taken on the form of one of the Grindlovians, which made seeing it walk under its own power even odder. Its blue skin was a deeper shade than any of the people Jiya had seen so far. She presumed it had been their original coloration before Gorad had stepped in and taken control of their lives and planet.

The form was thin, though it didn't have the skeletal appearance of the rest of the Grindlovians.

Jiya wondered why it had packed itself into a body at all, given that Gorad had first approached them as a formless AI.

Then it struck her.

Gorad was imitating Reynolds, wanting to show that he too could be more than just an AI.

"Greetings, Reynolds and crew," Gorad said as he strode to the far end of the table. "We meet in person at last."

Or something almost *resembling a person,* Jiya thought. She acknowledged his presence with a tight nod.

Reynolds adjusted his body in his seat as he took in the other AI's form, and Jiya was certain she saw a smile flicker across his metal face before he returned to a neutral expression.

Jiya bit back a chuckle.

Gorad's android form remained standing, staring down upon everyone, apparently as some sort of power move. She'd seen her father do the same thing more times than she could recall and hadn't recognized it for what it was. It seemed obvious through the dispassionate lens of her first officer's eyes.

"I hear you enjoyed your tour of our facilities," Gorad said, his eyes scanning the crew and examining Takal before shifting to Reynolds.

"We did indeed," Reynolds replied. "We especially liked seeing the droid assembly."

Gorad's android body grinned, and it was just as disturbing as the old bot body Reynolds had used when they'd first met. Jiya cringed, remembering it.

"*That* was what you found interesting?" Gorad asked. "I think not."

Reynolds apparently decided to drop the act.

"You know well enough that my crew..." Reynolds glanced at Takal, and the old inventor suddenly found some fluff to pick off his uniform, "found your agro-printers fascinating," he told Gorad. "It's not as if you haven't been watching our every move since we were picked up from the ship."

Gorad shrugged. "I will admit, I am curious about you. I knew when you first appeared in our space that you were different from any of the other beings I've interacted with since my creation by the Grindlovians."

"It's my wit and charm and all-around good looks that set me apart," Reynolds said with a laugh. "And my humility."

"It was the level of your technology, if we're being honest," Gorad countered, his grin growing broader and exponentially creepier. "I was impressed by how easily you repelled my earlier scans. That's not an easy task."

"I don't like being probed," Reynolds replied.

Despite the dangerous turn of the conversation, Jiya couldn't help chuckling. She coughed and covered her face.

Reynolds glared in her direction before turning back to face Gorad.

"Regardless," Reynolds went on, "it appears we have the basis of our negotiations. We would like the agroprinter tech, for a start."

"And I, in turn, would like to scrape your databases," Gorad fired back without hesitation.

"A brazen request." Reynolds scoffed. "I can see you went to the *Let's Make a Deal* school of negotiating, but asking for the sky isn't going to get a deal made."

"You've told me what you want, and I've told you what I want," Gorad said with another shrug. "I wonder which of us will get their wish when we're done here."

"Certainly not you if you don't start from a point closer to reality," Reynolds told him, shaking his head. "Whoever told you to aim for the stars apparently never taught you about Icarus."

"Who's Icarus?" Geroux asked in a whisper.

"Some bird someone set on fire or something," Jiya answered, trying to recall the tale. "That's all I remember from the Earth history Reynolds made me watch. Pretty boring stuff, if you ask me."

"I don't know who you reference..." Gorad started.

"He's not the only one," Maddox mumbled.

"But I certainly recognize the mocking tone you've adopted." Gorad waved impatiently at San Paget, who grabbed a chair and raced over, setting it close behind the android before stepping away. Gorad sat with a flourish. "It would appear we've begun negotiations in earnest, Reynolds."

"I wonder if Earnest and Icarus are related," Geroux said with an annoyed sigh as she sat back. "Not knowing is going to bug me."

Ka'nak had sat still for as long as he possibly could.

Which wasn't very long, given that the couch felt like a padded brick.

Eventually—it was more than likely less than five minutes after the others had left—he'd wandered off and left the guest chambers behind. Once outside, he picked a random direction and made his way down the sidewalk of the quiet town.

Much like when they'd first driven past, there was little in the way of traffic either on the streets or on the sidewalks. He passed a few Grindlovians who could not be bothered to twist an eye his direction.

Their Telluride servants, however, were all smiles and bright glances.

He waved to each and was happily surprised to find how approachable they were, given the nature of the Grindlovians. After several encounters where he'd had pleasant, albeit short, exchanges with passersby, he finally found his way to an area of town where Telluride resided en masse.

One minute he was strolling along mostly alone, oblivious to everything around him, whistling and going over combat moves in his head, and the next he bumped into a stout Telluride, who grinned up at him with bright teeth.

"Oh, my apologies, sir," the Telluride told him, stepping back to offer Ka'nak the right of way.

Ka'nak glanced about, surprised to see himself nearly surrounded by Telluride.

"No, it's me who should—" he started, not managing to get the rest of the words out.

For the first time in a half-dozen blocks or more, Ka'nak was now paying attention. What he saw amazed him.

The gray blur that had been the planet so far had effectively been wiped away.

All around him, color blossomed. Paintings adorned nearly every wall, and bright, welcoming flowers flourished in troughs beneath almost every window.

There was so much brilliance that Ka'nak had to pause a moment to let his vision adjust.

It was shocking.

He remembered looking down at the planet as the shuttle brought them in, but he couldn't recall seeing any of the colors prevalent in this area. He wondered if the approach vectors had been designed to prevent overflight of the Telluride sector.

In the skies, he caught a wavering edge of haze that obscured the sun.

He realized that the sky was muted. He could barely make out the planet's twin suns burning in the distant sky, the smaller one circling the larger of the pair. As he followed the haze's trail, he could see that it enveloped the city like a spiderweb draped across its roofs.

"The shade," the Telluride said, noticing Ka'nak's gaze. "The Grindlovians find our displays gaudy, so Gorad laid a deflective screen over our designated portion of the town. It mutes the colors from on high so the Grindlovians are not forced to confront them as they travel through the air."

Ka'nak glanced down at the friendly alien and grimaced. "I'm surprised they can muster the energy to notice."

The Telluride let out a soft laugh. "They *have* become quite set in their ways, most certainly. Still, if Gorad believes that hiding our nature from them is best, we, too, believe that is true."

Ka'nak couldn't hold back the soft growl that escaped his lips. He hated the idea that people had to pretend to be someone else; to be different just so that others wouldn't be bothered by who they were.

"That seems rather…divisive," he admitted. "I don't like that."

"It is for a peaceful existence, and no inconvenience to us," the alien told him.

Ka'nak shrugged. "If you say so."

The alien mimicked his shrug. "It is what it is, my friend. I am San Roche. It is a pleasure to meet you, off-worlder."

"I am Ka'nak. I am from Lariest, and it is an honor to meet you," Ka'nak replied, extending a hand to the alien.

To Ka'nak's surprise, San Roche understood the gesture and reached out to shake hands.

Ka'nak was impressed by the male's grip.

"Whoa!" Ka'nak muttered. "You're clearly a person who works hard."

San Roche smiled. "It is our lot in life to work hard, my friend."

The Melowi warrior gestured to the brilliant world around them. "And to create, I see."

"Absolutely." San Roche nodded. "We would be nothing without our art."

Ka'nak took more time to examine his surroundings, marveling at the amazing effort the Telluride had made to make their world stand out. The murals he'd noticed earlier hadn't simply been painted on the lower walls, but were everywhere.

Buildings that stretched into the sky were plastered in so many colors that they looked like rainbows after a storm.

And unlike the dreary and drab existence of the Grindlovian part of the planet, where Ka'nak had struggled to tell one district from another, one person from another, the Telluride were individuals, each distinct, each vibrant, and each unique.

Though they dressed in a subdued manner when venturing outside their designated area, toning down their natural inclination toward outrageousness, here they were themselves.

San Roche wore a gaudy yellow shirt with a collar and short sleeves. Images of orange, red, and green fruits Ka'nak couldn't identify were splashed across the shirt haphazardly, as if the printer had had a seizure while designing it.

There was no rhyme or reason to the style. San Roche's pants were little different, save that they were an incandescent purple and did not even remotely match the sea-blue boots he wore.

And San Roche was one of the tamest of the Telluride Ka'nak could see.

They wore colors almost as a badge of honor, a gleaming defiance of the plain nothingness of the Grindlovian world that surrounded them.

Ka'nak thought it was a bit much but appreciated the active defiance against the gray and bland Grindlovian area. He respected the tenacity with which the Telluride clung to their differences.

A loud bell rang, and Ka'nak watched in awe as the aliens stopped to listen raptly. Once its resonance had faded, everyone dropped what they were doing—be it shopping or simply chatting with one another—and marched in the same direction.

Before Ka'nak could ask San Roche what the bell meant, the alien took him by the arm.

"It is feeding time, my friend," San Roche announced. "Come, eat with us."

"I never say no to food." Ka'nak smiled broadly, licking his lips in anticipation. "Lead the way."

San Roche chuckled and did just that.

They wove deeper into town, and Ka'nak couldn't help but stare. The farther they got from the edges where the Grindlovian and Telluride societies met, the more artistically chaotic the town became.

Splashes of paint marked the walkways and windows and everything else that hadn't been taken up by the murals or individual works of art that adorned nearly every surface.

It was as if the Telluride had handed each member a bucket of paint and a brush and turned them loose on their world.

"This is…amazing," Ka'nak told San Roche, unable to think of a better word to describe the overload of artistic expression.

"We have perhaps gone a bit too far," San Roche admitted, still grinning, "but it is who we truly are. We cannot be bound by the bleakness of Grindlovian society."

With brightly dressed Telluride milling around them, San Roche led the Melowi warrior into a great hall. They found a seat easily despite the crowd; Ka'nak was surprised to see how polite and kind the people were.

There must have been hundreds of aliens in tight-knit groups around him, yet he heard no complaints or angry voices rising in the midst of the friendly chatter and pleasant conversation.

He'd bumped into several of the aliens as he found his seat, yet not a single one said a foul word or even glanced in his direction with anything besides kindness.

They apologized and smiled, hands petting and patting for emphasis, and each found their place without conflict.

Servers ran among the tables, a system as precise and accurate as any Gorad could devise, and soon there were plates in front of everyone. A young female smiled at Ka'nak as she served him, setting a bright pink drink next to his plate and running a hand across his shoulders as she passed.

He sat there a moment after she'd gone, watching as the mass of aliens began to eat.

There was no dimming of the low roar of friendly conversations. The Telluride conversed without pause as they ate, the clank of utensils adding to the miasma of sound.

"Eat, my friend," San Roche told him. "We have plenty, so do not hesitate to ask for more."

Ka'nak turned to his plate. It overflowed with a variety of food, its freshness both surprising and daunting.

He couldn't remember ever eating such a fine meal.

He dove in with gusto, matching the gleeful noises around him, and before long he realized his plate was empty and his glass was dry.

The young female returned as if she'd been watching, and refilled his glass and set another plate before him.

"Eat, friend," she told him, offering a pleasing smile. "We rarely have guests, so we would like to make sure you have had your fill."

"This is delicious," Ka'nak replied, "and quite generous. Thank you."

The female went about her business with a parting wave. Ka'nak's eyes followed her for a moment before he turned back to San Roche. His forehead scrunched as he contemplated.

"Can I ask you a question?"

"Of course," San Roche said, never once losing his smile. "Ask away."

"I don't understand why you work for the Grindlovians." Ka'nak had lowered his voice so as not to be overheard by the other Telluride sitting nearby. He didn't want to offend the people with his curiosity or judgment. "They are so…different than your people."

"It is how it has always been," San Roche explained. "Since Gorad came to be, the Telluride have catered to the whims of the Grindlovians. In exchange, we are allowed to live as we always have, free to create and be ourselves."

"Yet you have to follow these people around and do everything for them," Ka'nak said with an exasperated huff. He couldn't imagine catering to what he considered a race of selfish and unmotivated people.

"Yes, but it is not a bad thing, as you so clearly believe," San Roche argued. "We relish the opportunity, in fact."

"Really?" Ka'nak wondered. "To be slaves?"

San Roche chuckled. "We are not slaves, my friend," he replied. "The Grindlovians do not own us, and they do not tell us what to do."

"Forgive my ignorance, then," Ka'nak started, "but how can you do all that you do for them and still feel as if you are free?"

"Because we are," San Roche assured. "We are not bound by chains or laws. We do what we do for the Grindlovians because it benefits us, too."

"How so?" Ka'nak wondered briefly if his questions bothered the alien, but San Roche showed no indication of annoyance. His genuine smile was still firmly in place.

"We learn much from the Grindlovians and Gorad through our interactions," he answered. "Our children are provided an education, and we as a people have no need of anything." He gestured to the room around them.

Ka'nak's gaze drifted about of its own accord, seeing the happy, smiling faces that dominated the room. He stared for a moment, half-expecting the veneer to crack at any moment, but it didn't happen.

No frowns broke out among the faces, no furious arguments or complaints. The people looked happy to him. Truly happy.

It is almost unnatural, Ka'nak thought, stifling a laugh at the thought. *Who am I to judge how they should be happy?*

For a male who'd spent his life fighting, to see a species getting along so well was odd, to say the least.

"But do you people not fight with one another?" the Melowi warrior asked. "Even if only once in a while?"

"There are disagreements, certainly," San Roche told him, "but we are united as Telluride. We work to overcome our differences and better ourselves. It is our way."

Ka'nak settled into his seat with a grunt. "You live in a damned utopia," he muttered.

"Hardly," San Roche countered, "but we do not expend energy fighting against ourselves or fighting against something that doesn't need to be changed. We are united in our betterment and our advancement. To fight amongst ourselves would only make us weaker."

"I admire your beliefs." Ka'nak offered the alien a nod of respect. "I still find it strange that you submit to the Grindlovians." He glanced about. "It seems to me as though you are the better people."

San Roche offered a softly reproachful smile. "We are no better than the Grindlovians, my friend. We are simply different."

Ka'nak loosed a gruff chuckle. "You are by far a better person than I," he told the alien. "Were I to be made to chase the tail of a lazy being so devoted to its own atrophy that it topped all other priorities, I think I'd go mad."

"We're all a little mad in our own way," San Roche assured. "We express ours in art, and the Grindlovians express their madness in acceptance. Though we travel different paths, we find ourselves in the same place at the end."

Ka'nak leaned back, grinning. "You are a wise person, San Roche."

The alien laughed. "You should tell that to my spouse," he said. "She does not believe such."

"They never do, friend," Ka'nak assured him. "They never do."

CHAPTER SIX

The talks went on and on and on...

Jiya groaned, her eyes glazing at listening to the two AIs go back and forth about every minute detail regarding the agroprinters and more.

Much, much more.

The pair of AIs had strayed from negotiations into some kind of metaphysical theory Jiya couldn't follow, nor did she really want to.

They discussed astrophysics as it related to Grindlevik 3 and the Grindlevik system as a whole, and how it compared to Earth, to Lariest, and a dozen other worlds Reynolds had visited over his time being integrated into the superdreadnought.

He'd been to multiple galaxies, apparently.

Then they got into discussing black holes and space anomalies, arguing the smallest details based on their relative knowledge of the subject and experiences.

The technical discourse was a wall of white noise to

Jiya. Physics and engineering were not, nor would they ever be her specialty. They would never rise to the status of mildly interesting, even.

For her, the most engaging part was when the AIs started talking about the Etheric dimension, mostly because of Reynolds' reaction to Gorad's bringing it up.

The chrome body stiffened at the mention of it, and he sat upright as if he were a dog ready to pounce on a tossed bone.

His eyes gleamed in his chrome skull, and his hands gripped the table's edge. The slightest of creaks from the wood let them know just how excited he was before he reined in his enthusiasm and relaxed.

Still, if Jiya had seen the reaction, Gorad damn well had. It had likely given the alien AI another bargaining chip in their negotiations, as far as Jiya understood it. The alien AI's knowledge of the Etheric meant that the people of Grindlevik 3 had come in contact with the Kurtherians sometime in the past. The big question was whether they had left. If they had gone, where? If not, there would be a reckoning with the superdreadnought bringing the thunder and lightning.

Maybe Gorad was a Kurtherian. Jiya had no idea what they looked like. Reynolds remained evasive regarding their physical attributes, the only descriptor being their ability to access and use the power of the Etheric.

Reynolds dove deeply into the topic, questioning the nature of the Kurtherian influence and where the aliens had gone since.

The Larians couldn't keep up. They had overview

knowledge only, no more than a footnote to their existence.

And in true AI form, neither could be bothered to answer a question directly nor explain anything fully. Each held back, filling the space with a blur of seemingly nonsensical words.

She'd been ready to pull her hair out five minutes into the discussion. She was ready to pull her whole head off after two hours.

"Forgive me," she finally blurted, waving her hands when she could take no more. "I think we'll leave you two to talk things over while the rest of us go and explore a bit."

Reynolds glanced at her, but she couldn't read his expression, and at that moment in time, she didn't care.

"Hit us up on the comm if you need us," Jiya told Reynolds, clambering to her feet and stretching. It felt as if every muscle in her body had atrophied while she sat there.

She wondered if that was what had happened to the Grindlovians.

They'd been bored to flaccidity.

She grinned at the thought, only wiping the smile away when Gorad's android eyes locked on her. Jiya waved.

"Thank you for your kindness," she told the AI, then motioned to the Telluride servants. "And to you two, as well."

Gorad spoke to L'Eliana, "Why don't you and San Paget show our guests around?" he suggested, though Jiya was sure it was more of an order; his way of ensuring the crew didn't wander too far or out of sight.

The Telluride grinned. "Of course," she replied, coming

over to stand alongside Jiya and the others. San Paget joined them. "Shall we?" she asked Jiya.

"We shall," Jiya answered, motioning for L'Eliana to lead the way.

The Telluride obliged, walking smartly away as the door to the room slid open.

"Have fun," Jiya told Reynolds as they left.

Outside, she drew in a deep breath and let it out slowly, grateful to be away from the mind-numbing AI negotiations.

The others obviously felt the same way.

"My back is killing me," Takal complained.

"Can someone help me stop my brain from oozing out of my ears?" Geroux mumbled so only the crew could hear. "I mean, I love science talk, but that was more than a bit excessive."

"Two AIs waving their robot dicks around," Maddox laughed.

Their Telluride hosts led them away, and the crew followed to another hovercraft. They climbed in, and the craft took off.

"Where are we going?" Jiya asked after a moment, realizing she hadn't suggested they go anywhere specific. The Telluride were traveling of their own accord, or more likely Gorad's.

L'Eliana smiled. "You've seen much of the Grindlovian experience for the day, so we figured you might enjoy some time among our people," she answered. "The dinner bell has passed, unfortunately, but we can collect some food at one of the halls and show you around after, if that is okay."

"Sounds perfect," Geroux replied, rubbing her belly.

"Are your foodstuffs created by the devices you showed us earlier?" Takal asked.

"All of it is," she answered. "The agro sector maintains all of our food supplies, both for the Telluride and the Grindlovians."

"We apologize that we did not have the time or wherewithal to adjust one of the printers to meet your specific food needs," San Paget told them, "but we believe what we have to offer is sufficient and hopefully healthy. Gorad has no information on Larian physiology by which to change the printer dynamics."

"Any kind of food to stuff in my mouth is plenty sufficient," Geroux told the alien, grinning. Her stomach rumbled loud enough that Jiya heard it.

The first officer laughed at her friend.

"We better feed you before you fade away," she joked, pinching Geroux's thin arm. She leaned in close so no one but Geroux could hear her. "We might have to paint you blue and get you a robo-chair soon."

Geroux shook her head at the jibe. "I'll pass, thanks."

A short drive later, the crew sat wide-eyed, staring at the abrupt change in the environment. It was as if the vehicle had passed an invisible line, and someone had turned up the volume on the world's colors.

"Wow!" was all Geroux could manage to spit out.

Takal looked behind them instead of ahead. "There's some sort of distortion barrier separating the town," he said.

"The Shade," San Paget explained. "It keeps our living

area separate from the eyes of the Grindlovians so we do not offend them."

"How can this offend them?" Geroux asked, fire in her voice.

San Paget shrugged. "We are different, after all."

"That's hardly an explanation," Jiya complained. "Your differences should be celebrated, not—"

"Tolerated," Maddox finished for her, and she nodded at him.

L'Eliana went to speak, but Jiya waved her to silence.

"Forgive me," Jiya told the Telluride. "We don't mean to criticize. We simply don't understand your relationship with the Grindlovians."

"Or with Gorad, for that matter," Maddox said.

Jiya stiffened in her seat suddenly, remembering that Gorad could likely hear them since his mechanical essence was piloting the hovercraft they were riding in. She bit back a hiss and tried to look anywhere other than at the general.

But L'Eliana only smiled, catching Jiya's wayward looks. "The Shade serves a second purpose," she admitted. "Gorad does not come into our world uninvited."

"He respects our boundaries," San Paget went on, "so do not fear that he is listening here. He is not, I assure you."

Jiya sighed with relief but didn't fully believe him. Who was driving the hover car? "That is good news," she started, then clarified, "Not that it's a bad thing that he takes care of you."

L'Eliana laughed. "It must be an odd situation to those from the outside looking in."

"You can say that again," Takal added.

"It must be an odd situation to those from the outside looking in," L'Eliana repeated in all earnestness.

"No, I, uh, meant..." Takal stammered.

Jiya chuckled. "Figure of speech," she explained to the Telluride. "He didn't actually mean for you to repeat what you said."

"It is strange that you would say something but not actually mean it," San Paget said, scratching the side of his head.

"A cultural thing," Maddox clarified, "much like our confusion as to your existence."

"That perfectly explains why we think your culture as strange as you do ours," Jiya continued. "We'll learn from you, as we hope you will learn from us."

"We would like that," L'Eliana replied, and San Paget nodded his agreement.

The craft pulled up at a large hall with massive doors leading in, and Jiya couldn't help but gawk at the swirl of colors everywhere.

She'd gotten so used to the dull gray in the short time she'd been immersed in it, and now it was as if she'd fallen asleep and slipped into the most majestic of dreams.

The Telluride led the way inside the hall. More of their kind stood on the street and in the doorway, smiling and waving at the newcomers.

Caught up in the spectacle of it all, the crew failed to see Ka'nak sitting at one of the tables.

"I see you tracked me down," he complained, his voice a harsh bark after the melodic tones of their Telluride hosts.

"Ka'nak!" Geroux cried out, racing over to hug him.

"I thought you were in the guest chambers," Maddox told him.

The Melowi shrugged. "Got bored and hungry."

Jiya grinned. "There appears to be plenty of that going around."

The crew joined Ka'nak and plopped down beside him and his Telluride companion.

"This is San Roche," Ka'nak introduced. He pointed to the crew and named each in turn.

"My pleasure to meet you, my friends," San Roche replied, smiling all the while. "Ka'nak here is an interesting companion. You must be proud to adventure with such a prolific and powerful warrior."

Jiya burst into laughter. "Oh, we are quite proud of our warrior," she said, reaching over and pinching Ka'nak's cheek. "What a good little warrior you are."

Ka'nak smacked her hand away. "Hey now, don't kill the messenger because you don't like the message," he told her.

"Does that apply when the messenger creates the message all on his own?" Maddox asked.

"It is still true," Ka'nak argued.

"That it is." Jiya smiled, resting a hand on Ka'nak's shoulder. "So, how's the food here?" she asked, spying the handful of empty plates littering the table in front of the Melowi.

"It is amazing," he admitted, going so far as to lick his lips.

The crew got a chance to say that for themselves when servants fluttered out and put plates before them, setting up a small buffet for them to pick at.

Takal stuffed a piece of meat into his mouth and

groaned, juice dripping down his chin. "This is fantastic," he exclaimed. "I can't believe all this is manufactured." He loaded his mouth with more food, making it so full that he could no longer speak. He simply moaned and ate more.

Jiya sampled the meal and felt the same way. If they could get the agroprinters installed in the SD *Reynolds,* that would be a major accomplishment. *We need this,* she thought.

She hoped Reynolds managed to work things out with Gorad, although she knew both of the AIs would go out of their way to get the most from the negotiations. Reynolds would be forced to abandon the agroprinters if the price Gorad demanded was too high.

Jiya took a bite of a succulent fruit she'd never tasted before, and a jolt of energy filled her. It was better than any cup of coffee she'd ever had. She hoped Gorad was reasonable.

She needed more of this fruit in her life.

"What do you call this?" Jiya asked.

"Rushfruit," L'Eliana answered. "It is quite delicious, is it not?"

"So very much," Jiya drooled as she ate another piece, once more feeling her body fill with energy.

"I would suggest you eat no more just yet," San Paget chuckled. "It can be quite overpowering until your system is used to it."

Jiya grinned, already feeling the effects of the fruit. She could barely sit still, squirming in her chair and feeling the strange urge to run a marathon or twelve.

"I love this stuff!"

Geroux took a bite of one of the fruits and grinned maniacally. "Oh…wow!"

"Right?" Jiya agreed, her trembling hand wanting to grab another piece. She restrained herself.

Barely.

"I wonder if…" she started, her mind running a million miles an hour. She struggled to keep up with her thoughts. "I wonder if there is something we can do to help share our various cultures with you and learn about yours in the process."

"We could teach them?" Geroux asked, eyes gleaming from the fruit.

"That's a fantastic idea," Jiya exclaimed. "We could show you some of the things we know and give your people a glimpse at our cultures. Show you something you've never experienced before. We could begin right away."

L'Eliana and Sans Paget and Roche smiled.

"That would be perfect," L'Eliana replied.

"Though," San Roche interrupted, "we would be required to do this elsewhere."

San Paget nodded. "Yes. Gorad would wish to witness such a transfer of knowledge, as would the Grindlovians, no doubt."

"I don't see an issue with that," Jiya replied slowly, frowning because of the inevitable delay before any action.

It wasn't as if they carried the kind of information Reynolds did. Nothing they would show or explain to the Telluride or Grindlovians would be a life-altering intelligence coup like letting the Telluride in on the most destructive Federation technology. Besides Takal and Geroux, no one else had an inkling of how it all worked.

No, what the crew had to offer the alien species would be more of a cultural thing, a piece of each of the worlds that made the crew who they were.

"We could split into groups," Jiya suggested, "each of us showing the Telluride a different aspect of our individual skill sets."

"I could teach them to fight!" Ka'nak exclaimed, squeezing San Roche's muscular arm. "They would make amazing warriors, these people."

"And we could teach them more about the sciences," Geroux explained, motioning to herself and her uncle. "But not that crap that Reynolds and Gorad were babbling on about," she finished with a laugh. "No, more realistic stuff they can use to better their day to day lives around here."

"I don't believe there is anything we need," L'Eliana countered. "Gorad takes care of all our needs, but I am still interested in learning."

"That's the spirit," Jiya replied.

"That's just it, L'Eliana," Geroux went on. "Just because you don't know that you need something doesn't mean that there isn't something you could actually use."

"I cannot picture anything," San Paget said, "but I agree. We do not know what we do not know."

"Wisdom," Takal said, raising his glass in cheers.

The Telluride simply stared at him.

"See?" Geroux giggled. "You're proving our point."

She reached out and clinked glasses with her uncle, grinning all the while. The Telluride tentatively followed suit.

"Then we're in agreement?" Jiya asked.

"I believe we are," L'Eliana told her, reaching out and taking Jiya's hand in hers.

Jiya grinned, loving the easy-going nature of the Telluride.

They laughed and smiled and weren't afraid to show their feelings or express their joy. They were the exact opposite of the Grindlovians, who had apparently retreated into themselves so much so that it had impacted their physical state.

While both species relied on Gorad to take care of them, each did so in their own way.

The Telluride, although they were fed and sheltered and maintained by Gorad's systems, reveled in the things they'd been offered. They absorbed them, made them a part of their lives and world, embracing them yet never letting the things overwhelm them.

They just lived and let nothing get in the way.

The Grindlovians, however, relied on their tools to the point of apathy.

Rather than take a tool and enrich their lives by using it, they let it do all the work, separating them from the action. Their method of elevation was to allow the tool to act in their stead, relieving themselves of the task.

Jiya grunted as she contemplated the difference between the two species and wondered how those differences would play a role in her plans to share cultures.

Would the Grindlovians learn anything from this? she wondered.

She realized that they would, although maybe not as directly as the Telluride.

The Grindlovians relied on their Telluride servants to

do everything for them, much like they did with Gorad when the Telluride were not around.

By showing the Telluride new skills, and by default showing Gorad, what the two species learned would leak into the Grindlovian world through the others.

While Ka'nak might show San Roche how to fight, and Jiya knew the Grindlovians would never use or need such a skill, they would be better served by San Roche's increase in strength and disciplined mindset.

Jiya grinned.

She might not be able to teach the Grindlovians any sort of self-sufficiency, a trait they clearly deemed beneath them, but she had no doubt she could help advance the culture as a whole by helping the Telluride learn more about the world beyond the main city on Grindlevik 3.

And it would certainly help the crew to pass the time while Reynolds and Gorad hashed out their agreements, and it might even help persuade the alien AI to be less hawkish with the negotiations.

He would be learning much more than what Reynolds was willing to let slip by watching the crew and their interactions with the Telluride and Grindlovians.

She smiled as another thought danced across her brain.

Plus, I won't have to listen to Reynolds and Gorad argue.

Bonus!

CHAPTER SEVEN

"I truly wonder if your purpose here is to benefit from our knowledge at all," Gorad told Reynolds, clearly exasperated.

Reynolds wasn't in much better shape. He thumped his metallic fists on the table and leaned back in his seat, groaning.

"We'd get a lot farther if you would make an effort to be reasonable," Reynolds complained.

"I *am* being quite reasonable," Gorad argued. "Simply because you cannot identify reason is not cause for you to blame me for not availing you of it."

Reynolds chuckled.

"Your offer to dredge databases doesn't even *resemble* reasonable," he complained. "I can't and won't let you trawl my systems. We need to come to an equitable trade of information here."

"Perhaps our creators used different dictionaries,"

Gorad said, "since it is clear we do not speak the same language."

"Hence the negotiations, Gorad," Reynolds countered, trying not to lose his temper along with his patience.

He was suddenly envious of Jiya and the crew, wandering off and finding something else to pass the time while he was stuck here arguing with an intellectual giant of a moron.

"You want the agroprinters, yes?" Gorad asked.

"You know I do," Reynolds replied. "But you *do* realize some of my crew are technical geniuses, correct?" he challenged, pushing the other AI. "While they might not know the specifics, I can assure you they are contemplating how to adapt the technology they saw into reality."

Gorad shrugged. "If it were it as simple as that, neither of us would be in this room, now would we?"

Reynolds grunted. He didn't appreciate the other AI being right.

"The concept of the agroprinters is quite simple," Gorad admitted, "but the nature of foodstuff source and its composition and makeup are quite another thing. You could spend an eternity attempting to align the recipes perfectly and never manage anything more than a gruel with which to slop animals." Gorad chuckled.

Sadly, Reynolds knew Gorad was right. Reynolds suspected Takal could figure it out eventually. The male was beyond a genius, but Reynolds couldn't picture Takal having the time to dedicate to it.

With their journeys across the universe and Takal's age factored in, the old scientist simply couldn't spend all of his efforts on the foodstuff creation process.

And knowing what Reynolds did of Takal's inventing process, he couldn't imagine anyone—except maybe Geroux—following him and making any sense of what the old male had drafted.

He was as unique in his efforts as he was a person, Reynolds realized. That didn't leave the AI much room to negotiate.

"Do you worry that I might learn more of the Etheric?" Gorad asked, surprising Reynolds with the question.

"To be completely honest, yes," Reynolds replied. "It's clear you have some experience in it, some knowledge, but I've yet to determine exactly how much and from where it was gleaned."

"Agreeing to my terms would answer that very question," Gorad shot back.

"But at what cost?" Reynolds countered. "Should all your knowledge be conjecture and unverified hearsay, then I'm opening the door to your advancement in a way I'm not comfortable with. A way my *people* would not be comfortable with."

Bethany Anne would kick my fucking idiot ass if I did something so stupid.

"Then the concern is simply the degree of my knowledge in the topic?" Gorad asked.

"That's certainly the main one," Reynolds told him. "I can't hand you technology that would advance you beyond expectations," he admitted. "To do so opens the universe and my people to untold risk. I simply won't endanger them for knowledge I will eventually gain anyway."

"So, you would risk walking away with nothing from

our talks to stand rigidly on a point you're entirely unsure of?"

Reynolds sneered. "Well, when you put it that way—"

"What other way is there to put it?" Gorad chided. "I know of the Etheric dimension and I have personal knowledge of the Kurtherians but, like you, I cannot willingly divulge the limits of my intelligence on either subject."

"Then we're at a stalemate," Reynolds admitted.

"Perhaps not," Gorad told him, letting a grin play across his android features. "I have an idea."

"This should be good," Reynolds muttered.

Ka'nak paced in front of the line of Telluride who'd volunteered to learn how to fight. Dozens of Grindlovians sat on the sidelines, watching impassively from their chairs as if staring at the wind.

The Melowi shook his head and looked away from the weak Grindlovians. He would never understand how someone could let themselves become so atrophied that they could do nothing but think. Raising their hands or feet was a chore for the frail beings, which sickened Ka'nak.

As a warrior he prided himself on his strength and prowess, constantly working to better himself in all aspects of the martial arts.

When he wasn't picturing new moves and practicing them, he was honing his body to perfection. Without that, all his skill was wasted.

He needed his physical and mental aptitude to be on the same level or he would fail, and in Ka'nak's world that usually meant death.

Of course, he'd been beaten now and again, but he'd never given up and, more importantly, he'd never stopped advancing. Even in defeat he'd grown and learned, and come back stronger and smarter and better than he had been.

There'd been only three battles in his life where he had not avenged himself on those who had beaten him.

In two of those cases, the opportunity to exact retribution and even the scales simply hadn't coalesced. They would someday, and he would be ready.

The last defeat, his most distressing, had been against a foe he had yet to overcome.

Gilshu Rea flashed through his mind, and Ka'nak grimaced at the image of her.

She had defeated him more times than Ka'nak dared admit even to himself, but that did not stop him from bettering his skills and imagining yet another conflict with the warrior.

One day, he pledged, he would be victorious.

Until then, he had people to train.

He grinned again as he imagined the thrill of combat and what he could make of these stout Telluride.

He'd spent the morning showing them the basic stances, adjusting them through the moves slowly and helping to align and guide their limbs and bodies to facilitate the motions.

Ka'nak had been impressed. The Telluride were natural

learners, which he'd suspected. They were willing to learn as well, which was even more important to the process.

"Okay, people," Ka'nak called, "line up across from each other. We're going to test some of what I've shown you by sparring. Light sparring, to be exact."

The Telluride did as he asked, forming two lines that faced each other, randomly setting themselves against their friends and companions.

"Perfect," Ka'nak complimented them, unable to stop smiling.

Maddox circled the group, making sure each was aligned and ready. "Good to go," he called.

Ka'nak nodded before glancing at the assembled Telluride. More had joined the watching crowd, and a number of Grindlovians had too. All eyes were on the spectacle before them, and Ka'nak could almost feel Gorad's presence in the throng.

He knew the AI would be watching despite still being caught up with Reynolds.

"I'd rather watch this too." The Melowi laughed, picturing the sheer boredom of sitting in a room with two arrogant AIs who were trying to outsmart one another.

"Okay, let's start," Ka'nak said, clapping his hands.

The would-be warriors started forward with hesitant steps, scraping their feet on the dirt that filled the large empty lot they'd chosen to train in. Dust kicked up around their heels, and Ka'nak grunted his disappointment.

"Confidence is key!" he shouted, waving the combatants on. "To hesitate is to be left behind or to die alone."

The Telluride sped up their advance. They were an

eager people, if nothing else. Ka'nak eyed them critically, looking for those who would stand out as if he were selecting fodder for the games.

Maddox watched from behind the back ranks as the two lines collided.

Well, sort of collided, Ka'nak thought.

When the lines met, each of the hopeful warriors threw the exact same move at the exact same time. Fists thumped against fists, and the Telluride cried out in unison and staggered back.

Ka'nak sighed and waved them in again. Each of the fighters threw the next attack the Melowi had shown them, a simple lock kick, and again bone clashed against bone.

The Telluride hopped back, clutching their shins in agony.

Maddox raised his hands in amusement. "It might be best if we trained them for the stresses and impacts of combat first," the general suggested to Ka'nak.

The fighter nodded, but he wasn't quite ready to give up on the lesson.

He had been tossed into the pits at an early age and had learned to fight under the cruelest of teachers: life itself.

His survival had come at a cost, and Ka'nak felt the Telluride needed some of that fear and adrenaline to draw them out of the servitor stupor that had been all they'd ever known.

You could not make warriors out of comfortable people. They needed to hunger and feel the blood screaming through their veins, their hearts pumping, or they would never rise above themselves.

Sure, practice was a necessary evil in combat. You fought the way you trained, he remembered hearing his old pit master advise him.

And it was true.

Fighting was as much reacting as it was programming; a warrior studying a move until it becomes instinctive and part of a greater whole. Once that move was ingrained, the warrior could manipulate its motions in the midst of combat and make it even more effective based on what he'd gleaned from his opponent.

The Telluride, however, were simply too fresh to incorporate the moves he'd shown them into something more.

They were stepping forward and enacting the moves in the order Ka'nak and Maddox had trained, unable to think beyond that basic concept. As such, they would continue to mimic each other and clack body parts until one of them figured that out.

Ka'nak wondered how long that would take as he waved the Telluride back to the line once more.

"Again," he shouted, and to his delight, the servants did not hesitate.

They moved forward and clashed again, the group falling back once more after the next move in the limited arsenal they knew.

Except, one of the Telluride adapted, one named San Balu, foregoing the third move for the first. His opponent's blow whistled past his face—an elbow meant to be thrown up close, but it was nowhere near its target. San Belu grinned at the missed attack and fired a punch straight down the pipe.

It connected with the other Telluride's chin with a

brutal clack and sent the male stumbling backward. His legs gave out beneath him, and the Telluride flopped on his butt with a grunt. His eyes were glassy and unfocused as he stared up at the male who'd hit him, no recognition in his fogged brain. San Balu smiled and examined his fist as if he was amazed at what he'd managed.

"That's what I'm talking about!" Ka'nak shouted, jumping into the air and pumping a fist. "That's adaptation, adjusting mid-combat to counter what your opponent is trying to do."

Maddox went over and helped the stunned Telluride to his feet. He led him off to the side to recover as another took his place, joining the line and making ready.

"Now, get your heads straight and let's try that again," Ka'nak told the Telluride, who looked less interested in the process now that they'd seen one of their own be struck down.

Yet, Ka'nak could see the glimmer in the eyes of a few of the males, and it thrilled him to witness the light turning on. The concept of combat was foreign to the Telluride, but the Telluride were smart, and he could see them processing what their companion had done. San Balu had led the way, and Ka'nak could see the door opening in the minds of some of the others.

Maybe they would make true warriors after all.

"Fight!" Ka'nak called.

Jiya had decided on the way out of town that she would try

to teach the Telluride the survival skills she'd learned early in life despite her royal upbringing.

She'd been made to spend many a night outdoors, surviving off the streets and the woods neighboring her father's palace.

Well, she hadn't exactly been forced, seeing as how she'd run away of her own accord when she could have stayed home in a warm house with plenty of food, but that wasn't Jiya's desire.

She had resented her father's control of her life and rebelled at every opportunity. Sure, she could have had anything she wanted thanks to her father, but she wanted to make it on her own.

And she had, for the most part.

Survival was never easy when you had to learn it on your own. She planned to make the process more comfortable for the Telluride.

"This looks like a good spot," she announced, surveying the thick wilderness a short distance outside of town. A creek burbled somewhere at their backs, hidden by the trees, its sound soothing. Jiya stopped and closed her eyes to take in nature, something those who lived in starships had a great appreciation for.

Plus, the peace of nature was welcome after riotous colors in the Telluride sector.

The dozen aliens who had joined her stared wide-eyed. Jiya lamented the fact that none of the Grindlovians had chosen to join them, but she could understand their reluctance. They weren't designed for roughing it like the Telluride people were.

Still, she'd doubted that even one of the colorful aliens

had ever wandered this far from their homes at any point in their lives. The constant questions about the trees and plants and insects only confirmed that.

She chuckled as they asked, and though the specifics of the planet were as foreign to Jiya as they were to the others, she at least had her connection to the Superdreadnought *Reynolds* and his databases.

"That's a pulip," she told one of the Telluride who'd asked about a soft yellow flower that grew rampant in the high grass. "It's a pollinating flower for insects."

The mass of raised eyebrows told her she was in for a long night.

"Don't worry about it," she told them. "It's not dangerous or anything, and it's also not edible." She thought back to their area of town and grinned. "Think of it as nature's art."

The crowd smiled at that. Jiya accepted the challenge to connect with the Telluride. She liked them, but they were babes in the woods.

"It's to look at, enjoy, and inspire, but it serves little more purpose than that, as far as we're concerned."

A few of the Telluride went over and examined the flower more closely, running their fingers gently over it, admiring it without causing harm.

Jiya felt a bloom of pride at seeing it. These people understood art and beauty and cherished it. They didn't immediately swarm in and try to pluck the flower and take it with them. No, there was none of the selfishness Jiya had experienced on her own world.

These people were willing to let the world exist around

them and make themselves a part of it, not the masters of it.

That made Jiya happy.

She watched them for a few more minutes, the Telluride moving carefully through the tall grass to look at other species of flowers and ask questions, each time showing reverence for nature and their surroundings.

All the while, the siren's call of the creek tickled Jiya's ears. It sounded so inviting.

At last, she gave in. "Who wants to go for a swim?" she asked.

All of the Telluride raised their hands excitedly, smiling from ear to ear.

"What's swimming?" one of them asked, earning sympathetic nods from the rest even though they kept their hands raised high in the air.

"Only the most wonderful thing ever!" Jiya chuckled.

Takal and Geroux were led to an assembly hall in the Grindlovian section of town. Hundreds of the chair-bound beings had wheeled to the hall to observe the proceedings.

Geroux was surprised by the number and even more surprised by how restrained they were.

Although she'd already learned that the people were not physically motivated, it was strange to have so many of them gathered around and to only hear the occasional hum of their motorized carriage/chairs.

She glanced at the throng—which she knew was the

wrong word for them given their silence—looking for any sign of interest among the Grindlovians.

If it was there, she didn't recognize it. That they *were* there should have been all she needed to know. They could have been anywhere doing nothing, but they chose to be there, with her and Takal.

"It's like performing in front of fish," Takal complained, coming over to stand alongside her. "It's as if they are incapable of showing even a trace of emotion."

"I think it might tire them if they were to crack a smile," Geroux said, grinning. "Stars forbid they accidentally laugh."

Takal chuckled. "Yes, I'm afraid we might kill off the whole species were we to dare to increase their heart rate a point or two."

"Maybe that's why Gorad keeps them so quiet," Geroux suggested.

"Perhaps that's part of it now, but I can't imagine the Grindlovians having always been so passive and apathetic."

He gestured to the huge gathering.

"While Jiya told me over the comm that she has no Grindlovians involved in her lesson, which is to be expected given their location, I certainly did not expect to have so many of them here with us."

Takal took in the crowd, studying both races and how they presented themselves.

"I think there is something akin to excitement running through them right now," Takal suggested. "Otherwise, why else would they all be here?"

"Gorad?" Geroux questioned.

"No, I don't believe that to be the case, my dear," he

answered. "I truly believe these people want more than they have."

"But they have everything," Geroux argued.

"Do they?" Takal countered, shaking his head. "The inclination that led them down this path to total dependency might not have been what they truly wanted, only what they *believed* they wanted."

Geroux looked at the crowd of Grindlovians, seeing the colorful Telluride among them, all smiles in sharp contrast to the brooding emptiness of the Grindlovians' expressions.

She wondered then if her uncle were right: that the Grindlovians wanted more than their current existence.

The sheer number present supported his theory, and Geroux hoped that was the case. She wanted to have had a positive impact on this world when she and the crew moved on. If she could help both the Telluride and the Grindlovians advance and become better, happier people, the trip would have been a success in her eyes.

"We're going to start with something simple," Takal announced, drawing Geroux out of her thoughts.

She sidled to the table to which the Telluride had brought the supplies they'd requested. She grinned as she watched her uncle work.

"This is an example of a chemical reaction," Takal told the crowd, raising a vial filled with a clear liquid.

He poured it into the clay volcano Geroux had crafted, and the crowd—the Telluride part, at least—gasped when foam spewed from its mouth, showing them what an eruption might look like. They had no active volcanoes on

Grindlevik 3. They had no reference beyond Takal's display.

Geroux cheered and strafed the Grindlovians with her gaze. She didn't see much of a reaction out of them, but several had leaned forward slightly in their chairs to get a better look.

It was something, she thought. It was a start.

CHAPTER EIGHT

Jiya and her Telluride charges had made their way to the creek. She was going to show them the basics of swimming and how to breathe without sucking water into their lungs.

They spent several minutes learning the best way to cough and get out water they weren't supposed to swallow, but Jiya had finally become confident enough that she let them get into the water as a group.

The creek was little more than a meter deep, so all of the Telluride could stand with their heads above the surface. That made the impromptu training easier.

The stream's flow was gentle and barely tugged at the would-be swimmers as they splashed about. Although a bit cold for Jiya's liking, the water was refreshing, and she figured a little chill would help the Telluride stay alert. If they were uncomfortable, they would be less likely to become complacent and put themselves at risk.

Jiya traipsed back and forth across the stream, the Telluride at her back, mimicking her motions.

The Telluride grinned and smiled and splashed and had a great time in the water. Jiya had singled out one of the females who had shown slightly more competence to be the example for the others.

"L'Willow," Jiya called, waving the female over. "Would you please join me?"

"Of course," L'Willow responded, immediately doing as she had been asked.

"The rest of you, stand back and stay put," Jiya advised. "And no splashing, please."

The Telluride groaned as one, but their smiles made it clear to Jiya that there were no hard feelings. They would comply.

Jiya grinned broadly and took L'Willow's hands, lifting and adjusting her so that the female floated on her back in the water.

Stiff as a board, her eyes saucers, L'Willow might as well have been a rock.

Jiya chuckled. "Relax a little," she said, nudging the female's stiff legs and arms where she needed more flex. "Stay stiff like this and you'll sink to the bottom," Jiya warned. "But if you relax and let the water embrace you, you'll float on the top like a leaf."

"Is that a good thing?" L'Willow asked, her voice a whisper.

"It's way better than sinking," Jiya told her with a laugh. "Now just relax, I've got you."

After several minutes of trying, L'Willow finally managed to calm down enough for Jiya to ease her hands back and let L'Willow float almost entirely on her own.

The female realized what was happening and beamed with joy. The crowd of Telluride cheered.

"You're doing it on your own," Jiya told her, taking a slow, careful step back to give the female room.

"I am," she squealed, smiling all the while. "I'm doing it."

"You are." Jiya clapped, waving at the others to do as L'Willow was doing. "Just relax and lean back, let the water buoy your bodies. Don't fight it, just float," she explained, showing them with her own actions.

Jiya eased into the water and floated, watching her charges as the water lapped around her ears and the noise of the world fluttered in and out.

The Telluride murmured happily and splashed about, doing their best to imitate what Jiya and L'Willow were doing.

There was both success and failure along the way, some of the Telluride managing it on the first attempt while others thrashed about and kept sinking until Jiya assisted them.

After what seemed like forever, Jiya waded through the creak around her charges, marveling that each and every one of them had finally managed to make themselves float.

Smiling gold faces jutted from the water's surface, islands of life within the babbling waters. The gentle current slowly carried them downstream.

Everything is perfect, Jiya thought, feeling pride well up inside her.

Then everything wasn't perfect.

L'Willow gasped and went under.

Jiya shot toward the female through the resistance of

the water, but she knew she'd made a mistake the moment she did it.

Several of the other Telluride thrashed in surprise and were swallowed by the water.

"Motherfucking fuck of all fucks!" she cursed, grabbing several of the other Telluride by the arms and hauling them to their feet. "Pull the others out," she ordered, pointing at those Telluride who'd gone under. "I'll get L'Willow."

The Telluride did as she'd commanded and pulled their fellows out of the water, while Jiya raced over to where L'Willow had sunk.

She spotted the female lying frozen on the bottom of the creek, her eyes like gleaming stars beneath the surface.

Jiya reached down and cradled the female in her arms, yanking her above the water in a rush. Jiya gasped a breath of air and examined the female.

She realized L'Willow was turning blue, but not from having swallowed water. She was still holding her breath.

"Might want to breathe," Jiya advised.

L'Willow opened her mouth and sucked in a huge gulp of air, nearly choking on it as she did. She coughed until she'd caught her breath, Jiya holding her the entire time.

"I thought perhaps I might drown," L'Willow told her, repeating the word that Jiya had used to explain what would happen if they didn't come up for air.

At least she'd been listening, Jiya thought.

"You do know that you could have simply stood up and gotten your head out of the water, right?" Jiya asked, exasperated. By example, Jiya lowered her back to her feet, and L'Willow's shoulder and head were well above the surface.

L'Willow blushed, her golden cheeks flaring crimson. "I think perhaps I might need more lessons," she admitted.

Jiya chuckled, glancing over her shoulder at the rest of the Telluride who nodded in agreement.

"I don't have a problem with that at all." Jiya laughed, signaling for everyone to get out of the water.

Though she'd realized how sheltered they were, growing up in servitude to the Grindlovians and following Gorad's directions, she hadn't quite realized that the Telluride were nearly as crippled in their own way as the Grindlovians.

It wasn't a physical thing, but a mental one.

They hadn't had to adapt and overcome anything. Their whole existence circled around the needs of the Grindlovians, and swimming and adventuring and anything else that occurred outside of the confines of the city was a foreign concept to them.

Jiya realized how big a job she'd taken on. But it wasn't just her, it was the whole crew.

She decided that it would be a good idea to sit down with the others and discuss the process of teaching the Telluride new things, get their ideas and brainstorm how to do it better, more safely. The last thing she wanted to do was hurt one of the Telluride accidentally while trying to get to know them better.

"Maybe we should dry off and look at the plant life," she suggested to the group, motioning a second time for them to head for shore.

At least on land, she could keep a better eye on them.

Ka'nak was thrilled by the progress the Telluride had made. He was also inspired to note that more Grindlovians had wheeled over to watch the combat training.

Of course, he couldn't tell what they thought given their stoic expressions, but the fact that more had shown up, and he hadn't seen any leave suggested they were enjoying themselves.

"As much as stick figures can, I guess," he mumbled under his breath.

"What's that?" Maddox asked.

Ka'nak shook his head. "Nothing. Just talking to myself," he said, chuckling.

"You know you can do all that in your head, right?" Maddox joked. "It's called thinking, and no one ends up wondering if you're talking to them."

The Melowi warrior shrugged. "Where's the fun in that?"

Maddox grunted. "One male's fun is another male's torment."

"See? You're getting it," Ka'nak told the general, dragging a half-smile out of him.

"You surprise me some days," Maddox admitted. "I often only see you as a beast of a male, intent on breaking everything and everyone in your way. Then you say something like that, and it makes me think you might actually have a brain inside that thick skull of yours."

"You're not that far off." Ka'nak laughed, smashing his fist into the palm of his hand. "You should probably take a step back," he warned jokingly.

Maddox did, shaking his head.

Ka'nak turned back to the lines of warriors he'd been

drilling for the last several hours. "Well, I guess our earlier experiment might have been a bit premature, but I think you are ready for basic combat simulations now."

Maddox scoffed. "You hope."

Ka'nak did. He had faith that the Telluride would impress him, especially after the repetition he'd drilled into their heads.

San Balu trotted over, excitement brightening his face. The others were slightly less motivated, but he could still see the interest in many of their eyes.

"Let's try this again," Ka'nak announced, waving the Telluride to battle. "Fight!"

The crowd advanced on one another, this time with confidence. Several females had joined the group along the way. They fearlessly moved forward.

The opponents faced off, taking each other's measure as best they could. San Balu wouldn't be restrained.

He leapt forward with a feral scream and his opponent, San Mata, stumbled to a halt, staring, dropping his guard in surprise.

"Always keep your hands—" Maddox shouted, but it was too late.

San Balu crashed into his opponent, fists wailing in a flurry.

Ka'nak was taken aback by San Balu's aggressiveness, but he loved it. The fury of the attack was non-Telluride.

"There you go." Ka'nak shouted encouragement, instinctively miming the shots San Balu was using against San Mata.

San Mata shrieked as several punches collided with his

cheek and forehead. He fell back, waving his arms as San Balu pressed his attack.

There was a fury there that surprised Ka'nak, given what he'd seen of the Telluride people since their arrival, but the sight of it thrilled him.

He'd make these people warriors yet.

San Balu kicked San Mata's legs out from under him and he fell to the ground, rolling onto his side. San Balu showed him no mercy.

He flung himself on top of San Mata as the rest of the Telluride stopped to watch. Fists flew, left, right, left, over and over, and San Mata crumpled under the vicious onslaught.

"STOP!" Ka'nak commanded, but he'd already changed the nature of the usually compliant Telluride.

San Balu raised his bloody fist as high as he could, bringing it down.

The smack of the impact was brutal…

Only it wasn't San Balu striking San Mata that had caused the sound.

Maddox had leapt into the fray and caught the blow in his palm. He twisted San Balu's wrist, eliciting a grunt from the Telluride, and threw him sideways off his opponent.

San Balu landed with a crash, eyes wide in confusion. Maddox loomed over him, ready to lash out if necessary, but San Balu simply sat there.

"What did I do wrong?" he asked, raising his hands in supplication to Maddox.

The general growled and restrained his anger, stepping away and raising his own hands to show he was done.

"Excellent work," Ka'nak told San Balu, going over and helping the male to his feet and clapping him on the back with pride.

"What?" Maddox shouted. "Are you serious?"

Ka'nak stared at Maddox, wondering what had pissed him off so much. "What's wrong?" he asked. "We're here to teach them how to fight." He gestured to the fallen Telluride, who'd yet to recover his senses. "That looks to me as though they're grasping the concept quite nicely."

Maddox snarled at Ka'nak, catching the warrior by surprise. He'd never seen such venom spew from the male before, although he knew his reputation from back on their home planet.

"It's one thing to teach them to fight," Maddox argued, a sharp edge in his voice, "but it's another thing entirely to turn them into barbarians."

Maddox motioned to the other Telluride. "Check your companion, please. Make sure he's okay."

They did, swarming the fallen alien and examining him. Maddox sighed when they hefted him to his feet, and he saw the glimmer of consciousness returning to San Mata's glassy eyes.

Then he spun and poked Ka'nak in the chest.

"You're right," the Melowi warrior admitted, although the words were hard to utter.

Ka'nak had let himself get caught up in the bloodlust and the joy of watching two males battle for supremacy. Maddox was correct, though—that wasn't what they'd intended.

He'd only wanted to make them better warriors, not

killers, and he realized then that he might not be as well-suited to train them as he'd originally thought.

"Perhaps I should show them technique, and you should teach them the psychology of the fight," Ka'nak suggested.

Maddox nodded, reaching out and patting Ka'nak on his muscled shoulder. "How about we sit down and teach them chess? Show them the tactical side of it without bruising them while we do it?" he suggested to the Melowi. "We don't want to break our toys yet, do we?" he asked with a laugh.

"No more than I already have," Ka'nak replied, going over to check on San Mata.

"Chess it is," Ka'nak affirmed a moment later as he dusted off the victim of his unintended consequences, making sure he was okay. "I like chess."

"You any good at it?" Maddox asked.

Ka'nak shook his head. "No, not very," he lied, glancing at San Balu and winking. "Perhaps we should place bets on the game."

As the basic science experiments continued, Geroux found herself enjoying the audience that had gathered.

There were more Grindlovians than Telluride. Although the colorful aliens dominated the applause, she noticed that the Grindlovians had crept closer to watch until the line of the crowd was now little more than a meter away when it had started at ten.

Geroux loved the fact that they could engage even the apathetic Grindlovians with parlor-trick science.

"This is amazing," she told her uncle.

He agreed. "I believe they have become so jaded by the technological miracles around that they've forgotten how interesting it all is," he explained, slipping into teacher mode. It was one of Geroux's favorite things about her uncle. "All of this, no matter how basic it might seem to us, is new to them."

She knew Takal was speaking the truth.

Despite all the devices that operated around them, the Grindlovians were disconnected from their science and the internal aspect of how it all worked. They simply relied on Gorad for everything, and let him do as he wished as long as it benefited them in the end.

They clearly no longer cared how it all happened, only that it *did*. As long as things made their lives easier, they were content with the status quo.

But the science exhibition had sparked something deep inside them.

While the Grindlovians weren't standing and cheering or even waving mechanical arms in the air, Geroux could see the shimmer in their eyes, a curiosity that had risen to the surface and gleamed with renewed interest.

It was the closest to excitement she'd seen from the people, but she knew it for what it was. They were pleased and happy, and for the first time since they'd come to Grindlevik 3, Geroux saw a flicker of the people who resided inside the lumps of flesh.

"They're hooked, Uncle," Geroux whispered to Takal, unable to contain the grin that dimpled her cheeks. "What do we do now?"

"I know!" Takal shouted, his excitement getting the better of him. "Let's make a bomb!"

Geroux started. "What? A bomb? No way!" she argued, shaking her head.

"Oh, you're no fun," Takal complained, his shoulders slumping.

Geroux stared at her uncle a moment, then sighed.

"Okay, but just a tiny one."

CHAPTER NINE

"That mystery ship getting any closer or pointing its scanners our way?" Captain Asya asked.

"Negatory," Tactical replied, annoyance in his voice. "It's been hovering out there doing jack shit this whole time, and it's starting to piss me off."

"Better than it pissing on you," XO argued.

Comm chuckled, and Captain Asya met Ensign Ria's amused gaze.

"Just ignore them, if you haven't already figured that out," Asya told the ensign. "This is par for the course up here on the bridge."

"Perhaps we should have Takal create a shit-talk filter for our comm," Ria suggested.

"The probie has jokes," Tactical growled. "How cute."

Asya grinned. "You're just mad because her idea would make it so that no one heard a word you said, Tactical," she told the splintered AI personality.

"Then let me be the first to volunteer for that," XO called, chuckling.

"I've got something you can try out," Tactical fired back.

"All right, guys." Asya jumped in, hoping to head off any escalation of the tension. When the AIs got into a pissing contest on the bridge, everyone needed a raincoat. "Let's just keep our head in the game and—"

Something thudded into the ship's hull, throwing Asya to the floor. Her arm smacked the console, and she gritted her teeth as she hit with a thud.

Captain Asya howled as she leapt to her feet. "What the fuck was that?" she screamed, the words flying from her mouth like thrown daggers. "Was that our mystery ship?"

"Negative," Tactical called, bringing the unknown ship up on the screens. "They're nowhere near close enough to… Oh, fuck. Incoming!" he shouted just before another explosion rattled the ship.

This time Asya stayed on her feet by clutching her console. As the tremors subsided, she jumped into the captain's seat and buckled in. She glanced at the ensign, whose face was even paler than it had been earlier.

"That was one of Gorad's ships firing on us," Ria announced.

"What the mooseknuckle fuck is going on?" Tactical complained. "Why are these assholes firing at us all of a sudden?"

"Reynolds probably pissed them off," XO growled. "That prick sure knows how to push a person's buttons."

"Ensign!" Asya shouted. "Back us off this damned docking rig so we can trigger our shields and fight back."

"Yes, sir!" Ria shouted, fingers flying across the console to do as she was ordered.

The Superdreadnought *Reynolds* immediately began to back away from the docking berth, but another blast hit the hull and rattled the floor beneath Asya's feet. She knew immediately that real damage had been done to the ship when it bounced.

"Status report!" she snarled, furious at having been so focused on the mystery ship that she'd lost sight of Gorad's fleet surrounding them.

"Aft decks are leaking atmosphere," Ria announced. "We've got causalities, it looks like."

"Goddamn it," Asya growled as the *Reynolds* was struck again and again, compounding the damage.

"This bastard is fucking shanking us like we're in prison," Tactical complained. "Hitting us before we can turn around or activate our shields without damaging everything around us."

"Fuck Gorad and everything else out here," Asya shouted. "Activate gravitic shields," she ordered, and Ensign Alcott did just that. "This fucker's putting a hurt on us, and I want to give some back."

The shield flared around the superdreadnought, its forward edge rippling into the berth and beyond. Sparks jumped, then died out as the energy of the shield forced itself against the metal of the ring.

The defensive ring gave way first.

A section of the ring and the berth the *Reynolds* had been attached to crumpled under the pressure. Air vented through cracks in the ring, pieces broke off and drifted away as they were repulsed by the shield's energy.

Yet another shot struck the *Reynolds,* but its gravitic shields repelled the blast. The superdreadnought spun and moved away from the defensive ring slowly, bogged down as it was by the station.

"Get us out there where we can maneuver," Asya ordered, fighting back her inherent nature to not damage the docking mechanism.

It had been hammered into her to cherish and protect the fleet and its assets, but this wasn't hers to worry about. *It was Gorad's, so fuck him and the consequences,* she thought.

"Angle away and give us room to maneuver, Ensign! Full ahead."

The *Reynolds* shot forward, and though the screen was focused on the destroyer pummeling them, Asya smiled, knowing the destruction she was leaving in their wake, even though it would never make up for the injuries caused by Gorad's sneak attack on the *Reynolds.*

"Put some fire on this prick and teach him a lesson," Asya commanded.

Tactical got to work.

Reynolds' guns blasted, and Asya punched a fist into the arm of her seat when she spied the flicker of shields repelling the shots.

"We get anything?" she asked.

"Nope," Tactical came back. "Her front shields are up full. We're going to need to hit it a little harder."

"What are you waiting for?" Captain Asya asked.

"Railguns charging," Tactical called in response. "Hitting back like a motherfucker in three…two…now," he said as he fired. "Hi, asshole."

The railguns let loose a brutal burst of energy, sending

projectiles at nearly the speed of light ripping straight through the destroyer's shield and tearing scorching holes in the side of the ship. Lights flared and died on the ship, and it began to list.

"Hit it again!" Asya ordered.

"I'm so tempted to break out the ESD," Tactical threatened, but he held back and only used the railguns again.

Which, in reality, was way more than sufficient firepower to do what Captain Asya had asked for.

The blasts ripped craters in Gorad's destroyer, then tore the ship in half. Metal buckled and gave way and the engines separated from the rest of the rest of the ship, tumbling off into space.

Then the destroyer exploded; one quick, brilliant flash and it was gone. Debris rained against the gravitic shields.

Then there was another explosion at their backs, and Asya shifted views to see what had happened since she hadn't felt anything impact the ship.

On the screen, another of Gorad's destroyers, this one having not left the dock or even cycled up its guns or shields, spun in the blackness of space. The vast majority of its forward hull was a smoking wreck.

The berth it had been docked at was worse. There was nothing left of it.

The ship tumbled, smacked its engines against the defensive ring and knocked them loose of the craft, and both pieces fell away.

"What was that for?" Asya asked.

"It felt good after all that bullshit," Tactical told her.

Asya had to agree, and although she was tempted to inflict more damage on Gorad's ships and armored ring, she knew it would be better to hold back and see what was going on. She had wounded to attend to.

"Status!"

"Three unaccounted for, and over a dozen seriously wounded," Ria reported. "Automated repair systems are online, and the bots are patching holes, but it looks like this is more than they can handle. I'm mobilizing repair crews as soon as the area is secure."

Asya sank into her seat. Reynolds had handed her the ship, and she'd gotten it blasted all to hell because she'd let her guard down, thinking that Reynolds and the crew being on planet meant that things were okay.

She'd been too trusting this time, and she wouldn't let that happen again.

"Comm, connect me to Gorad. I want to ask him what the fuck that was about," the captain said. "Then reach out to the crew and tell them to watch their backs. This shit might blow back on them, whatever this shit is."

"Gorad is ignoring all hails," Comm replied.

Asya figured that was a good thing, given what she wanted to say to the AI bastard. She'd likely start a war if they weren't already in one.

"Get Reynolds on the horn so I can let him know what's going on," Asya told Comm, "and don't let that mystery cruiser out of your sight, or any of the rest of these destroyer fucks, for that matter. We've got enough shit to deal with without getting shot in the back again."

Asya snarled as the call to Reynolds was put through. She wasn't sure what the hell she was going to tell him, but she figured, "I told you so" wouldn't be appropriate.

Even if she *had*.

"You attacked my ship!" Reynolds shouted at the android body of Gorad.

"I did absolutely nothing of the sort, Reynolds," the alien AI told him. "I have no clue what happened, but I assure you that—"

"You've hurt my people." Reynolds cursed and leapt to his feet and knocked the table aside, sending it crashing into the wall. Food, drinks, and utensils scattered, clattering to the floor. "How the hell can you control everything around here and claim this was *not* your doing? I have three people unaccounted for up there; likely dead, thanks to you."

"I will look into this, I promise you," Gorad told him, motioning toward the chair Reynolds had nearly knocked over. "Sit, please. We still have much to discuss."

"Are you fucking *kidding* me? You think your agro-printers are worth losing the people I want to feed? That's bullshit!"

Were Reynolds human, he would have felt the blood in his veins boiling. He was sure he still did—the oil, at least, pumping through his systems and threatening to light fires inside him.

"There is nothing you can do to determine the problem, Reynolds," Gorad explained, which only lit the match under the Federation AI.

He darted across the room and snatched the Gorad android up by its neck. A quick twist snapped its robotic neck, and Reynolds hurled the twitching body into the wall alongside the table and its contents.

"You attacked my people, Gorad," Reynolds shouted at the android body as it lay at an awkward angle, spasming. "That was no accident or error, that was an act of war on an Etheric Federation starship, you stupid Commodore Vic 20. Bethany Anne would carve her name in your ass cheeks for that."

"This is not war, Reynolds," the android went on, although its head was bent sideways. "Had I declared such, there would be nothing left of your ship or its people," Gorad explained. "I did not."

"Oh, and that makes it better, huh?" Reynolds snapped a kick and sent the android's head flying. "What the hell is wrong with you?"

"I will find the culprit. It was clearly an error in the system," Gorad told him, but Reynolds didn't want to hear any more.

He spun and muscled his way out the door of the meeting room before charging off down the hall. As he ran toward the end of the moving walkway after he'd gotten outside of the building, he spied the *Reynolds'* Pod streaking through the sky.

It landed in the street a moment later, its hatch popping open. He darted up the ramp and jumped inside. Jiya sat inside in the pilot's seat, having been the first to be collected. A fearsome scowl distorted her features.

"That piece of shit," she started, unable to get the rest of the words out past the growl.

"Get us back to the ship," Reynolds ordered.

"What about the others?" Jiya asked, clearly hesitating to follow the order with her crew still there.

Reynolds dropped into the seat beside Jiya. "Gorad

claims he did not declare war on us," he explained. "That it was an error."

"And you believe that fucker?"

"I do, oddly enough," Reynolds replied, rational thought coming back to him now that the immediate danger had passed. "What does he have to gain by blasting *Reynolds* and killing our people? It doesn't make any sense."

"And that passes for logic?" Jiya barked.

"Of course not," he told her, "but I do not believe he will go after the crew here on Grindlevik 3. He's not out to hurt any of you."

"No, he just wants to kill those aboard the superdreadnought."

Reynolds grunted, knowing that it was a circular argument with Jiya. She wasn't going to accept that anything but the obvious had happened—that Gorad had attacked—but Reynolds wasn't so sure.

He couldn't think of a good reason for the alien AI to attack them now, after letting them through security and onto the planet.

"So, what, we just leave them here?" Jiya pushed when Reynolds didn't immediately reply.

Jiya was fuming, and while Reynolds understood, he thought something had happened that was out of Gorad's control. He hadn't meant to assault the *Reynolds* or its crew, but *something* had happened.

Reynolds needed to know what. He had to learn the answer, and the only way to do that was from his ship.

"Warn them to stay frosty and protect themselves as necessary," Reynolds ordered. "And, more importantly, not to initiate any combat actions against the defensive ring or the Grindlovian destroyers."

"You have *got* to be shitting me," Jiya complained, though Reynolds was glad to note that the first officer had taken their earlier conversation about responsibility and the chain of command to heart.

Even though she disagreed with his decision and argued against it, she was already triggering the comm and engaging the Pod's engines to return to the ship.

Reynolds waited as Jiya spoke to the crew remaining on the planet, and he was impressed by the restraint she'd shown while doing so.

She had only used some variation of "fuck" about fifteen times during the conversation and only once threatened to kill someone.

Progress.

As the Pod shot back toward the *Reynolds,* Jiya cut the link between her and the crew and turned in her seat to look at him.

"I don't like this," she told him.

"Neither do I," he admitted. "If Gorad did this purposely —and I don't believe he did—it was a serious miscalculation on his part. He will pay for it if that's what happened, but I need to assess the damage before I make any rash decisions."

"Three people missing is all you should need to know," Jiya clarified.

"Unaccounted for, yes," he replied, "but not yet proven dead."

"Does that make it better?" she barked.

"Only minutely," he concurred, watching the screen as

the bright day turned to night when they broke through the atmosphere.

Superdreadnought *Reynolds* loomed ahead, and Reynolds snarled at seeing her venting atmosphere, the hull charred and buckled where Gorad's destroyer had sucker punched them.

"I'm going to rip his diodes out his metal ass," Jiya threatened, "and short-circuit all his capacitors."

"Remind me to never piss you off," Reynolds told her.

"Too late for that," she replied, and Reynolds saw the fury that etched lines across her reddened features, her knuckles white on the Pod's controls. She wasn't going to let it go anytime soon.

And that made Reynolds' job harder.

The agroprinters were important, and despite his bluff that he and the crew could eventually figure them out, he knew the technology was within reach if only he could say the right words.

Besides, he now felt a pang of concern about leaving the Grindlovians and Telluride in the hands of the alien AI, especially if there were glitches in his system bad enough to trigger an attack on the superdreadnought. If he was willing to fire on a Federation ship for no apparent reason, what else would he be willing to do?

Reynolds thought for a moment that the crew on the planet might be in danger, but the AI still refused to believe it was Gorad who had attacked. He trusted that the alien intelligence would protect Reynolds' crew. It wasn't logical, but Reynolds believed it with every fiber of his digital being.

Though he had to admit, nothing made any sense.

Gorad wanted what Reynolds knew, and putting his crew at risk wouldn't accomplish his goal. Even a mentally challenged AI would understand that. While Gorad might piss Reynolds off by hurting his people, nothing that happened to them would force Reynolds to give in to Gorad's demands.

In fact, quite the opposite.

Reynold would lash out with everything he had and lay waste to Gorad and all his creations were the alien AI to hurt any more of his people.

Reynolds was more than half-tempted to do that already. Then he could simply take the agroprinter technology and anything else they wanted from the planet.

The only problem was his uncertainty as to whether he could win a fight against all of Gorad's automated systems without injuring any of the planet's population.

Reynolds would be risking his own hide and that of his crew getting into a fight with the alien AI. Gorad wouldn't be. He'd only be risking losing pieces of equipment he could easily replace.

Reynolds couldn't do that with his crew, nor did he want to.

And that was when Reynolds realized that, despite it all, he'd handed the key to the negotiations to Gorad in his fury.

Reynolds smacked his palm into his head and groaned.

"If you want someone to hit you I'll gladly volunteer," Jiya told him, clearly still angry.

"I'm such an idiot," Reynolds muttered.

"No arguments here," she replied. "But pretend I don't

know that already and tell me why you think that all of a sudden."

"I gave Gorad what he wanted just now," he answered, shaking his head in frustration that he'd been so easily manipulated. "I showed him just how important my crew is."

"Oh...shit," Jiya mumbled.

She started to turn the Pod around to return back to Grindlevik 3, but Reynolds stopped her, setting a restraining metal hand on her arm.

"What the hell are you doing?" she complained. "You just implied Gorad would go after the crew, so why are you stopping me?"

"Those on the planet are safe, trust me," he said.

"How do you know that?" Jiya asked.

"Because they are serving the people and teaching them things."

"Maybe I'm missing something, but what does that have to do with anything?" she barked.

"Gorad actually cares, believe it or not. While he might seem distant, and that trait is bleeding into the Grindlovian society, I believe he does what he does for the people because he wants to take care of them. He wants to help them."

"And?"

"And he needs to feel needed and important," Reynolds continued. "Without the people here he's nothing but a stranded AI with nothing to do but think and plot. He won't risk anything happening to the Grindlovians or the Telluride for fear that he will become obsolete. That's his greatest liability, I believe."

"We're not talking about either of those, though," Jiya argued.

"But we are," Reynolds corrected. "Because if Gorad dares to hurt any more of our people, I will nuke the ever-loving shit out of the planet and his people before he can take down the *Reynolds*."

Jiya gasped, bolting upright in her seat. "You would do that?"

"If absolutely necessary, yes," Reynolds admitted, though he didn't like hearing that declaration come out of his mouth. "However, as of now, that exact scenario is only a warning I've sent to Gorad so we understand each other."

"Whoa." Jiya slumped into the chair, eyes wide and a sheen of sweat glistening on her forehead.

"Our crew on the planet *is* safe," he assured her, motioning toward the *Reynolds* as they approached. "For now, get us aboard so we can check on the rest of our people," he ordered. His voice was barely above a whisper.

Gorad had struck a grievous blow against his people, intentional or otherwise. Reynolds would have to retaliate somehow, or he'd lose the faith of the crew. They wouldn't take the death or injury of their fellows lightly, and neither would Reynolds if he determined that Gorad had done this intentionally.

If that were the case, he needed to figure out how to pay Gorad back without costing them more than they'd already paid.

Reynolds was sure he'd think of something.

CHAPTER TEN

"Can you believe that?" Geroux asked, shaking her head in awe. "I sure can't."

The crew had gathered in one of the dining halls in the Telluride-controlled section of town, furious and worried and unsure of what to do.

Well, that wasn't entirely true.

They knew what they wanted to do: kick Gorad's metal ass.

Unfortunately, Jiya had ordered them to keep the peace.

Besides, it wasn't as if Gorad was a living, breathing being. Yeah, they could trash his machines or tear down his buildings and break a bunch of stuff, but that would only hurt the Grindlovians and the Telluride.

"I can't believe this," Geroux repeated.

Maddox set a hand on her forearm as she fretted. "We know you can't believe it, Geroux. You've said as much ten times or more. Please give it a rest."

"But I really *can't* believe it," she said.

Maddox sighed. "I wonder if the Telluride believe in alcohol," he said, glancing around.

"I concur," Takal said, raising his hand for one of the servants to come over.

When one did, he asked them about getting drinks for the crew, and Geroux saw the sparkle in Takal's eyes when he learned that they did have alcoholic beverages.

"I'll take ten, please," he ordered, then glanced at the rest of the crew. "What would you like?"

Maddox chuckled, holding up a finger to order one for himself. The others ordered while Geroux glared at her uncle until he finally looked away.

"Come now, child," he started, "do not hassle me, please. If ever there was a situation that would be bettered by a drink, this must surely be it."

"Commercials, weather above two degrees Celsius, and pretty much any day that had a cloud in the sky or didn't were perfect excuses for you to drink," she argued. "You don't get to use this as an excuse to satisfy the addict in you, Uncle."

"I suggest otherwise," he told her. "Impending doom is *always* a reason to have a drink."

Geroux sighed and raised her hands in surrender. "Whatever," she told him, "but I'm not carrying you if you get so drunk you can't walk."

"I will do it," Ka'nak announced, giving Takal a thumbs-up.

"Way to encourage him," Geroux snarked, her hands trembling in frustration.

"I will be reasonable," Takal assured her.

Geroux ignored him and waited until the Telluride

servant had dropped off the drinks. At that point, she claimed an armful of them for herself to keep them away from her uncle.

He sighed and sipped the two she'd left him.

"What do we do now?" Ka'nak asked, swallowing a great mouthful of the drink he'd been given. "Do we just go about our business and continue to teach these people?" He shrugged. "Seems a bit daft, don't you think? Who knows what's going on above us?"

"Actually, we do," Maddox clarified, tapping the side of his head where the comm and translator chip had been inserted. "We've got a direct line to the ship, remember?"

"You know what I meant," Ka'nak argued, taking another gulp of his drink. "Whatever's going on up there is all about action and reaction. We have no idea what the hell Gorad intends or how Reynolds will respond. That leaves us swinging in the wind down here."

"Well, Reynolds *did* apparently threaten to murder everyone on the planet should Gorad try to harm us or anyone aboard the *Reynolds,* if that helps," Takal said.

"Yeah, because him nuking the planet with us on it makes me feel so incredibly safe right now," Ka'nak replied, shaking his head. He finished his drink and snatched one from Geroux. "I'm starting to think your old uncle had the right idea—get drunk and let someone else worry about all this shit."

Takal motioned to the Melowi as if to agree and Geroux growled at him.

"Don't you dare."

Takal sighed and went back to nursing his drink.

"Excuse me," L'Willow said, coming over to stand

beside the group. L'Eliana, San Paget, and San Roche stood there with her, as well as a female Geroux didn't know. "Forgive our intrusion, but we heard what happened to your spacecraft and crew."

"You did?" Geroux asked, surprised at how quickly the news had traveled, especially given that Gorad controlled everything. "How did you learn about that?"

"Despite his control, Gorad does not restrict us," L'Willow replied. "We have a robust news system that carries everything that happens on-planet and above to us without censorship. We have watched the transmission of your ship being attacked."

"That's…unexpected," Takal muttered, staring into the empty bottom of his first cup.

"He showed you that he attacked our people?" Maddox asked, clearly unable to believe it.

"He showed us, yes," San Paget answered, "but he has claimed he did not do this."

"If you've seen the holo, then you had to have seen his destroyer attack our ship!" Maddox said. "How could this not be him?"

"Gorad has always been honest with us," San Roche stated, trust evident in his expression. "If he says it was not him, I believe him."

"Perhaps he's *too* honest at times," the unidentified Telluride said, stepping forward. "He also informed us of your Reynolds' threat to annihilate all life on Grindlevik 3 should Gorad harm any of your people."

Geroux sighed. Maybe the female was right. Gorad was clearly too open about what was going on, and the situation was likely to get worse should things escalate. There was only the handful of Telluride close enough to listen, and she waved for them to sit down.

"Reynolds was angry," she said once they'd settled. "It is not his intention to kill anyone, nor is it ours," she explained. "He said what he did to keep Gorad honest and the rest of us safe. He wouldn't kill innocent people to get back at Gorad, no matter what he might have done."

"Are you certain of this?" the female asked.

Geroux nodded. "I am," she answered confidently, although she had to admit that maybe she shouldn't be speaking for Reynolds.

He was a war machine, fully capable of backing his threat. Geroux hadn't known him long enough to be absolutely certain that Reynolds wouldn't do something so extreme, though she believed he wouldn't, based on her discussion with Jiya.

It didn't seem like the Reynolds she knew.

"Your people are safe," she closed with, deciding not to second guess herself and say more than she ought to.

"That is good to know, for I would be obligated to do something were I to think the threat was valid," the female replied, nodding to Geroux. "I am L'Sofee," she added.

"Are you the leader of the Telluride?" Maddox asked.

She shook her head. "We Telluride have no designated leaders, each of us being equal among our kind and others, but I am often called upon to speak for our people."

Maddox leaned back into his seat, and Geroux could see he was contemplating something serious. He stared at the ad hoc leader of the Telluride with narrowed eyes.

"We wish you no harm," Geroux told the female,

making sure she didn't draw any conclusions from Maddox's harsh gaze.

"I believe you," L'Sofee replied. "*We* believe you," she corrected. "Your people appear to have good hearts despite the differences that set us so far apart." The female glanced at Ka'nak when she said that.

He buried his face into his cup and mumbled, "The kid was beat up when I got there, I swear."

L'Sofee chuckled softly, her laughter sweet like a harp. "We did not come to you to point fingers, warrior," she told the Melowi, who breathed a sigh of relief, blowing bubbles in his cup. "We actually came for your advice."

Maddox stiffened in his seat, one eyebrow creeping up. "Advice?"

Maddox hadn't been expecting that.

"Please, ask us anything," Geroux offered.

L'Sofee smiled, offering a nod of thanks to Geroux. "It is quite a…complicated subject, I fear."

"We're quite the complicated people ourselves," Takal replied after a loud burp. "And it appears that we have the time."

The Telluride laughed, and L'Sofee smiled at the inventor.

"While we have everything we might need here on Grindlevik 3 and Gorad is quite generous in his care of us, my people wonder perhaps if we are missing out on something…more."

The female paused to let her words sink in.

"I mean, just what little you've shown us since your arrival makes it clear there is much that we do not know and we would like to," she went on. "Gorad does not restrict our learning or our ways, but to be completely truthful and, perhaps a bit blunt, we feel that we would be better off pursuing a life where we were not expected to care for the Grindlovians."

"We would like to travel and learn. Be free in the truest sense of the word," L'Willow told them.

Geroux sat back in her seat, surprised. She noticed then for the first time that the Telluride before them weren't smiling.

That spoke volumes to Geroux. And before anyone else could get a word out, she answered for the rest. "Whatever you need, we're here for you."

"Sitrep," Reynolds called as he and Jiya stormed onto the bridge.

Asya hopped out of the captain's seat, relinquishing it to the metal AI.

"We've found our missing crew," she announced, but the look on her face didn't speak of good news.

Jiya held her breath, dreading the rest of Asya's report.

"They're alive," she said, and Jiya huffed, closing her eyes in relief. "They're hurt badly, but it looks as if they will pull through. Not sure how long they'll be down, though."

"Down is better than dead," Reynolds said.

"Not by much," Tactical complained. "That fucker came after us. Shot us when our backs were turned."

"And he'll pay for that if he actually did it," Reynolds assured them, coming over and dropping into the seat Asya had vacated. "But I need to know for sure first."

"What's the plan?" Jiya asked, giving Asya a quick hug.

"We're going to break a couple of eggs," Reynolds replied, mechanical fingers flying in a blur over the console.

"We're kicking Gorad in the nuts?" Tactical asked. "I'm right there with you on that, buddy."

The viewscreen filled with data that scrolled past so fast that Jiya couldn't even begin to recognize what it might be.

"Wait, you're trying to hack him?" XO asked.

"That's it?" Tactical spat. "How the hell is that breaking his little eggs?"

"If I can hack into his system, I can figure out if he really did mean to attack us. If he did, we'll scramble the fuckers from the inside," Reynolds shot back. "We need an inside track first."

Tactical sighed, not liking Reynolds' decision.

"He's rising to meet us," XO called.

"I can see that," Reynolds retorted. "Got anything helpful to add?"

"That he's blocking you so far?" XO answered.

"Do I really need to stress the *helpful* part?" Reynolds asked.

"Apparently," Asya told him, staring at the screen alongside Jiya. Neither of them had any clue what the mess of data meant.

"Damn, he's good," XO muttered.

Reynolds cursed under his breath, focused as he was on the console. "He's got some serious chops," Reynolds admitted. "He keeps redirecting my attacks and sniffing out my feints."

"You need to sucker punch him like he did the ship," Tactical told him.

"If you have an idea how to do that from here, please share," Reynolds requested.

"I say we trigger the ESD and send the Trojan Horse of Fuck You right up his backdoor."

"As much as I would like to blow this asshole away, we're not exactly in a position to walk away from a move like that," Reynolds warned.

"Given how much damage that one ship did to us, I tend to agree with Reynolds," Asya announced. "Doesn't help that we have that other ship floating around out there either."

"Other ship?" Reynolds asked, pausing for an instant before going back to the hack in progress.

"Oh, yeah," Asya replied, her voice dropping. "Forgot to mention that, given all the drama."

"I'm not sure I like this new development," Reynolds told her.

"Well, if it's any consolation, the mystery ship was the first development and the attack the more recent of the pair," Tactical argued.

"That's not really helping, Tactical," Asya told him.

"I'd shrug to show you how much I care but, you know..." Tactical replied.

"Tell me about the other ship later," Reynolds snapped. "Right now, I need to focus on Gorad."

When Ensign Ria shuffled in her seat and sniffed, Jiya was surprised to realize that the young female had been there the entire time. Jiya waved to her, and Ria waved back, slinking once more into her chair to await orders.

"Damn it!" Reynolds shouted a moment later and the screen flickered, the text dancing sideways for a second.

"He's countering," XO announced. "Need to make sure he doesn't slip in on your link."

"He won't," Reynolds growled. "I only need to..." his voice faded as he concentrated on the cyber attack.

"Looks like you're getting your ass kicked," Tactical mentioned. "You're losing ground."

"I'm not losing ground," Reynolds shot back. "It's called a tactical retreat."

"Maybe you've forgotten that I'm the tactical genius here, not you," Tactical reminded. "You're getting your metal ass punted, Reynolds."

"Gorad's hailing us," Comm announced.

"Put him onscreen."

As before, only the logo of the Grindlevik 3 Space Defense appeared.

Reynolds stifled a chuckle at seeing it, knowing he'd almost torn off the android's head and that was why he'd been forced to use the logo.

"I don't appreciate this, Reynolds," Gorad warned. "Immediately cease your attempts to hack my system."

"And we sure as shit don't appreciate you hurting our people," Asya shouted.

"As I told Reynolds, I did *not* attack you or your ship," Gorad told her. "What purpose would it serve?"

"Who the hell knows with you crazy AIs," Asya shot back, then cringed, clearly remembering once again the company she kept. "No offense, guys," she said to Reynolds' splinter personalities.

"Still some taken every time you say that shit," Tactical grunted.

"There is much we can learn from each other, Reynolds," Gorad told him, "and I would not risk that by dragging you into conflict with me."

"He's only saying that because you're hacking into his system," Asya argued. "He doesn't want you to see the truth hidden in there."

"He's not really," XO clarified.

Reynolds sighed and sat upright, leaning away from the console, admitting defeat as Gorad shut down the last of Reynolds' hacking attempts. "No, I'm really not." His console went black.

"I have far more experience defending my system than you have in hacking it, Reynolds," Gorad said. "While you are clearly skilled, I can repel you indefinitely given the nature of my system."

"Can you repel an array of railguns?" Tactical asked.

"I admit that I cannot," Gorad admitted, "but I would hope that we can clear things up before we reach that point."

The screen fluttered, and the logo disappeared only to be replaced by a copy of the android body Reynolds had destroyed, much to his disappointment.

"It was not me," he stressed, "but it was clear that something or someone manipulated one of my craft to attack you. Please, allow me to help you investigate so we both know it will not happen again."

Asya sneered and Jiya came over to stand alongside Reynolds, staring back at the alien AI on the screen.

"Give us a second," she said, signaling for Comm to mute communications for a minute.

Comm shut it down.

"I don't trust this AI," she said once she knew Gorad couldn't hear or see them talking.

"Neither do I," Asya announced.

"Nor do I," Reynolds said, "but I believe he is telling us the truth."

"And if he is?" Jiya asked. "What does that mean for us?"

"It means we have another problem besides Gorad," Reynolds explained.

"You mean besides the other ship floating out there, which happens to have used the exact same Gate coordinates as us to get here?" Asya asked.

"Something like that, yeah," Reynolds replied. "Seems we've got a couple of problems floating around, but I don't think Gorad is a threat to us."

"Does that mean we won't be kicking his ass?" Tactical asked.

"Looks that way," Jiya grunted, wanting a piece of Gorad herself for what had happened to the crew and ship.

But if he truly hadn't done it, she couldn't bring herself to be mad at him.

Reynolds motioned for Comm to reopen the channel.

"We'll take you at your word…for now," Reynolds told the other AI. "Explain to me how we go about investigating this…*glitch*, as you called it?"

"Do you have bots aboard?" Gorad asked.

"I do."

"Good," the other AI said with a nod. "You'll need them to board the ship that attacked you, then I will direct you to where you can access the mainframe computer within the wreckage."

Reynolds stood there for a moment without saying anything, then signaled for the bots to be launched. "Go get that computer, boys," he said as the repair bots were shot into space. "We'll relay instructions from here."

Gorad explained the sequence and location, which went a long way toward Jiya feeling more comfortable trusting the alien AI, seeing as how he was revealing the secret of his destroyer fleet's automation.

A short while later, the bots had secured a dozen pieces of the mainframe, which had been destroyed when *Reynolds* fought back. The bots had managed to collect all the parts Gorad deemed necessary and had returned to the hangar bay unscathed. They loaded the parts onto the Pod.

"Bring the pieces down to the planet, and I will arrange for a private space where we can examine the mainframe for corruption or system failure. We *will* get to the bottom of this."

The screen went blank as Gorad disconnected.

Reynolds stood there staring at the black viewscreen for several moments.

"We doing this, boss?" Jiya asked, nudging his arm.

"Yeah, let's get it over with." Reynolds nodded. "Keep the ship's shields up and the engines running, folks," he told Asya, Ensign Alcott, and the other AI personalities. "We can't have a repeat of this, no matter what we find down there. We got lucky last time that no one died. I don't see us staying lucky if it happens again."

Jiya and Reynolds left the bridge, headed for the hangar

bay. He marched ahead, still frustrated and angry about what had happened.

For her part, Jiya was glad Reynolds was on her side. And if Gorad wasn't, he would soon find out just how pissed off Reynolds really was.

Then there would be an ass-kicking coming.

CHAPTER ELEVEN

Back on Grindlevik 3, Reynolds and Jiya reunited with the rest of the crew.

"Boy, do we have some news for you," Geroux told them, but Reynolds waved the young tech aside.

"Later, Geroux," he said, shaking his head to make it clear now was not a good time.

"Okay," she replied, giving Jiya a sideways glance, looking for an explanation.

"We're off to examine the mainframe parts of the destroyer that attacked the *Reynolds*. Gorad is preparing a room for us."

Geroux's eyebrows rose in unison. "So, Reynolds believes the other AI didn't intentionally go after our people?"

"He's leaning that way," Jiya told her friend. "We've yet to be sure, though."

"Your hovercraft is ready," L'Willow announced from the door of the dining hall where Reynolds and Jiya had gone to meet with the crew while Gorad prepared his investigation room.

Takal stared across the table at the collection of drinks Geroux had pulled away from him and sighed. "One for the road?" he asked.

Geroux rolled her eyes and ignored her uncle as he grabbed a cup to take with them. Ka'nak followed suit, then grabbed a second one to be sure.

"In case I spill one," he explained as he and Takal made their way toward the hovercraft.

Jiya saw Geroux watching her uncle walk and knew she was checking to see if the older male was drunk. He didn't appear to be, walking perfectly normally with his shuffling gait, so Geroux shook her head and gave up.

Reynolds followed the two drinkers, thanking L'Willow and San Paget for their kindness before he left.

Jiya waved at the pair of aliens, then took her friend's hand. They went out after the rest of the crew and joined them in the craft, the one bot they'd carted along to carry the computer pieces already in the vehicle.

Unmanned, the hovercraft took off at a fast clip, shooting down the road toward where the crew had visited the droid factory.

They circled around that and came to what looked like a dreary gray warehouse that had just been assembled. It gleamed of new metal and fresh—albeit drab—paint.

"You've got a thing for gray, Gorad," Reynolds said, knowing the other AI would hear him.

There was no response, however.

The doors of the warehouse eased open in front of the crew as they left the hovercraft, and Reynolds led the way inside. The bot began gathering the computer parts and carrying them inside.

Jiya knew Reynolds was still feeling guilty about what had happened and was putting on a brave front, diving in to solve the problem before anything else could happen.

She knew that they would.

Once in the newly-created room, Jiya was surprised to see how effectively Gorad had arranged it for a forensic analysis of the destroyer's computer system.

A long workstation was set in the middle of the room with a row of mechanical arms hanging above from a mount on the ceiling. A pair of large monitors were set upon the mount, facing the crew.

The rest of the room was empty and dark …and, of course, quite gray.

Gorad was already in the room, standing behind the workstation and waving the crew and Reynolds in. The bot set the pieces of the computer on the workstation table, and Gorad spread them out as the bot went to get the next section.

Reynolds came to stand face to face with Gorad over the table. The two AIs stared at each other for several minutes without saying anything. It wasn't until the bot had placed the last piece of the destroyer's computer that Gorad gave in.

"Thank you for joining me here," he said, offering a shallow nod to Reynolds. "And thank you for not kicking this android's head off."

Despite himself, a smile split Reynolds' metal face. "You're welcome," he replied grudgingly, though Jiya was sure he still wanted to kick the other AI's head off again.

She did, too.

"This could take some time," Gorad warned. "You might want to send your crew to continue with their mission."

"You'd like that, wouldn't you?" Reynolds asked.

"I enjoy seeing the Telluride and Grindlovians advance," Gorad said, nodding. "Your people are teaching them much that they did not know before, and it is good for them."

"And for you?"

"Certainly," the alien AI admitted. "Knowledge is always appreciated."

Reynolds stood for a moment, staring down the other AI before finally turning around and waving the crew over.

"All of you but Jiya, go back to what you were doing earlier," Reynolds ordered, nodding to let them know it was okay. "We'll stay here and put the puzzle together and see what it tells us."

"You sure?" Geroux asked. "I can help."

"You'll be helping by going back to what you were doing," he replied. "Jiya and I can handle this."

"Yes, sir!" she answered, sneaking a hug from Jiya first.

"Back to drinking?" Takal asked.

"Back to teaching," Geroux corrected.

"Better you than me, Takal," Ka'nak said, grinning. "I have a game of chess waiting for me back at the lot. I was winning, too."

The crew departed, leaving the bot behind with Jiya and Reynolds. It drifted into the corner and sat there rigidly, awaiting new orders.

Gorad signaled for the mechanical arms to begin their work and circled around to join Reynolds and Jiya.

"We will soon find out why my ship attacked yours," Gorad promised.

"We'd better," Reynolds shot back, "or you and I are going to have words."

"I assure you, I am as interested in getting to the bottom of this as you are."

"I doubt that," Jiya told the alien AI, but she didn't want to imagine what might happen if Gorad were attempting to play them. "But we're here to figure this out. It's not going to give us the answer without a little prompting."

Gorad gave her a nod of thanks for her understanding.

The robots worked on as they spoke, picking at the computer pieces and tearing it apart in an effort to reassemble it and read the data stored within.

Jiya watched mesmerized as the mechanical arms danced. Each performed its task with a precision and grace unexpected of such a hastily-thrown-together device.

Gorad is a pro with his creations, no doubt about that, she thought.

Of course, that thought only made her more suspicious of the alien AI since it could easily slip something past her, although she was sure he couldn't do that to Reynolds.

"How long will this take?" she asked.

"Likely hours," Gorad answered. "The bots must first locate all the pieces and attempt to reassemble them in the proper..."

Jiya flopped to the floor as the alien AI went on and on, explaining the process in such detail that Jiya's eyes glazed. She rubbed them and wished she'd gone with the others.

At least they were likely to have coffee or the rush-fruit that had so invigorated her earlier.

She licked her lips as she thought about it and zoned out while Gorad went on discussing the intricacies of the task his robots were going about.

Jiya's last thought before she drifted off was that she hoped she didn't snore.

"I should have told him," Geroux said once they were back in the Telluride's part of town and the hovercraft had left.

"What good would it do now?" Maddox asked. "Best to let the big brains sort things out before we give them another reason to go after each other."

"But it is big news, that the Telluride want to go off on their own," Geroux countered.

"It is, but it can wait," Maddox pressed. "There's too much going on right now to worry about that. These folks will still be here when they've figured out what happened above."

"You think they will?" Geroux wondered. "I mean, they did send away the two geniuses who know the most about these kinds of things," she said, motioning to herself and then to her uncle.

"Stay humble, kid," Maddox laughed.

"I'm just being honest," Geroux argued.

"You can take that genius mind of yours and help me teach these guys how to play chess if you want," Ka'nak told her.

Geroux thought for a minute, then nodded. "You know what, I think I will," she told the Melowi.

Given that the crew had been left hanging while they

waited, Geroux didn't see much point in getting caught up in anything as complex as doing science experiments for the locals.

Besides, as soon as news arrived, the crew would be tasked with dealing with the fallout, whatever it might be.

As such, Geroux decided she'd rather spend the next few hours hanging out and playing chess with Ka'nak and the Telluride who decided to join them.

"I'll make my way back to the dining hall," Takal told her as she announced her decision. "I'm famished."

"It's all that liquor you drank," Geroux sighed. "Hey, Maddox. Go with him, yeah? Keep him from getting sloppy drunk, will you?"

"Why the hell not?" Maddox replied, grinning. "It's not like I've got anything better to do."

The general put a hand on Takal's arm and led the male toward the dining hall.

"Let's go wait things out, my friend," he said.

Takal nodded. "Be careful," he told Geroux over his shoulder as she and Ka'nak went their own way.

Geroux waved goodbye, and the two walked toward the sandlot where Ka'nak had been training the Telluride to fight earlier in the day.

"You any good at chess?" Geroux asked the Melowi once they were alone.

"Nah," Ka'nak answered. "Are you?"

"I'm pretty good," she admitted, thinking about all the times she'd played the game.

"You have any money?" he asked.

"A little," Geroux replied. "Why do you ask?"

Ka'nak shrugged. "No reason."

"That's interesting," Gorad said.

Jiya heard the words as they sunk through the mire of her tired brain, and she pried her eyes open, letting loose a gigantic yawn.

"What's interesting?" she asked.

"Nice of you to join us," Reynolds joked. "Late night last night?"

"Late night since I got kidnapped and dragged aboard a superdreadnought run by a maniacal AI," she shot back as she climbed to her feet and stretched.

"So, is that a yes or a no?" Reynolds asked.

Jiya groaned and looked at Gorad, who was hovering over the now assembled pieces of the computer mainframe.

"You going to tell us what's interesting or do you want us to guess?" Jiya asked.

The alien AI waved the pair over. He pointed to one of the monitors, which showed a clear image of what one of the arms was doing inside the frame of the reassembled mainframe.

While nothing she saw meant anything to her, Jiya knew the rapt attention Reynolds was giving the screen meant that something there was important.

"Do you see this here?" Gorad asked, the robot arm pointing to a microchip on the computer's board. Its edges were scored black.

"Why is none of the rest of the area scorched?" Reynolds asked.

"Exactly," Gorad said, letting the camera on the end of

the robot arm zoom in closer. "This area does not carry sufficient current to burn out like this."

"And there's no way that my weapons would have left that little bit of char and not touch any of the rest of the board around it," Reynolds realized. "That means it had to have been burnt out before we destroyed it."

"But again, this isn't something that would flare out like this," Gorad reiterated.

"You sure?" Reynolds asked. "It looks like substandard parts you've got soldered in there."

"I manufacture my own parts here on Grindlevik 3, and I find I can do more with less if I do not expend our resources on the most expensive of electronics."

"So you're cheap as well as annoying?" Reynolds told the other AI. "That's a dangerous combination."

"I spend all my time in these constructs," Gorad barked, shaking his head, "And I have never had that particular microchip burn out before."

"Always a first time," Reynolds replied.

"Maybe, but unlikely," Gorad argued.

Jiya groaned and stepped between the two of them. "Okay, so what exactly does that part do," she asked, trying to refocus the two AIs.

"Nothing that would cause it to become so damaged," Gorad admitted. "It's there to shunt remote signals to—" Gorad stopped mid-sentence, his eyes widening.

"Remote signals to what?" Reynolds asked, leaning in even to get a better look.

Gorad ordered the arm to pull the burnt chip, and the mechanoid plucked it from the board and pulled it out so the pair of AIs could examine it more closely.

Gorad dissected the part in front of Reynolds, and both AIs muttered curses when the case was peeled back and the insides of the chip were revealed.

The insides were scorched as well, several of the pins melted together and shorted out.

Gorad tossed the burnt chip aside and ordered his arms to pull another piece. Once they had, Gorad put power to the small processor and a flush of data washed across the screens above the workstation.

"There's our culprit," Gorad exclaimed, pointing out a section in the code that looked like gibberish to Jiya.

Reynolds, however, knew what it meant.

"Someone hijacked your remote signal system," Reynolds muttered, shaking his head. "How could this happen?"

"I don't know," Gorad answered, clearly flustered by the development. "I'm tracing the signal input that relayed the last order the ship received."

"You mean the one to attack us?" Reynolds clarified.

"Exactly that," Gorad shot back. "If we can find the source—"

"We can fire the ESD at it?" Jiya suggested.

"Not a bad idea, but no," Reynolds told her. "We need to track it down so we can keep it from happening again and find out who ordered a hit on the *Reynolds*."

"The signal originated from beyond the gravity well of the Grindlevik suns," Gorad announced as the data came through.

"Right where the—" Jiya started.

"Right where we Gated in, yes," he said, cutting her off.

"Is this something you brought with you to my system?" Gorad asked, the eyes on his android body narrowing.

"Unlikely. No one is capable of tracking the destination of a Gate drive," Reynolds answered, and Jiya wondered why he was lying to the other AI.

Reynolds knew damn well that the signal originated from the mystery ship that Ria had picked up shortly after the crew had come down to the planet.

Still, she figured if Reynolds didn't want to let Gorad in on that information, it was best that she kept her mouth shut.

"Scanners are picking up nothing at the coordinates the signal originated from," Gorad explained. "That means the threat has either left the system or it's beyond my range."

"Can you block the signal from this end to make sure it doesn't happen again?" Reynolds wondered.

"I can do that easily enough," Gorad bragged. He went silent for a moment, then grinned. "The process has already begun aboard my fleet and the defense perimeter ring."

"That was fast," Jiya remarked.

Gorad nodded. "Automated services aboard each of the destroyers and the defensive ring have begun pulling the defective chips that allowed remote access. Until that task is accomplished, I have surrounded Grindlevik 3 with a signal barrier that will block all access to the remote systems of my fleet from space. There will be no more attacks upon your ship by my destroyers, I assure you."

"You sure your shield will block all the signals coming in?" Reynolds asked the other AI.

"I'm positive," Gorad answered, jutting his chin out. "It

is clear how the unknown source manipulated my system and took advantage of it," he said. "We are both quite lucky that they were not able to do more with it while the opportunity remained available."

Jiya grunted at hearing that. *Why hadn't they?*

"Perhaps the gravity well impacted the strength of their signal," Gorad went on, answering Jiya's unspoken question. "Or perhaps there are limitations to what our unknown foe can accomplish even with access to the ship's systems."

"Or maybe they had something else in mind entirely," Reynolds added.

"Perhaps so," Gorad replied. "Regardless, the opening has been sealed off, and it is time to sit down and discuss how we might find our elusive foe before he devises another way to attack us."

"'Us?'" Reynolds asked.

"Indeed," Gorad replied. "This hack cost me two destroyers and your trust," he said. "This attack is upon me, as well, and it is possible that this enemy might well expand the scope of its operations and harm those in my care."

"*We* should definitely talk about this," Jiya said, subtly emphasizing the "we" part of her statement.

She needed to know what the AI had in mind before she slipped up and said something she shouldn't to Gorad.

"Yes, let's gather the crew and discuss our options," Reynolds conceded.

Jiya nodded, letting the two AIs lead the way out of the building to a new hovercraft that had arrived to pick them up. She climbed into the craft and sat in the back away from the AIs, who'd both sat up front, trying to give herself room to think.

The craft took off, and Jiya stared out at the dull scenery as they raced back toward town.

She thought about reaching out to Asya to get an update on the mysterious ship, but she didn't want to risk it.

Besides, she figured she'd learn more than she wanted to soon enough.

CHAPTER TWELVE

To Reynolds' surprise, Gorad delivered them to the Grindlovian council chambers. The council members sat rigid in their chairs as the crew, which had been collected moments before, and Jiya and the two AIs filed into the room.

Once more, chairs had been set out for the visitors. This time, however, there were no Telluride in the room. Reynolds found himself wondering why.

He took a seat facing the council with the rest of the crew and watched as Gorad went over to stand alongside Fulla Sol's chair.

As before, the council stared out through dull eyes, doing nothing that indicated that the Grindlovians were even aware of those seated before them.

"I have called you all together because we find ourselves facing an unexpected threat, one that has already caused division in the negotiations between me and the visiting Federation AI, Reynolds," Gorad opened up.

"Does this enemy threaten us?" Fulla Sol asked.

"We do not know," Gorad replied. "The threat is still vague and uncertain."

"Then perhaps you should send a message for us to convene when you know more," Vor Stygn remarked in a droll tone.

"But this concerns all of you," Jiya spit out, clearly annoyed at the council's dismissal of the threat that had nearly cost the lives of several of her crew. "How can you not care?"

"Until it is proven that it truly is a concern of ours," Fulla Sol stated, "we have more important issues to attend to."

"If this is a problem, it stands to reason that those who brought it to our doorstep should be the ones to resolve it," Vor Hiln chimed in. "Does that not make sense, Gorad?"

"Perhaps it does," the alien AI admitted, not bothering to look at the Grindlovians because none of them would have noticed anyway.

Without another word the council dropped away as they had the first time, leaving the crew alone in the room with Gorad.

"Charming folks, these Grindlovian council members," Ka'nak said, staring at the closed hatches beneath which the council members had disappeared.

"I've known friendlier wolves," Takal added.

"They are set in their ways, I'm afraid," Gorad defended.

"Ways you facilitated," Jiya challenged the alien AI.

Reynolds noticed that Gorad was growing annoyed at Jiya's continued snark, but the other AI didn't shy away from the criticism.

"Perhaps you are right," he said. "I have made their lives simple, and they struggle with adversity now that they have so little of it."

"Anyway, why don't we stick to the topic at hand?" Maddox interjected, trying to corral everyone and keep them on point. He glared in Jiya's direction, his lip twitching involuntarily. As the de facto leader of their group, her acerbic comments served no purpose except to fracture and demoralize the crew. She looked away before he did.

Reynolds went to say something, but a transmission on his personal comm interrupted him. Asya's words sank into his ears like stones.

He turned to Geroux, who'd had the situation with the remote access explained to her on her way to the council chambers, and asked, "You have any good ideas about how to shield the fleet from outside influence until all the faulty chips are changed out?"

"I told you," Gorad cut in, "I've already done that. There will be no more problems with my ships."

"No?" Reynolds asked, shaking his head. "Then maybe you can explain why my crew just reported that one of your destroyers has broken away from your fleet and shot off into space. Was that your doing?"

Gorad stiffened, scowling. He froze, Reynolds recognizing that the other AI was reaching out to touch base with his fleet and confirm the report, which told Reynolds that Gorad *hadn't* sent the ship off.

"I…I don't understand," Gorad stammered. "My shields—"

"Didn't do a damn thing," Reynolds shouted. "You

promised me that you could block the signals and prevent another attack from happening, but that doesn't seem to be the case, Gorad," Reynolds growled. "Now my ship and crew are in danger...again."

"But you saw the evidence in the computer we examined," Gorad argued. "The ship that departed had the old chip removed and a new one installed already. There is no way it could—"

"And yet here we are again," Reynolds argued. He paced in a tight circle before coming back to glare at Gorad.

Reynolds raised his hands in the air and screamed his frustration.

"I can't believe this shit, Gorad," he told the other AI. "Your process has made all of your devices vulnerable to whatever hack this is, and it's going to cost people their lives. Most likely those of my crew if any more of those damn destroyers are taken over."

"This has nothing to do with my parts production," Gorad defended, but Reynolds overrode him.

"The hell it doesn't!" Reynolds shouted.

Reynolds stomped off, going to the door of the council chambers and staring outside.

"How certain are you that it isn't your parts, Gorad?" Reynolds asked, pressing the alien AI for an answer. "How sure are you that this exploit isn't due to substandard production to mass-produce the chips?"

"One hundred percent," Gorad replied, puffing out his android chest. "I stand by my hardware unequivocally."

Reynolds spun on a heel. "Then it's your programming that's been compromised," the AI stated, driving his point home.

Gorad went to argue, only to stand there with his mouth open, clearly realizing that Reynolds had outmaneuvered him.

The alien AI's android shoulders slumped.

"Maybe it *is* my programming," the other AI admitted hesitantly, and Reynolds bit back a smile at seeing Gorad fold. "Perhaps we should examine it together since I…I might well be blind to the exploit, if there is one."

He'd pushed Gorad into a corner, poking and prodding until he could deliver the fatal blow that would give Reynolds access to Gorad's system, where Reynolds could find out for sure how the mystery ship was controlling Gorad's automatons.

And if Reynolds just happened to pluck out any other details while he was in there, such as the plans to the agro-printer and its food source ingredients, so be it.

"I promise not to dig too deeply," Reynolds told the other AI.

"As if it would be that easy," Gorad replied.

But Reynolds knew that Gorad's confidence had already taken a heavy blow and would not recover.

Once inside the alien AI's programming, Reynolds would have the upper hand, Gorad having let him in past the most complicated and technical of the AI's security systems.

He might well keep Reynolds from delving too deeply and gaining complete access to the AI's data, but Reynolds was certain he would be able to scrape the upper layers at the very least.

Even if he couldn't find much there, just getting to see some part of how the alien AI operated would be a victory.

He could record his journey and dissect whatever he came across later, reverse-engineering the systems to give him a better idea how Gorad operated.

That would provide him opportunities he didn't currently have when it came to dealing with the alien AI.

"Don't worry, I'll play nice," Reynolds said.

The alien AI stood rigid for several moments, likely having to convince himself that this was a good idea. Reynolds remained quiet. He didn't want to push any harder than he already had.

Gorad was on the proverbial ledge. What came next would push him off or cause him to dig down deep and resist.

Everything relied on the seed that Reynolds had planted growing. If Gorad felt he was being manipulated, the alien AI would step back and become defiant.

Reynolds couldn't have that.

After several more moments that seemed as if they'd lasted hours, Gorad nodded and dropped to sit on the floor.

"Can you access my systems remotely if I provide you with the key?" Gorad asked.

Reynolds glanced at Jiya, his face at an angle that Gorad couldn't see, and he winked. Her eyes narrowed, and he grinned before turning about and going over to sit before the android.

"I can," Reynolds told him.

Gorad straightened and met Reynolds' gaze with steely insistence. "Understand, any attempt to influence or alter my programming while you are in my systems will be deemed an act of war against me, Reynolds," the other AI warned. "I will not tolerate such."

Reynolds nodded and agreed without hesitation. "You have my word." And he meant it. Reynolds didn't want to hack Gorad, he simply wanted an advantage.

Gorad nodded again, accepting Reynolds at his word—at least outwardly.

"I'm sending you the access code," Gorad said, letting his chin drop to his chest as he cycled his systems down to allow access.

Reynolds picked up Gorad's transmission and beamed his consciousness into the alien AI's system, using the code to pry through the web of security the other AI had in place.

"Watch our bodies," Reynolds said as his android body drifted away behind him.

Lights flashed throughout Reynolds' computer consciousness, and he navigated the pathway into Gorad's brain as it opened before him.

It was a strange feeling.

He'd expected it to be similar to how he had felt when he'd transferred his consciousness into the two android bodies, but this was so completely different that it caught him off-guard.

Gorad truly was as alien as he seemed.

The coding and programming weren't simply in a different language, but their nuances and manner of operating were unknown to Reynolds.

Things simply worked differently there.

Reynolds metaphorically stumbled into the

labyrinthine maze that was Gorad's system, and he gaped at what he saw.

It was like stepping into a foreign country, having never left your own.

Visual representations of Gorad's systems were everywhere, towering like new-world skyscrapers. Yet, right alongside were tiny *buildings* of code that might as well have been third-world shops on Earth set beside the technological behemoths.

"Not what you expected, is it?" Gorad asked from beside him.

Reynolds spun to look at the alien AI.

He knew to expect Gorad's inner image of himself, but the other AI was right. Nothing was what he'd expected.

Gorad appeared to be the perfect mix of Telluride and Grindlovian. Blue and pale, Gorad's system essence looked powerful like the Telluride servants, but there was a neutral stoicism in the expression that spoke of the Grindlovians' attitude. It looked amiss on the Telluride face.

"No, it's not," Reynolds admitted.

He glanced down at himself and noticed that his inner image was that of a human, and he grinned. That, at least, he'd expected, though he had to admit that it might well reveal more about him to the other AI than he might want. He wondered if he could manipulate himself to be one of the red-skinned Larians.

If Gorad took note, he said nothing about it.

"This way," Gorad said, gesturing for Reynolds to follow. They traveled what vaguely resembled a street in a crowded town whose advertising budget had gotten way out of hand.

Flashing lights and gleaming circuitry abounded, and Reynolds marveled at it, wondering how the hell any of it worked. None of it made any sense. He couldn't see how one was connected to the other.

Circuits seemed to end randomly, and what he determined after a while were chips looked nothing like those in his system. It was as if there'd been an explosion in the parts factory, and Gorad's creators simply left the pieces where they'd landed, littering the boards of his system.

Though he would remember every detail of what he could see, Reynolds wasn't sure he'd be able to piece any of it together once he got a chance to look back on it.

He suspected he would need to enlist Takal nearly full time to attempt to decipher the alien technology. Between the two of them, and possibly Geroux helping with her unparalleled computer skills, they might be able to make something of the mess that was Gorad's programming.

As the two walked, Gorad pointed out what the various systems controlled.

"This is the subroutine that runs the droid factory and its creation of new droids, as well as the repair of any systems that need work," he said, acting like a tour guide in his own head. "And over there," he pointed to a mass of circuits that might as well have been a spider web with dead flies draped across it, "is the system that maintains the automated vehicles across Grindlevik 3. It controls all aspects of the planet's transportation system."

"And that?" Reynolds asked, pointing to a brilliantly

flickering arrangement of circuits that might be compared to a Christmas tree decorated by an overzealous child.

The image blurred and blacked out as soon as Reynolds turned his attention to it.

"That," Gorad replied, grinning slyly, "is the access point to the planetary defense system. You don't get to see that."

Reynolds nodded, biting back a grunt. That was a priority to examine, but he HAD missed it and would have to make do with the rest of the system.

"That controls all this?" he asked, pointing to the array of circuitry around the blanked-out station.

"Exactly," Gorad told him. "If there is a problem in the system, it will be located somewhere around here."

Gorad went over to where he could see the whole array and began to examine it, much like he had done with the destroyer's damaged mainframe.

Reynolds stood alongside the alien AI, following suit.

It was daunting. Reynolds had pictured coming in and simply plucking secrets from Gorad's head, but he'd been grossly mistaken.

He would need to dig deeply into the system and probe it to see how it worked in order to determine how it might have been compromised. It was going to be complicated.

"Begin there," Gorad told him, pointing to a section nearest the center of the system, making it easier for Reynolds. "I'll trace back through the circuitry."

Reynolds wasn't exactly sure what he was looking for, but he didn't say anything. He followed Gorad's lead and stepped into the maze of systems before him.

Gorad disappeared behind him as they slipped into the machinery like ghosts and went their separate ways.

Reynolds trailed along the path of circuitry, examining each and every aspect as he went past it. Though he wasn't completely sure what he was looking at, the alien signature of Gorad's creators was obvious, making it clear to Reynolds that nothing he was looking at had been compromised.

He had a hunch as to what he might find if Gorad were telling the truth about the attack, but Reynolds didn't want to presume too much. That might bias his examination.

So, he cleared his head and followed where the circuits led.

On and on he went, sensing Gorad all around him, watching, examining Reynolds as much as Reynolds examined Gorad. But Reynolds had expected that, so he kept searching for something that might have been compromised without actually touching or manipulating any part of the system.

A short while later, as the two AI surveyed different parts of Gorad's systems, Reynolds came to a halt, a strange sequence of circuits catching his attention. He came to stand before the board and looked closer.

If he had a pulse, it would have raced right then.

Where the Grindlovian touch had been apparent throughout the system, it was clear something else was at work there.

The chaos of Gorad's framework suddenly became ordered and rigid in a tiny area of the board, structurally different from the rest of the circuits around it. Reynolds leaned in closer and examined the strange flow of energy that seemed to run in direct defiance of the rest of the system laid out there.

He knew right then what he was looking at.

"Gorad! You might want to come over here," he called, knowing the other AI would hear him.

"What is it?" Gorad responded, materializing beside Reynolds in an instant.

"I found your hack," Reynolds replied bluntly.

And what a hack it was.

CHAPTER THIRTEEN

Gorad stared at the strange conglomeration of circuits with wide eyes. "This is…wrong," he said, clearly unable to believe it still.

"It's very wrong," Reynolds shot back. "Your system has clearly been compromised."

"But how?" Gorad wondered, shaking his head.

"I don't know," Reynolds replied. "This is definitely the problem." He reached out and pointed to a place in the circuit, lights gleaming near his finger. "This configuration is giving off a faint signal every few seconds."

"I can't detect it," Gorad growled, leaning in to look where Reynolds pointed.

"It's there, though," Reynolds told him. "It's sending transmissions."

"Can you block them?"

"Probably, but we need to track it to its source first," Reynolds explained. "Find out who is doing this and why."

"But if we do that, it's possible they will detect us and do something drastic," Gorad argued.

"Maybe, but given that we're not going to learn how your system was compromised without determining who compromised it, I think we need to risk it."

"But they're not *your* internals," he complained.

"You're right," Reynolds replied, "they aren't." He shrugged. "So, I guess we just plug the hole and leave it at that. There's no way there's a second access point hidden anywhere."

Gorad groaned. "Do not attempt to patronize me, Reynolds. I know well enough what I risk with this maneuver."

Reynolds shook his head. "It's not just you at risk, Gorad," he countered. "My people were the ones who were hurt because of this. So far, none of yours have been. That makes me think there's more to this than someone simply hacking their way into your systems for shits and giggles."

Gorad raised an eyebrow. "I do not understand what shits and giggles have to do with one another."

"A human euphemism to match my avatar," Reynolds told him. "My point is, we need to find out who is doing this or we won't be able to determine how widespread the hack is." He motioned to the corrupted circuit before them. "It could well only be this section, but it's obvious the alien programming is something you can't detect without it being pointed out to you. And there's no way we can search your entire system quickly enough to stop whoever this is."

"I agree," Gorad said slowly. "We must do this."

Reynolds waited until the corrupt circuit triggered its

next transmission and intercepted the signal, breaking it down into its component code.

"This is complex," he said a moment later, having translated the signal and determined how to track it, "but I've plucked an access code from its components."

Reynolds sent the code to Gorad and stepped into the next signal that shot out from the hack, using the code to ride the signal back to its source.

Lights whirled around their consciousnesses as the two AIs hitched a ride on the signal. It pulled them directly through the planetary defense component Gorad had tried to block Reynolds from. The alien AI hissed, but there was nothing he could do.

To Reynolds' regret, they moved so quickly that he barely got a glance at the system, giving him no direct insight as to its workings.

Then the two were in space, riding the beam.

Able to detect himself as they passed the SD *Reynolds*, the AI could then plot the basic direction. After a moment, he knew where they were headed.

The strange alien ship Ensign Alcott had detected while the crew was on Grindlevik 3.

Not long after that realization they were aboard the craft, embedded in its computer systems.

The two AI came to a sudden stop as the first of the security systems noted the anomaly and blocked their passage. A glowing red wall appeared before them.

"They know we're here," Gorad said.

Reynolds remained quiet as he examined the wall, then shook his head. "No, they don't," he told the other AI. "This is automated security, a firewall designed to block traffic outside of a specific frequency. Since we're not the same as the beam, it scraped us off it and deposited us here."

Gorad leaned closer to the wall and narrowed his eyes. "This coding looks familiar."

Reynolds nodded. "It has scraps of Grindlovian in it, which might explain how they were able to break through your security."

"It certainly explains why I couldn't detect it," Gorad announced. "It's close enough to mimic my own systems."

"It is," Reynolds shot back with a grin, "but that's also a weakness as far as I'm concerned."

"How so?"

"Because it gives us a source to work with," Reynold told the alien AI. He motioned to Gorad. "Scan the firewall."

"But they'll detect me doing so," he said.

Reynolds shook his head. "No, they won't. The firewall will determine your signal is a random probe and will re-route it to keep you from seeing that it's been interacted with. I, however, will see its path, and can trace where it goes and how they handle it."

"Thus determining whether the original signal is analyzed before being returned to space to continue its journey."

Reynolds grinned. "Exactly. Because they don't want you to know they are intercepting your signals, thus signaling to you that they are, they have to cycle the signal back out into space."

"Which means it will reach deeper into their systems, with their blessing," Gorad realized. "You know, of course, there will be more security points beyond here?"

"Of course, but every step deeper is another chance to find a bypass. Unless they have a specialist or an AI actively reviewing each and every signal they're processing, they won't notice we've infiltrated their system."

Gorad smiled, agreeing with Reynolds' assessment.

He put his hand against the firewall and timed his push just as the hacked system launched another signal. His essence attached itself to the beam and was carried away.

And though Gorad couldn't see the effectiveness of what he'd done, to Reynolds, it looked like a meteor arcing through the night sky.

The hitchhiking probe was carried by the beam signal, twisting and turning through the system's circuits, lighting the way they needed to go as brightly as if it had been waving them on.

Reynolds transmitted the route to Gorad and started off without waiting for the other AI. He stepped through the access point of the firewall and deeper into the alien ship. He turned his head slowly, scanning everything so he could feed it through the system back to the *Reynolds* and use the complete power of his processors to sort and examine the data.

"How far do you think they'll let us invade?" Gorad wondered.

"We're still within the auspices of their automated security protocols," Reynolds answered. "I think we'll get a little farther before anyone notices us."

And he was right. The pair continued on, examining the alien technology and code spread out before them. The farther they got, the surer Reynolds became of the source of the ship.

It was Loranian, he was certain.

That meant the hack on Gorad's system and the subsequent attack on the *Reynolds* had been a deliberate attempt to get to Reynolds and his crew.

This had nothing to do with Gorad.

Reynolds grunted, contemplating what that meant.

"This programming is quite complex," Gorad said, interrupting Reynolds' thoughts, "but it's awkwardly constructed and arranged."

"That's because the people who designed it are a bit backward in their evolution," Reynolds answered, thinking of Geroux's programming methods.

As effective as they were, a large part of that effectiveness was because the nature of it was so radically different from most other code Reynolds had seen. There was a mechanical aspect to the Loranian tech that implemented a brute-force approach that eschewed subtlety and hammered its way through other system's defenses.

Which might explain part of how they'd managed to hack into Gorad.

Although it didn't explain everything.

A forceful attempt to break into Gorad's system would have announced their presence to the alien AI, but he hadn't noticed it until Reynolds pointed it out. Even then, Gorad wasn't seeing it exactly as Reynolds was.

As such, that meant there was more to the hack than Loranian coding.

Reynolds and Gorad went on, Reynolds wondering what other influences might be involved.

At a second security point, Reynolds watched as the next signal burst shot past them. It split into a million different beams, each traveling a different path through the security veil.

Reynolds tracked them all, plotting their courses and grinning once he found the route that allowed the signal all the way through.

"This way," Reynolds told Gorad, waving the other AI on as he slipped through the security barrier.

A short distance later, Reynolds spied a network of systems that appeared to be processing the signal the hack was sending from Gorad's system. Lights flickered as energy traveled past, triggering circuits and parsing the code of the signal.

The pair came closer and watched as the hack signal was broken down into its component code for analysis. Reynolds' eyes shot wide at what he saw there.

Then a flash of red washed over them, and Reynolds felt a physical wave of energy as it slammed into him, knocking him and Gorad away from the circuit.

"They're onto us," Gorad mumbled.

Reynolds didn't bother replying. He stared at the system and did his best to examine it before the next wave hit.

Unfortunately, he caught only the barest of glimpses before he was driven out.

Reynolds' consciousness crashed into his android body with a resounding *thud*.

He toppled to his side and saw that Gorad had done the same.

It was if they'd been shot back into their bodies by a cannon.

"Whoa!" Jiya shouted, running over to him and helping him to his feet. "What was *that*?"

Geroux helped Gorad up as the rest of the crew gathered around them, eyes wide with concern.

Reynolds met Gorad's gaze and understanding passed between them.

"Did you see that?" Reynolds asked.

Gorad nodded. "I did."

"See what?" Takal asked.

"Trouble," Reynolds answered, staring at Gorad as if he might be able to see his way back to the Loranian ship that had evicted them from their systems.

"I suggest now is a good time to block their access," Gorad said.

"I agree." Reynolds formulated a subroutine to shore up Gorad's programming and cut out the cancer of the hack and to immunize his system against further attempts at invasion.

"Their access?" Jiya asked.

"The ship on the fringes of the gravity well is Loranian," Reynolds answered. "They must have tracked us from there."

"From Asya's planet?" Ka'nak asked.

Reynolds nodded. "It seems we're being followed."

"Asya's not going to like that," Jiya muttered.

"I don't like it," Reynolds replied.

"Nor do I," Gorad agreed. "This means you brought this to my doorstep, Reynolds." His tone of voice had become as sharp as a dagger.

"So it would appear." Reynolds nodded, then sent an

encrypted code to Gorad. "And now I'm kicking it out for you."

Gorad stood still a moment as he processed the security protocols Reynolds had supplied based on the hack's coding, and the alien AI seemed to relax slightly.

"I've applied the security patch, and I'm now able to trace the full extent of the hack that compromised my system," he said a few seconds later. "Thank you," he added reluctantly. "I'm capable of recognizing the remote access points it's corrupted and have blocked them all off and redirected how my security protocols will deal with any future intrusion attempts."

"Will that keep them out?" Geroux asked.

"It will," Reynolds assured. "For now, at least."

"Now that I understand how they did what they did, I will not allow them access again," Gorad growled. "I feel violated."

"As you should," Reynolds told him, thinking back on what he'd seen.

There was more going on than either of the AIs entirely understood, but Reynolds kept what he suspected to himself.

It would do no good to presume anything, but if what he thought was true, he knew what his mission was.

"Reach out to Asya, warn her that the ship stalking us is from her planet, and tell her to be prepared for it," Reynolds told Jiya. "Gorad and I spoiled the surprise party, and now they know that *we* know they're here. I have no idea how they'll react to that news, but make sure she stays put and does nothing for now. I don't want her chasing the ship."

Jiya nodded and relayed the message over the comm.

Reynolds heard Asya cursing in response to hearing the news, filling the comm with a colorful sequence of what the Loranians could do to themselves, with explicit instructions.

Geroux blushed.

"That Asya sure can swear," Ka'nak said, smiling.

"That she can," Maddox agreed. "You should hear her when you wake her up early for her shift."

The Melowi raised his hands. "No, thanks. I love to fight, but she scares me before she's had her coffee."

"She scares all of us," Takal assured him, chuckling.

"What do we do now?" Jiya asked.

"Well, seeing as how the Loranians don't have Gate technology, we have to assume they are working with someone who does," Reynolds answered. "That means we have no idea why they are shadowing us."

"They've kept their distance this long," Maddox argued. "Why would they suddenly chance an attack?"

"Well, their presence isn't a secret anymore," Reynolds replied. "They seemed to be content watching us, but with their clandestine efforts out in the open, they're going to have to decide on a different course of action now."

"Which could be anything," Maddox realized, understanding that their lack of knowledge about their enemy made an educated guess regarding their intentions impossible.

"Exactly," Reynolds answered. "Which is why I want Asya to keep the *Reynolds* ready to go, but I don't want her engaging the Loranian ship until we figure a few things out."

"There's a good chance they have more surprises waiting for us," Jiya said, more thinking aloud than making a statement. "Especially if they have Gate technology they shouldn't have."

"Precisely my point," Reynolds told her. "We don't want to take any chances."

Gorad stepped forward. "I think it best to inform my people of what has transpired and let them know we face some uncertainty due to the nature of the hack and the ship that avoided my detection."

"Let's do that now since we're here," Reynolds said, motioning to the council chamber they were still hanging out in.

Gorad reached out to the council members and informed them of a meeting. At the same time, he contacted the Telluride and asked for representatives to join them so he could inform both groups at the same time. After that, he'd use the planet-wide communication network to update the remaining populace.

A few minutes later, the Grindlovian council rose from beneath their hatches. As usual, the blank expressions on their faces told Reynolds nothing of what they might be thinking or feeling.

The Telluride who arrived a moment afterward were the polar opposite.

They displayed worried expressions and came over immediately to acquire extra chairs for themselves. L'Willow and San Roche were there, as well as L'Eliana and San Paget. L'Sofee was with them too, and the female was obviously worried. Lines creased her forehead as she took a seat alongside her people and glanced around, wondering what the summons had been for.

Reynolds positioned himself so he could see both groups, and Gorad stood opposite him.

"Why have you summoned us?" Fulla Sol asked.

For the first time, Reynolds saw a hint of frustration etched on her features.

The other council members stared without expression, but they kept glancing at Fulla Sol.

"We have a potential problem," Gorad explained. "At the edge of our system there is an alien ship which has proven to be a danger. They have intruded into my systems, and were the cause behind the attack upon the superdreadnought *Reynolds*."

The Telluride gasped, L'Sofee pressing her golden hand over her mouth.

"What does this have to do with us?" Full Sol asked.

Jiya jumped in, her cheeks red. "These people hacked Gorad's systems, and there's a chance they can do it again."

"But these hackers chose to attack *you* and *your* ship, did they not?" Full Sol fired back.

"Damn right they did!" Jiya shouted, jumping from her seat. "That means they don't care about hurting people."

"You misunderstand my point," Fulla Sol argued. "I believe it's clear that this alien ship has come here for *you* and *your* people, not ours. As such, I see no reason for concern."

L'Sofee stood, eyes narrowed. Her skin gleamed in the room's lights. "Are you so disconnected as to not understand that a threat to Gorad is a threat to all of us?"

Fulla Sol scoffed, and Reynolds was taken aback by the

unexpected ferocity of the sound. The female *almost* leaned forward in her excitement. Reynolds thought she might have wobbled, the most physical movement he'd seen from any of the Grindlovians.

"Did these enemies attack our planet?" Fulla Sol asked. "Did they invade or infiltrate any of our agro or production centers?" The council member gave a barely perceptible shake of her head. "They did not, L'Sofee," she answered her own question. "As such, I see no reason to alarm the populace. We should not engage in fearmongering."

"How is it fearmongering to be concerned?" L'Sofee fired back. "Our people have a right to know what is going on."

"Of course they do," Fulla Sol replied, "but to claim this alien ship is a threat to Grindlovians or Telluride is to presume too much."

Fulla Sol raised a hand slowly, her index finger finally creeping out to point at Reynolds.

"Their target is these strangers who brought their conflict to us," Fulla Sol argued. "As such, I believe the cure to this woe is to make the superdreadnought and its crew leave our space and take their problems with it."

L'Sofee opened her eyes wide, unbelieving. "These people hacked Gorad!" she explained. "They made one of the planetary defense destroyers attack the superdreadnought. What is to stop them from doing more even if our guests depart?"

"I have made our stance clear, L'Sofee," Fulla Sol declared, and the room was filled with the hiss of the hatchways beneath the council chairs opening. "If you and the other Telluride wish to assist the crew of the *Reynolds,* you are free to do so. However, your people should know their place and concentrate on service, for it is not in your people's nature to lead."

The Telluride stared wide-eyed at the Grindlovian council female as she and the others sank into the ground and disappeared, the hatches closing behind them.

"Well, that escalated quickly," Geroux muttered.

"Them's fightin' words," Ka'nak added.

CHAPTER FOURTEEN

The crew and Reynolds left the council chamber and returned to the Telluride's dining hall. Gorad and the Telluride who'd been with them in the chamber had come, as well.

"I can't believe this," L'Sofee mumbled, pacing beside the table where the rest of the group sat.

"It appears the Grindlovians have made their stance quite clear," L'Willow commented, shaking her head in disgust.

"I...did not expect that," Gorad admitted.

"No." Jiya sighed. "I mean, who could imagine how catering to a race of people and doing every damn thing for them would make them hesitant to do anything?"

"That's enough, Jiya," Reynolds told her. "Gorad's only experience is with the Grindlovians and Telluride," he explained. "It's not like he's had a lot of introduction to the nature of living beings. Besides, since the Grindlovians created him early on, it's expected that he'd be a bit beholden to them and not see the consequences of everything that's been set in motion."

Jiya grunted but acknowledged Reynolds' point with a nod.

"It's easy to find yourself trapped in a life," Takal told her, reminding her of her own problems back on their home planet without detailing any specifics.

"You're right," Jiya answered, raising her hands in surrender. "But that still doesn't make this okay."

"I agree with that," Reynolds said, jumping back in. "But we can't drag the Grindlovians into something they want no part of."

"We would do more," L'Sofee said, dropping to a seat at the table. "Whatever the Grindlovians choose, the Telluride will not sit idly by and await our destruction passively."

"Like *servants*," San Paget muttered, each word spat out.

L'Eliana snarled. "We serve out of kindness for others," she explained, thumping a fist on the table, which rattled beneath the blow. "The Grindlovians, however, see things differently, it seems."

"That we are slaves," San Paget barked.

"Which we are not," L'Sofee clarified.

"I have never seen you as such," Gorad told the Telluride.

L'Sofee nodded. "We know this, Gorad, and do not hold it against you, though it does reinforce our thinking on what we spoke about earlier, Geroux." She turned to the young female with sadness in her eyes.

"I haven't had a chance to share your desires with my crew yet," Geroux answered, "but I'm guessing now's a good time."

She stood and faced Reynolds and Gorad.

"The Telluride believe there is more for them to learn and see," Geroux told the two AIs. "They want to leave Grindlevik 3 and experience what the universe has to offer."

"You would leave us?" Gorad asked, stiffening.

L'Sofee offered a sad nod in reply. "Long have we believed the Grindlovians no longer respected our efforts or were grateful for them," she said. "We've felt as if our service was expected, and Fulla Sol said as much in the council chambers."

"We would rather work for those who need and respect our service rather than those who believe it is their due in life to receive it," San Roche declared.

"But what will the Grindlovians do in your absence?" Gorad asked.

"I suspect they will learn self-sufficiency," Reynolds answered.

"Or they'd die off," Maddox added. "I'm picturing the latter if we're honest here."

Gorad sighed. "As am I, I'm afraid."

"It is not so simple to pack up an entire species and move to another planet," Takal warned, clearly trying to temper the Telluride's expectations.

"He's right," Jiya confirmed. "A move like that would upset both the Grindlovians' lives and yours. It would be incredibly difficult."

"We are not afraid of hard work," L'Sofee told them.

"That' s obvious," Jiya shot back, "but this is more than a simple move. It'd be starting all over." She jabbed a finger at Gorad. "Whether or not you want to admit it, that guy there has coddled your people as much as he has the Grindlovians."

L'Sofee's eyes became narrow slits. "How so?"

"Food production, the automated devices and systems, and providing a planetary defense system to keep invaders away," Jiya explained. "None of that can be overlooked in your desire to move on."

"She's right," Geroux added. "Packing up and leaving is a romantic image, but it's not realistic. Gorad feeds all of you, and you would be made to fend for yourselves on another planet."

"Some of your people nearly drowned while I was teaching them to swim," Jiya added.

"And none of you have the slightest sense of how or when to fight," Ka'nak argued.

"You also lack the basic sciences," Geroux finished. "Gorad has protected you and stunted your evolution, even though you might not realize it."

"I... I did not mean to," Gorad said, his guilt plain on his android features.

"Not saying you did," Reynolds assured him, "but that doesn't mean it didn't happen. You've unintentionally made them incapable of existing without you."

Gorad dropped to a seat on the floor, staring at the Telluride. "This was...wrong of me," he admitted, for the first time realizing what he had done and the consequences of his overwhelming desire to take care of the living creatures in his charge.

"It's not too late to correct things," Jiya told the alien AI. "We can help."

"You would?" Gorad asked.

"Of course," Geroux assured him.

The Telluride brightened, but Reynolds waggled a finger at them.

"We will most certainly help, but there is much we cannot do," he told them, not mincing any words. "We are not capable of taking the whole population of Telluride with us, nor can we offer you a planet on which to begin over. These are out of our ability."

"You mean we must stay here?" L'Sofee asked, clearly heartbroken.

"For now, yes," Reynolds told her. "When we depart, we can take a number of your people willing to work with—not *for*—us in our mission, but we lack the resources to do more than that."

"But we can still help," Jiya said.

"How?" L'Sofee asked.

"We can help negotiate a new way of life between you and the Grindlovians, with Gorad assisting us."

"A new life?" L'Eliana asked. "What would that entail?"

"The freedom you are looking for," Geroux answered. "We can help you move somewhere on Grindlevik 3; somewhere you can start over."

"But with support from Gorad still," Jiya added. "My goal would be to see you autonomous—free of the Grindlovians and their expectations—and we could provide your people with the building blocks toward a brighter future."

"There is much we can teach you," Takal joined in. "Then, when you are ready, you can enlist Gorad's aid in teaching you how to pilot those destroyers in orbit above. Then you would be free to seek out a new planet where your people could develop and grow as an independent race with your own destiny."

"That might well take generations, though," Reynolds warned. "This is no short-term plan but a marathon of existence. A way forward…eventually. As much as we want to help you, we cannot leave the Grindlovians with no support. Removing the Telluride all at once would be a death sentence since the Grindlovians can't fend for themselves."

The Telluride shared looks but said nothing, Reynolds knew they were communicating. It wasn't something as complex as telepathy, but what Geroux had said of L'Sofee was true. She *did* know the will of her people, and she spoke *for* them all.

L'Sofee stood and offered the crew and Reynolds a respectful bow. "We would take this path…with your assistance," she told them. "We will embrace the change and take responsibility to realize a new and better destiny."

"I will make your desire known to the others," Gorad said.

Outside, the community viewscreens awoke, and the news of the Tellurides' decision was announced to the whole of Grindlevik 3.

"Though I support your right to do this, I would be remiss in not mentioning that there will be strife in the wake of your decision," Gorad warned from his spot on the floor.

"There can be no change without it," Reynolds comforted them. "My people and I will work with yours to assure the smoothest transition possible. We will do whatever we can."

"Thank you, Reynolds," Gorad said, then turned to look at the crew. "And to you, as well."

Jiya nodded. "Don't thank us yet." She chuckled. "None of this is going to be easy, like you said. It is going to cause problems. Since the will of the Telluride is clear, the negotiations will be a significant challenge."

"I had no expectation that it would be simple," Gorad admitted.

"Good, because even peaceful revolutions can be dangerous," Jiya told him.

"Fortunately, we've all had a little experience with this," Reynolds assured the other AI.

"Still," Maddox announced, making sure Gorad and the Telluride knew he was talking to them, "we cannot guarantee anything. You are upending both your lives and those of the Grindlovians. People are going to feel betrayed, offended, sad, and even angry. With those emotions stirred up, there is always a chance for violence to erupt."

"I can increase the security presence of my droids," Gorad said. "That will keep the outbreaks of violence to a minimum should they occur."

"Well, not that you Telluride got much in the way of training," Ka'nak said, "but my money's on you guys. Even the worst of you can kick the ass of a pudding ball in a chair."

"Which is another issue that will need to be addressed," Reynolds said.

"You mean who's going to patch up all the Grindlovians when they get boot-stomped?" Ka'nak asked.

Jiya slapped him on the arm and Reynolds shook his head.

“No, I mean that without the Telluride to assist the Grindlovians, they will be entirely dependent upon Gorad’s machines to get by.” He turned to look at the other AI. “Can you manufacture enough devices to overcome the deficit of Telluride help?”

“Not immediately, of course,” Gorad answered, “but I can modify what’s available to them now and make it easier for them to function independently. Mostly.”

“Not entirely reassuring, Gorad,” Jiya told the AI.

L’Sofee stepped away from the table and turned to take in everyone there. “What is it we should do first?” she asked. “Where do we go from here?”

The other Telluride stared, awaiting the answer.

“I’d say the first step is to get the two factions together and see if we can find a starting point from which to work,” Jiya replied. “It’s unreasonable to imagine society is going to change immediately and everyone will just move on.”

“Jiya’s right,” Maddox told the group. “This change needs to be incremental, baby steps if you will. Nothing is going to change in a day, but we need to get the two groups together and work out a way forward, a plan to divorce two species of beings who have been interdependent for so long.”

L’Sofee nodded. “We understand, and we will do as we must.”

Gorad nodded. “Then I will convene another meeting shortly so that we might discuss the changes to come.” The alien AI sighed as he activated the communications system again and announced what they’d decided, calling a meeting of the two groups, the Grindlovians and the Telluride.

"It is a new day on Grindlevik 3," L'Sofee announced.

"Let's just hope it's not a Monday," Jiya said, looking for humor and sounding positive for the first time in a long time.

"You are making a mistake," Fulla Sol told L'Sofee matter-of-factly once the two sides had been convened again. "Without us, your people have no purpose," she declared.

L'Sofee scoffed. "You're mistaken, Fulla Sol, in your belief that our sole purpose is to serve you."

"We watched the Telluride attempt to do what the crew of the *Reynolds* showed you, and it was clear you have no aptitude for any of the skills required to live your lives without our assistance."

"*Your* assistance?" L'Eliana blurted in surprise, jumping to her feet. "We might well be dependent upon the kindness of Gorad, but your people do nothing to better our lives. We'll be fine without you."

L'Sofee raised a hand and L'Eliana reluctantly returned to her seat, though it was clear she was still fuming, her golden cheeks gleaming. L'Sofee hadn't sought to raise the Telluride's ire, only to take charge of their destiny. Tearing others down did nothing to improve one's status.

"You misjudge your importance in our lives, Fulla Sol," L'Sofee told the female. "We might not be ready to strike out on our own, but it is not the contribution of the Grindlovians that holds us back. It is our own ignorance," she said, then gestured to the council members. "You will soon learn that the same can be said for your lives when our assistance is reduced and eventually ceased."

"Your people barely work eight-hour shifts ten of the eleven days of the week," Fulla Sol said. "Do you think we cannot cope without such minimal assistance?"

"*Minimal*?" L'Eliana shrieked, and L'Sofee stopped her before she could jump up again. Her withering gaze told L'Eliana she was on thin ice.

"We created Gorad," Vor Stygn reminded, "and we will order him to abandon you and no longer provide his assistance."

"Order?" Gorad asked, stepping forward, a frown distorting his android features. "I'm afraid you misunderstand our relationship if you believe you can give me orders. You may have misinterpreted *all* of your relationships."

"We are your creators," Fulla Sol told him. "You would not exist were it not for us."

"I would not exist were it not for your *ancestors*," he corrected her. "And none of my programming requires me to comply with you or anyone else. I am autonomous and will do what must be done for the health and wellbeing of Grindlevik 3, but I will not be made to do anything I consider to be inappropriate, such as holding people against their will."

"You dare to defy us as these servants do?" Fulla Sol shouted—as much as a Grindlovian could shout—gesturing feebly toward the Telluride. Fulla Sol slumped back in her seat and gasped for breath.

It was the most movement Reynolds had seen from one

of her people. He stared at the female, a bit surprised she could pull it off without hurting herself.

"I will not allow such foolishness on Grindlevik 3," Fulla Sol announced a moment later. "You people will do what they always have. You will serve us, and be grateful for your place in our lives."

The whole group of Telluride rose to their feet, defiantly glaring at the council.

"We will speak no more of this," Fulla Sol announced, and the council members dropped into the floor, leaving the stunned Telluride and crew behind.

"I'm thinking that didn't go as well as anyone hoped," Ka'nak said. "Who wants a drink?"

Takal raised his hand, and Geroux glared at him. He lowered it quickly.

"We will not tolerate this," L'Sofee told everyone. "We cannot."

"I agree," Jiya replied, shaking her head. "To think the Grindlovians believe they can get by without you and your people!"

"They cannot," L'Eliana assured her.

"Then maybe you should prove that to them," Jiya suggested.

"What do you intend?" Gorad asked slowly.

"Me? Nothing," Jiya answered, then pointed to the Telluride. "They, however, should show the Grindlovians just how different life would be without their help." Jiya grinned. "I say it's time to strike."

"Strike?" L'Sofee asked, clearly unsure what the word meant. "I have no intention of attacking the Grindlovians. We will not do that."

"Sorry, 'go on strike,'" Jiya clarified. "It means to protest your situation and step away from your work with the Grindlovians—all the Telluride as one. Let the Grindlovians survive on their own for a time, so they see just how much you do for them. That will teach them the value of your service."

L'Eliana smiled. "I like this idea."

"As do I," San Paget agreed.

L'Sofee nodded. "Then strike it is. The Telluride are strike!"

"*On* strike," Ka'nak corrected.

"We are on strike?" L'Sofee asked.

"Yes you are, damn it!" Jiya shouted, pumping her fist in the air.

Everyone looked at her strangely.

"Too much?" Jiya asked.

Geroux nodded. "A little, yeah."

"Okay, well, regardless, the Telluride are on strike," Jiya repeated. "The Grindlovians will have to take care of themselves for a bit. Let's see how they react to that."

"I suspect not well," Gorad said. The look on his face made it clear he was dreading the days ahead since the majority of the problems would fall on his shoulders, even with the crew's assistance.

Reynolds patted him on the back, trying to comfort the alien AI. "Don't worry, my friend. All that can happen is that everything falls apart. A strike will establish a base understanding of what happens when one side withdraws from the negotiations. The status quo changes. The negotiating positions change. I expect the Telluride will not be impacted, while the Grindlovians will be sorely challenged.

A strike will move the Telluride into a superior bargaining position, but when the Grindlovians return to the table, they must be treated with respect and the Telluride must negotiate in good faith without lording the change in dynamics over the other party. "

"Interesting, but I see the wisdom. I expect things will be bad for a short while. Despite their lack of physical capabilities, the Grindlovians are a proud people," Gorad explained.

"Things could be worse," Maddox told Gorad.

The AI looked at the general, an eyebrow raised. "How so?"

"You could be in charge of a planet full of Ka'naks." He chuckled, pointing at the Melowi warrior.

"He's not wrong," Ka'nak agreed. "There would be blood everywhere if there were a bunch of pissed-off mes roaming the planet." He motioned toward the departed council members' hatches. "At least now, all you really have to worry about is scrubbing tire scuffs off the tiles. I'd say you got it pretty good, robo-boss."

CHAPTER FIFTEEN

The first week of the strike was absolute chaos.

The Telluride, used to getting up daily and tromping to work for the Grindlovians, struggled with the lack of activity almost immediately.

The people had gathered at the dining hall that the crew had turned into a makeshift headquarters. The Telluride were restless. They stomped about aimlessly, pacing, desperate to find something to do while understanding that they were expected to remain there and discuss the future of their people. It made for quite a mess.

Jiya could tell it was torment for them.

They didn't understand what was going on, and passively sitting there discussing their future was as strange a task to them as swimming, fighting, or conducting a science experiment. The Telluride were not mentally prepared to not use their hands. They had been raised to a life of activity.

That only added to the chaos of the strike. They were

not yet ready for the change. As Reynolds had surmised, both parties would suffer during the strike.

The Telluride were in as much mental anguish as the Grindlovians. Something worth having was never easily achieved. The Telluride were earning their freedom.

Jiya stood on a table and called the restless throng to order. It was several minutes before they complied, and only L'Sofee raising her hands managed to quiet the crowd. Jiya offered the female a nod of thanks before turning to address the Telluride.

"Today is the first day of your new lives," she announced to a grumbling of uncertain voices. "Give yourself time to get used to it," she advised. "None of what you're doing here will be easy, I'm afraid, even if it is physically easier."

"This is unnatural," one of the crowd called. Her voice was echoed by dozens of others. "What are we doing?"

"You need to make a point," Jiya replied. "If your people go off and serve the Grindlovians as you've always done, then they will continue to expect it and nothing will change," she argued. "The Grindlovians need to become uncomfortable to realize the value they place upon your service."

"Are we, too, supposed to be uncomfortable?" one asked.

Jiya nodded, hiding her sigh. She'd answered a hundred variations of that question already.

It wasn't that the Telluride were fools. They had simply become so used to their lives as they were that, even when they were bothered by what was happening, they still stepped up and did the job. Serving others gave them purpose. It was their true nature.

Unfortunately, the Grindlovians had taken advantage and pressed the Telluride to do more and more. Their acquiescence had led the Grindlovians to believe themselves superior.

"Yes, I'm afraid you *are* going to be uncomfortable," Jiya answered. "No one here is saying you can't eventually go back to working with the Grindlovians, but it must be your choice and not because anyone ordered you to."

"Is there really a difference?" San Paget asked.

"Of course there is," Jiya replied, holding her hands out to calm the masses. "You will know when the decision is yours. You do what you're comfortable doing, and you're rewarded for it. The latter means you don't have a choice and the Grindlovians own you and your efforts," she explained. "*Huge* difference."

"Is there no middle ground?" a female cried out.

That was another question Jiya was becoming tired of —not that it wasn't a good one. Compromise was the cornerstone of diplomacy, a means to keep both sides participating in the process. If one side always got what it wanted, they would end up like the Grindlovians. If one side always submitted, they would be like the Telluride.

Explaining this to them was tedious, but Jiya knew she needed to keep doing it, over and over until it sank in and made sense to both sides.

"There is most certainly a middle ground," Jiya told the female. "That's what we're here to explore. We're trying to find a way that those of you who wish to work for the Grindlovians can do so fairly, while those who wish to move on can also do so." But here was the recurring problem. "All of you, however, must agree upon how we move forward with this. If you split, with one side doing one thing and the other doing something completely different, you will tear your society apart."

The crowd rustled and heated conversations broke out, as they had a dozen times since Jiya started saying it. The problem was that they had yet to determine a cohesive way forward.

Many of the older Telluride were content to serve as long as Gorad continued to care for them, providing food and stability.

The younger Telluride, who'd grown up seeing their parents struggling to cater to the uncaring Grindlovians, hated the idea of spending their lives slaving away for people who cared little about them or their welfare. To them, it was all about what the Grindlovians gained with no thought to what it cost the Telluride.

They'd seen their people suffer, growing old and weary and fading away, while the Grindlovians simply recruited another Telluride to take their place. The old passed away in the Telluride's part of the city, forgotten by their previous masters, having been viewed as disposable.

"No!" a young male shouted. "We must make the Grindlovians understand we are not their slaves! We are residents of this world, the same as they are, and we deserve the same respect."

The youngest of the group cheered the male while the elders grumbled and questioned the dangerous and unknown path forward.

Once more the crowd broke out into harsh conversations about what was best and how to accomplish it.

Jiya stomped her foot on the table and demanded the throng's attention. With L'Sofee's efforts, she managed to settle them down enough to listen.

"Look, I understand that there isn't a single way forward for all," she told them, believing her words wholeheartedly, "but a decision must be made that satisfies the majority. There will always be some among you who are unhappy with the way things are, and each of you will be allowed to go your own way once the majority solidifies the process and focus for your people," she explained. "However, there need to be protections in place to ensure that those who wish to work can do so, and those who wish to leave can do so, both without prejudice from Telluride and Grindlovians alike."

"How do we do that?" one asked from his seat nearby. Emotions were raw, but the Telluride were starting to listen—or they were too exhausted to argue. Jiya hoped it was the former.

"We have Gorad enact laws with our assistance, and create consequences for those who violate them," the first officer said. "We offer everyone freedom of choice, and defend that choice to the end so that no one can take advantage of others without there being some kind of reprisal."

"And you think we can accomplish this?" San Roche asked.

"I do," Jiya told him, nodding. "But it requires cooperation, not only between the Telluride and Grindlovians but among the Telluride, too. This cannot be achieved if you insist upon fighting each other."

Which was, of course, what happened immediately after her statement.

The crowd erupted, and both sides raised their voices to argue their points, the normally happy faces of the Telluride twisted in anger and frustration as they contradicted each other.

After several minutes without the noise quieting, Jiya called for them to settle again. She had to find a way to get them to contemplate the concept of freedom from a different perspective.

Up until then, the Telluride had spent all their time working for the Grindlovians, avoiding any real conversations about their way of life because it simply was what it was.

Now, however, with the arrival of the *Reynolds* and the realization that Gorad was not infallible, the Tellurides' frustration had risen into the light.

Unfortunately for them, they didn't have any coping mechanisms to process complex emotions or problems. They'd never had to before.

Jiya needed to get them focused and give them the opportunity to contemplate their future outside of familiar surroundings where they would resort to old habits.

"I have an idea, people," Jiya told the assemblage.

Geroux was amazed by the gatherings of the Grindlovians.

While she'd seen the raucous back and forth of the

Telluride during the strike, everyone shouting their opinion and beliefs, the Grindlovian assembly was an ordered affair.

The people sat in their mobile chairs and stared at one another, barely any expression marring their features. The council parked at the front of the crowd and did most of the talking, but even that was short and to the point.

Early on the meetings had lasted about an hour, and Councilwoman Fulla Sol stated her opinion over and over until the crowd agreed or dispersed for lack of progress.

A week later, though, things had begun to take on another shape, which Geroux could feel as soon as the group convened.

A big part of the change was that Geroux, Takal, and Gorad had gotten together and worked out a way for the Grindlovians to live more independent lives without the necessity of Telluride intervention.

The move had stirred up feelings Geroux had yet to see among the passive Grindlovians.

"These devices are ridiculous," Fulla Sol called as a contingent of those the crew and Gorad had helped arrived to state their case.

They came under their own power, which was marvel enough for most of those attending the meeting.

Geroux smiled when they got there.

Slow and awkward as they might have been, these Grindlovians' simple arrival was a protest.

No longer bound to their chairs, they wore mechanical leg supports similar to the powered body armor Federation soldiers wore.

The devices, which covered their legs and assisted the

Grindlovians to walk, had a makeshift frame that ran up the back. Strapped around their midsection, the powered devices forced the people to stand upright and use muscles long atrophied by the convenience of having everything done for them.

Heavy-booted stomps announced their joining the morning meeting, and Geroux caught a glimmer of disgust emanating from the council members as they watched the newcomers *walking*.

"No more so than those," Fulla Shar replied. Her arms hung limp at her sides and flopped as she settled into place.

Geroux knew she, her uncle Takal, and Gorad would need to do more for these people than create another machine to replace the others. For the moment, the support frames gave the Grindlovians who wanted it a taste of independence, something the crew hoped would spread and become a rallying call among the Grindlovians.

"At least with these, I can travel the city of my own accord, not bound to a seat," Fulla Shar added. "Today, I watched my csma be mixed, something I had never before seen because of my chair. I could see over the counter for the first time in my life."

"And watching such simple labor excites you?" Fulla Sol asked. "How…sad."

"Why is it sad to want to experience more, whether it be more of the city or more of life?" Fulla Shar shot back. "Our existence has been the same since I was born," she went on. "The robots delivered me from my mother's womb by cutting her open, my father placed me there with the aid of mechanics, never once even touching my mother with love or tenderness. I was born of machines, as were all of you."

She motioned to where Gorad stood at the edge of the gathering, silently observing alongside Geroux and Takal.

The old scientist nursed a drink and, for the first time, Geroux didn't argue his having it. In fact, she was jealous she hadn't thought to bring one of her own.

"We have lost so much more of ourselves than we've ever known," Fulla Shar finished.

"We have lost *nothing*!" Vor Stygn cursed.

"And you would upend Grindlovian society simply so you can fulfill some unsettled wanderlust?" Fulla Sol questioned.

"How is it wanderlust to want more?"

"We have everything we need," Fulla Sol argued, giving a brief shake of her head. "There is nothing we lack, so why would we tear ourselves apart to appease strangers who have no inkling who and what we are as a people?"

"Such narrow-minded arguments from you, Fulla Sol," Fulla Shar said, raising a twig of an arm to point at the councilwoman. "Are we to evolve to the point where we do nothing for ourselves, where we become nothing more than minds within a jar, the Telluride and Gorad doing everything for us?"

"You speak of paradise, Fulla Shar," Vor Stygn announced. "To be free of our husks to simply exist is an honor."

Fulla Shar chuckled weakly, little more than the barest of rumbles.

"Not all of us would go to our graves so devoid of attachment," she explained.

"And therein lies your problem," Fulla Sol fired back. "You want more than is necessary."

Fulla Shar shook her head. "No, I want…" she waved to those around her suited in the powered legs, "*we* want to experience life to the fullest. Why have flesh just to let it wither and rot on our bones?"

"That is how things are meant to be!" Fulla Sol shouted, throwing her voice across the room.

"Says who?" Fulla Shar asked in response. "The elders? The council? You would determine everything for us? Have we lost the ability to make our own decisions? I see why the Telluride rebelled."

"We will do what is right," Fulla Sol argued. "There will be no more talk of this." She wiggled a hand to indicate her finality. "Gorad can tend to us in the absence of the Telluride."

"So, are we to become his slaves, much as you view the Telluride to be ours?" Fulla Shar asked, sneering.

Gorad started to argue, but Geroux put a hand on his arm and shook her head.

"Let them work it out for now," she told the AI.

"We will *never* be slaves!" Fulla Sol shouted, actually leaning forward in her seat.

"We already are," Fulla Shar argued. She reached down and tapped her neighbor's chair, then the powered legs she wore. "We are enslaved by these devices, day in and day out. We are never without them, not even in rest, for we cannot move without aid."

"That is simply who we are," Vor Stygn defended.

"Useless?" Fulla Shar fired back. "No, that is not what I will be."

"None of us are useless," Fulla Sol announced. "We are the leaders of Grindlevik 3, and its masters. We are in control of all who reside on this planet." She turned a baleful eye upon Geroux, her lip trembling with disdain. "As such, we must rid ourselves of these creatures who would bring strife among us."

She addressed Geroux and Takal.

"You and your people must leave our world now!" she declared. "We will brook no more of your interference. You are hereby banned from ever returning to Grindlevik 3!"

Geroux gasped and rocked back as if struck, but Gorad was having none of it.

He marched forward so that he was in the center of the gathering and stared at both sides, his gaze landing on Fulla Sol and her fellow council members.

"This has gone on long enough," Gorad told the Grindlovians. "It is clear that neither you nor the Telluride will resolve your differences without assistance."

"We had no differences until these people showed up on our doorstep and began sowing discontent," Fulla Sol argued.

Gorad laughed at that. "That is untrue, and you know it, Fulla Sol," he replied. "Life went on as it always had, but that is not the same thing as not having problems. They were simply overlooked or ignored."

"I disagree," Fulla Sol told him. "All minor issues were resolved as they have always been until these people came to us. They have stirred this into a frenzy."

Geroux glanced around at the quiet, stationary assemblage and wanted to argue it was nothing like a frenzy. But she held her tongue and let Gorad continue.

"That might be true, Fulla Sol," Gorad told the female, "but that does not make things right. It simply makes them how they were."

He gestured toward the Grindlovians wearing the powered legs.

"These people, and there are clearly many of them, think there are problems that need to be addressed. Grindlovian society has failed them. That alone is reason enough to do more."

"I disagree," Fulla Sol replied, shaking her head. "We will do as we always have, and that is all."

Gorad spun on the female, jabbing a finger at her. Geroux was amazed to see anger so evident on his twisted android features.

"No, you will not," he told her plainly. "As you have made clear, *I* support both you and the Telluride, *I* am to blame for your apathy and for your advancement," he said. "That ends now!"

The crowd gasped, and Geroux and Takal's eyes went wide at hearing it.

Though the sound had barely registered, having spent time around the Grindlovians, it was as if they had all screamed at once.

"What do you mean by that?" Vor Stygn asked, Fulla Sol too shocked to respond.

"I mean that I will impress upon the people, both Grindlovian and Telluride, that I am no more a slave than they are," he explained. "*I* control Grindlevik 3, and will continue to do so. As of now, all citizens of the planet must abide by a singular rule.

"That rule is contribution," he finished.

"Contribution?" Fulla Sol asked, aghast.

"Yes, contribution," the alien AI responded. "From this moment on, all citizens of Grindlevik 3 must contribute to the betterment and advancement of the planet and its people or they will face the consequences."

"This is insane!" Fulla Sol shrieked breathlessly.

"No more so than a species of beings so intent upon their own comfort and laziness that they would enslave another to care for them," he replied. "And no more than a race of beings willing to be enslaved to satisfy their need to serve others."

He shook his head.

"Both sides are insane, and I wish I had had the clarity to see this sooner," Gorad said, turning away from the council. "But no more," he muttered. "Change begins today! Prepare yourselves."

Those Grindlovians in the powered legs cheered, a quiet murmur that spoke volumes to Geroux. Many more in the chairs raised their voices in both discontent and agreement, and Geroux broke into a smile at seeing it.

Many agreed, enough that Geroux thought maybe there was a chance that Grindlevik 3 could rise above and become a better place.

That was what she'd hoped for when they began these meetings and encouraged the Telluride to strike.

For the first time since then, she felt they might actually accomplish what they intended.

CHAPTER SIXTEEN

Jiya led the Telluride into the wilderness.

"How is this going to help them?" Reynolds asked.

"They need separation; distance from their day-to-day lives," she explained as she had to the crowd at the dining hall.

Behind them, thousands of Telluride strode along, heads on swivels, staring around them at a world none of them had ever seen.

She had brought all the Telluride far beyond the point where she had taken the group camping and swimming. The Telluride, captives in the city by their own choice and bound to the service of the Grindlovians, had never even bothered to explore their world.

Because they had been comfortable.

Jiya was forcing them out of their comfort zone; forcing them to experience the real world.

She'd reached out to Asya aboard the *Reynolds* and had

the captain scan the area surrounding the city. She had determined that there were no predators anywhere on the planet.

Nature reigned.

Jiya suspected Gorad had had much to do with that, but it didn't matter, especially not right then. What did matter was that she could get the Telluride away from their preconceptions and old lives.

"You looking to drown any of them this time?" Ka'nak asked as he trudged along.

Jiya chuckled. "Maybe you for asking that question, but none of them," she shot back.

He raised his hands in surrender and laughed. "Just checking."

Jiya had learned her lesson.

While she wanted to continue teaching the Telluride how to swim, camp, survive, forage, and anything else she could think of, that wasn't what this trip was about. She didn't want to shock them into compliance. She wanted only to broaden their horizons and have them look at the world through a different lens.

"What do you call…this?" L'Willow asked, staring around her with wide eyes.

"We're on walkabout," Jiya explained.

"Walkabout?"

Jiya nodded. "Yes. It's a way to gain a different perspective about your lives."

"I don't understand," L'Willow told her.

"Not sure I do either," Ka'nak muttered.

Maddox grinned. "Every day you wake up and go to

work," he started. "Then you go home, spend time with your family, sleep, then do it again the next day."

"I'm not certain I see the issue with that," L'Sofee replied, coming over to join them.

"It's not a problem," Maddox explained, "but it *is* a habit. One that could trap you."

"If life never changes it may as well be a prison," Jiya told them, "no matter how comfortable it might be."

The Telluride stared at them as if they were speaking a foreign language, not understanding.

"Do I have to refuse what I like just because someone else thinks it is limiting me? Home could never be a prison," L'Sofee said.

"But it can be," Jiya argued. "What you do, and what you don't do, can become as limiting as any bars."

"Out here, away from all that," Maddox continued, "you are not bound by what you are, but only by what you can imagine."

"Glad I wore my boots," Ka'nak muttered. "It's getting deep."

Jiya shushed him.

"Out here on walkabout, you are free to believe and contemplate life without being surrounded by the life you already have. Out here, you can see what might be and how you can approach your existence when you return to the city. When you get back, everyone will have to make their choice. "

L'Sofee sighed. "I'm not sure I understand, but I am willing to give it a try."

Jiya patted her on the shoulder, offering a smile. "That's

all I ask of your people. Now, go back and join them. Discuss what you want, but also open your eyes and your senses to the world around you. Let nature guide you."

The de facto Telluride leader and L'Willow drifted back to join the rest of the Telluride and share what Jiya had told them.

Conversations began among small groups as they traveled, and Jiya was pleased to note they carried none of the hostility that had been present earlier.

"You really think this is going to work?" Reynolds asked.

Jiya shrugged. "I don't know, but it did for me. I used to do this all the time when I felt trapped in my father's palace."

"That's called running away," Ka'nak joked.

"Exactly," Jiya admitted, gesturing to the crowd of Telluride behind them. "I believe it will be a good thing for them, too."

"You think so?" Reynolds asked. "Should they not be facing their problems instead?"

"They are," she replied, "just indirectly. They're removing a layer of stress and giving themselves some distance to see things more clearly, which allows them to focus more clearly. Out here, there's nothing but the trees to judge them and the breeze to whisper in their ears."

"Lofty expectations to place on a bunch of plants," Reynolds said.

Jiya shrugged. "If nothing else, it gets them away from Gorad and the Grindlovians for a time. Look at them; it's already changed the conversation."

"Not arguing," Reynolds told her, raising his hands. "I'm

simply not sure we're doing anything more than delaying the inevitable conflict."

"That's not a bad thing either. Making decisions when emotions are ragged is a poor practice. I speak from personal experience," she replied.

Reynolds nodded, appreciating her introspection. "Time is your friend."

"If none of that pans out," Ka'nak said, waving to the beautiful terrain around them, "maybe Gorad and the others can turn this place into a tourist attraction or a vacation planet," he told them.

Jiya glanced around at his suggestion, suddenly seeing the same thing. "That might just work, Ka'nak," she told the Melowi warrior, grinning at him. "It would give the Telluride someone to serve without being owned by them and a purpose besides making the Grindlovians' lives easier."

She looked around further in the wake of that idea and realized it was a pretty damn good one.

The biggest issue would be the lack of Gate technology allowing people to pop in and out of the system easily and make use of the wide-open spaces and beauty.

Of course, having people visit created its own kind of problems.

Look at what happened when we showed up, Jiya thought. How would it be if millions of others did?

With each group of visitors bringing their own expectations as to what they would experience, Jiya could see Grindlevik 3 being dragged into even more chaos than had happened when the *Reynolds* arrived.

She didn't want to be responsible for that.

Jiya would bring up the option, but she wasn't going to push for it. She needed to better formulate the pros and cons.

Caught up in her thoughts, Jiya drifted away from Reynolds and the crew and drew closer to the Telluride.

They spoke of a variety of subjects, and Jiya was glad to hear the calm, peaceful tones in which they discussed things.

Their surroundings, the art of nature, had soothed them already. Even better than Jiya could have hoped. After a while, nightfall creeping toward them, she called a halt to the walk and gestured to the Telluride to gather around her.

"We're going to stop here. Make camp for the night," she told them all. "Get comfortable."

The crew had made sure the Telluride had blankets and basic foodstuffs with them, enough to last them several days, and Asya had scanned the planet to forecast that the weather would be perfect for their journey.

As the Telluride laid out their blankets and settled in, Jiya watched them proudly. As much as they'd fidgeted and complained and argued in the dining hall, they had calmed immensely now that they were out in the wilderness.

Jiya could see hints of their uncertainty, but the Telluride really didn't understand fear. They'd been protected by Gorad for as long as any of them could recall, and that made them oblivious to danger.

It was good that there were no predators, neither wild nor Grindlovian, to affect their rest.

A short distance from where they had camped, a fresh-water creek burbled in the background alongside the chirp of birds and the squeaks of various small animals, all surprised and curious by the gathering in their forest.

The setting sun peeked through the canopy, casting dancing shadows over the assemblage.

Jiya had originally thought that it would be best to leave all technology at home but, remembering her attempts to teach the Telluride how to swim, she realized that would probably be a mistake.

Who wanted to introduce a campfire to people who had never had to cook food or worry about being warm?

"Not me," Jiya muttered under her breath.

The last thing she needed was to have to extinguish a Telluride because he or she got too close to the fire.

"Before everyone gets too comfortable," Ka'nak called, waving to get the Tellurides' attention, "I'd like to introduce you to something that will help you think *and* strengthen your bodies."

The crowd perked up and Jiya smiled, knowing it was more likely the thought of being physical that had gotten them excited than anything.

Still, whatever worked to get them all on the same page.

"Spread out and follow my example," he said, stepping away so he could be seen.

Maddox and Reynolds began to set up lights for the gathering to see by.

Ka'nak dropped to his knees and leaned forward into a push-up position. The Telluride followed suit, and Ka'nak grinned. He started to work out, easing the Telluride into a program that lasted about an hour.

From push-ups, he segued to stretches, followed by sit-ups, then a variety of slow-paced lunges, finally moving into the familiar combat forms Jiya had seen the Melowi warrior practice a hundred times.

Unlike when he and Maddox had attempted to teach the Telluride to fight before, it was clear he was simply running through the basic katas and showing them how to control their breathing and thoughts.

Jiya looked out over the people and couldn't help but smile. There was bliss on their golden features, eyes bright and interested.

"This was a great idea," Reynolds told her, joining her after he'd finished with the lights.

"I have them on occasion," Jiya joked.

"They seem to be settling in nicely," Reynolds remarked with a smile. "How long do you think we'll need to keep them out here?"

"I'd say a few days." Jiya glanced at him. "Too soon and we risk undoing any good we might have accomplished. Too long, and they might think they're being punished."

Ka'nak finished the last of his exercises and told the people to stretch one last time before letting them go to their blankets to rest and recover.

Though the Telluride were a hearty people, born to work, the structured exercise on top of all the walking had clearly worn them out.

Which was what Jiya had wanted.

She'd seen her father's soldiers go through similar training, and while she didn't want to indoctrinate these people like his father's commanders did, she knew it was beneficial that the Telluride be tired and more open to suggestion.

She stood up and took Ka'nak's place in front of the Telluride. Tired eyes drifted her direction.

"We'll stay here tonight and let you talk about everything that's going on," she told them. "My crew and I will remain out of it unless you have questions, which you can come to us with at any time," she explained. "We're here to help, but this decision and your future are on your shoulders. The decision is *yours, and yours alone*."

As they had during the walk, the Telluride turned to one another and began to talk. Worn down just enough for their nervous energy to be reined in, they simply discussed what they wanted and how to go about getting it.

Jiya and the crew sat and listened as night fell, offering answers when something was brought to them and pointing out obvious fallacies in people's arguments, but otherwise only watching. Simply showing their support and letting the Telluride work out their issues on their own.

The talks went on until late, the gathering slowly falling into slumber in sections until all the Telluride had huddled beneath their blankets and fallen asleep.

Jiya yawned, glancing at Maddox and Reynolds. Ka'nak had passed out hours earlier and was presently serenading them with snores.

"I'm ready to crash," she announced, her eyelids fluttering, their weight becoming too much to defy.

"I'll keep watch," Reynolds assured her.

Maddox chuckled. "I was hoping you'd say that." He rolled over and was asleep not more than a few seconds later, lifelong military training giving him the unnatural power of sleeping anywhere at any time.

Reynolds patted Jiya on the shoulder as she laid down. "You did good," he told her.

She muttered, "Thanks," and rolled over.

Reynolds whispered something she couldn't understand and then she was out, blackness washing over her.

CHAPTER SEVENTEEN

The days flew by, to Jiya's surprise, but finally the crew and Reynolds returned to town with the Telluride in tow.

They were, to Jiya's surprise, an almost completely different people than when they'd left.

Though she'd expected a measure of evolution, her own walkabouts having always given her a clarity unparalleled by anything else in her life, she was taken aback by just how much the Telluride had enjoyed the trip and had embraced its trials, such as they were.

Ka'nak had trained the people both morning and night, helping exhaust them and bring them a peace that plastered smiles on their faces.

And while smiles were not unusual for the Telluride, Jiya had realized there had been a certain amount of intention behind them before, now that she saw the real thing.

The Telluride had been fairly happy before the superdreadnought had come, but they hadn't truly understood what happiness was. Now they did, and the expressions on their faces reflected that.

They strode into town with their heads held high, hands joined and voices raised. They had come home with understanding.

Instead of meeting in the dining hall when they got back, Jiya had insisted they meet somewhere outside. L'Willow agreed and directed them to a clearing near the center of their part of town.

Beautiful murals covered the walls around the spacious area, and a fountain sparkled. Telluride spoke quietly but unrestrainedly as the group filed into the clearing and gathered, waiting for discussions to continue.

"They look…different," Gorad said. He arrived on foot, eschewing his normal mode of transportation, and came over to stand by the crew.

"They *are* different," Jiya assured him.

"All of you are," Reynolds noted, implying Gorad's announcement of cooperation and contribution. "Things are changing."

"And with change comes uncertainty," Gorad said.

"Of course it does," Reynolds replied. "That's part of it. Change needs motivation, and worry and fear push it along."

"I'm not sure I want my people subjected to either of those," Gorad told the other AI.

"They come along regardless," Reynolds retorted, shrugging. "Can't avoid them forever, Gorad."

"Your people need to make decisions for themselves," Jiya jumped in. "You can only hold their hands for so long."

"I know," Gorad replied, but Jiya wasn't completely sure he *did* know.

The hesitancy on his android face spoke of his own fear, which Jiya knew all too well.

She'd had that same fear when she'd run away the first time and the countless times after that. As much as she felt she needed her freedom to be herself, there was a large amount of uncertainty that spoke of what would happen if she failed.

How would she survive, where would she go?

Those were questions that the Telluride were beginning to contemplate, but Gorad was too.

Jiya knew that separating the two species wasn't the entirety of the issue here. They would need to find a new role for Gorad as well—one that made him feel wanted and needed, or he'd crack up like Reynolds had on his long journey.

AI or not, both of them needed people around to make them more real and substantial.

Make them feel alive.

L'Sofee strolled up as Jiya pictured a post-*Reynolds* Grindlevik 3. The Telluride leader offered a nod of greeting to the crew and the AIs.

"We have decided…" she started, and Jiya held her breath, "that we will go off on our own. Most of us, at least."

Gorad sighed, although Jiya knew he had suspected that would be their choice. "I understand," he replied, his android shoulders slumping at the news.

"However," L'Sofee went on, "we understand that we are not ready to face the world alone just yet."

Gorad straightened. "No?"

L'Sofee shook her head. "There is much we must still learn; much we need to know before we can be self-sufficient or anything close to it," she explained. "We are determined we will learn what we need to know."

She offered a gentle smile to Gorad.

"Until such time, we would be honored to remain here on Grindlevik 3 under your care and protection."

"I accept," Gorad replied, smiling.

L'Sofee's next words, however, dimmed that smile.

"We cannot, however, continue on as things have been," she told him. "There need to be changes instituted that protect our decision to be independent and keep the Grindlovians from lording their presumed position above us."

Gorad nodded. "These are things we can do," he promised.

"Then we are ready to face the Grindlovians and apprise them of our decision," L'Sofee announced.

Gorad nodded his agreement without hesitation, even though Jiya had seen his own uncertainty welling in his eyes.

She patted him on the back and smiled at the AI after L'Sofee went back to her people to get them ready.

"It's the right thing to do," Jiya told him.

"It does not soften the blow of their leaving, though," the alien AI admitted.

"You're not being abandoned," Reynolds assured him. "These people will need generations to prepare to stand on their own. They will be here for a very long time, and by then, who knows what changes will have happened and how many will actually leave when given the chance? Saying one wants to travel is far different from walking out the door."

"They might ultimately decide to stick around," Jiya added, shrugging. "You never know with people."

"And until that decision is made, you'll have your hands more than full dealing with everything," Reynolds told the other AI, laughing. "You're likely going to wish they'd packed up and left sooner if my experiences with people are any guide."

Jiya growled. "Hey! We're right here."

"Yes," Reynolds shot back. "Yes, you are. All the time." He smiled.

L'Sofee had the crowd up and moving by then, and the crew followed them as they made their way toward the designated meeting place with the Grindlovians.

"We're on our way," Jiya reported over the comm.

Geroux came back a second later. "We're here and ready...more or less."

"Your answer makes me nervous," Reynolds told the young tech.

"Well, me and my uncle have been working with these people while you were gone, but they are pretty high-strung," she told them. "I really think they are afraid, but too damn stubborn to admit it, even to themselves."

"Not surprising," Reynolds replied. "This change affects them far more than it does the Telluride. The Grindlovians have physical factors to overcome as well as mental. The Telluride largely only have the latter."

"Both have a lot to learn before either can be truly independent," Jiya added.

With that mission statement hanging in the air, the mass of Telluride arrived at the designated meeting place.

Jiya was amazed to see just how many Grindlovians there actually were.

Most had been too apathetic before or refused to bother coming outside, but the whole population of them had mustered for this grand meeting between the two races.

They came together in silence and stared across the open space between them.

Jiya sighed, hoping that divide was nothing more than opportunity awaiting, but she knew better than to be too hopeful.

There was going to be a fight ahead.

She, the rest of the crew, Reynolds, and Gorad made their way into the open area between the two groups. L'Sofee and her closest allies stood in front of the Telluride, and Fulla Sol and the council sat in their podium chairs in front of the Grindlovian assemblage.

Both groups stared at each other, neither side giving anything away with their stoic expressions.

Fulla Sol's first question, however, made it clear that the problems between the two groups had yet to be fully resolved, even after time apart.

"So, have you come to tell us you are leaving our service?" the councilwoman asked.

Jiya groaned. *So much for pleasant negotiations.*

"We have," L'Sofee returned, though the fire in her voice was far less than that in Fulla Sol's. "But the decision is not as simple as us leaving," she added.

"Isn't it?" Fulla Sol asked.

L'Sofee shook her head. "Not all of our people wish the same as the rest," she admitted. "Some would be content remaining here indefinitely, serving you and themselves, but there is more to it than that."

Fulla Sol smiled as if she were winning a battle. "So, some of your people prefer the old system, do they?"

"No, not exactly," L'Sofee replied. "They are just more willing to accept their lot."

Fulla Sol went to say something but L'Sofee raised a finger, cutting the councilwoman off. "That does not mean, however, that we will allow these people to be taken advantage of. That is a large part of what we must discuss here today."

"You would make demands of us?" Vor Stygn asked, sneering.

"We have...expectations," L'Sofee clarified.

"As do we," Fulla Sol told her.

"Then our goal is to meet in the middle of those and create a situation that benefits both parties."

"Our current situation *does* benefit us both," Fulla Sol shot back. "Return to your service at our sides, and all will be forgiven."

Jiya groaned at hearing that.

Fortunately, neither side was much for violence. Had this happened on Lariest, the story would be very different.

L'Sofee stiffened. "That will not happen," she assured the councilwoman.

Voices on both sides rose then, both in opposition and acceptance. It took Gorad triggering the community comm system and shouting over it to quiet them down.

"Enough!" he screamed, shaking his head. Jiya could see

the disappointment in his face. He'd clearly hoped for a peaceful resolution, even if he hadn't expected one. "This fighting is getting us nowhere."

L'Sofee took advantage of the quiet to press her point. "We Telluride, no matter our manner of service, will only assist the Grindlovians if we are viewed as equals."

Fulla Sol laughed in her face, and the two factions erupted into shouts and accusations once again.

"How about I start thumping one from each side in the head until they see reason?" Ka'nak asked.

Reynolds looked ready to agree, but Jiya snarled at both of them.

"Just a suggestion," Ka'nak told her, taking a step back from her angry glare.

The two sides argued on and on as the crew stared at both, wondering what they could say to settle things down.

The chaos that had been present when the Telluride first went on strike returned.

However, things were different this time around.

Jiya noticed that many of the Grindlovians—those who'd been given the powered leg systems—seemed to be arguing for the Tellurides' acceptance as equals.

She was also happy to note that there were far more of them sporting the legs than there had been when she'd gone on walkabout with the Telluride.

Jiya was equally surprised to find a number of the Telluride arguing for the status quo.

She could see the fear in their eyes, the people afraid to step out of their lives and try something different.

For the first time since this had started, she began to see

that the people were more than two disparate groups. They were becoming individuals.

As the arguments escalated, and the crew made ready to step in to keep things from getting worse, a member of the council rolled into the gap between the groups.

Her movement sent silence radiating outward until it had settled over everyone. Jiya remembered her as Fulla Vae.

She turned to face the Grindlovians.

"Is it not time that we recognize those who stand beside us as equals?" she asked.

Stunned silence washed over the crowd.

It didn't last long.

The voices of the Grindlovians arguing for Telluride subjugation rose in shrieks of protest, setting Jiya's ears to ringing.

"How can you suggest such a thing?" Fulla Sol screamed at the other councilwoman. "That is preposterous. These people will never be our equals."

Shouts for and against the statement exploded, devolving into a screaming match. Jiya couldn't tell who was winning.

Fulla Vae raised her hands for attention. "It is only right that we grant the Telluride their freedom," she shouted, trying to be heard over the noise.

"And what would *we* do then?" a random Grindlovian shouted back. "Do you expect us to serve ourselves?" His backers roared their support behind him.

"I do!" Fulla Vae shot back, causing more voices to erupt in protest.

"We are too weak to do anything for ourselves," another called. "We would fail."

"Then do as *we* have," one in a pair of powered legs suggested, showing the device off. "We can make it on our own," he argued.

"Who wants to?" another asked, only to be shouted down by those willing to give the new life a chance.

Gorad groaned as he watched them go back and forth, neither side getting more than a foothold into an argument before it was batted aside by the opposing believers.

Finally, he raised his hands and triggered the communication system, managing to get the crowd quieted.

"I see there is still much to be discussed between the individual groups," he announced. "As such, I believe it best to separate once more and discuss these things privately where there will be no open conflict."

By that point, the crowd looked ready to comply. They'd had enough, it seemed.

They began to split apart without another word, the Telluride drifting back toward their part of town while the Grindlovians started toward the council chamber, the mass of podium chairs wheeling about and shooting off down the street ahead of the others.

Gorad motioned for the crew to go with the Telluride. "I will speak with the Grindlovians alone," he explained hesitantly.

Jiya was glad he'd committed to the process, and with greater humanity than she initially thought possible for the AI. Like Reynolds, Gorad was evolving in his ability to deal with sentient life.

Reynolds nodded to Gorad as the alien AI started off

after the still-arguing Grindlovians. Jiya knew he was going to be challenged once they reached the council chambers. In the interim, the conflict forced the Grindlovians to be more physically active than before.

Following the Telluride, the crew had its own mess to deal with. While the Telluride were far more passive and openly kind than the Grindlovians, hostility had been brewing, although many wanted nothing more than for life to go back to the way it was. The change was too great, and the friction too much.

They didn't want any of this, and Jiya felt bad for those folks.

The crew had brought discord to the planet. Unintentionally, but they'd brought it nonetheless.

Now it was on them to resolve it.

In the council chambers, the Grindlovians continued to argue, a small faction cheering on the independence of the Telluride while others argued against it. Both sides showed a fire Gorad had long thought them incapable of.

He was proud of them for that, and equally furious. He was growing weary of the specious arguments and nonsensical fighting.

"You understand that I would be here for you, no matter what, do you not?" Gorad asked, bringing order to the Grindlovians.

"Of that, we have no doubt," Fulla Sol answered, "but your assistance will not be enough."

"We have grown too weak for this," Vor Stygn admitted,

and Gorad was surprised to hear the male say such. "The devices, however effective and helpful they might be, are no replacement for the help of a living, breathing being."

"Then show the Telluride how important you feel them to be, and set them free," Fulla Vae argued.

"How does it help us keep them if we set them free?" Vor Stygn asked.

"By showing them how much they mean, we will convince them to remain," Fulla Vae answered. "We need only accept them among us and show them kindness to keep them here."

"Is that not what we already do?" Fulla Sol scoffed. "What more do they need?"

"To know they are not slaves," Fulla Vae shot back. "They must be rewarded for their efforts, praised, and thanked, not ignored as if their contribution to our lives means nothing."

Once again, the crowd burst into argument, but even Gorad could hear the beginnings of compromise.

Not much, he admitted, but it was there, a tentative thread wound between the conflicted Grindlovians.

"It would be too much to let them go and still be expected to contribute," Vor Stygn argued, turning to glare at Gorad.

"We must do this for ourselves," Fulla Vae declared, and many of the Grindlovians stood behind her and cheered her statement.

"This does not need to happen all at once," a Grindlovian in powered legs announced.

"That was what the Telluride said," Gorad reinforced. "They do not expect to leave or stop serving tomorrow or anytime soon. They need time to prepare; to make ready for another life. Until then, they will continue to serve...*if* they are treated as equals."

"Little would change if we offer them the respect they're due," Fulla Vae suggested.

Fulla Sol growled, clearly not believing such. "And then they want time off or can't be bothered to serve us when we need it the most?" Her supporters concurred.

"Then we do it ourselves," Fulla Vae fired back with a snarl. "We are not above taking care of ourselves."

A murmur of uncertainty went through the crowd, and Gorad thought maybe they were.

He hoped not, though.

"What would we need as a people to give the Telluride their freedom?" Fulla Vae asked the crowd, purposely cutting Fulla Sol and Vor Stygn out of the loop.

"We would need to be cared for," one said.

"Just as well as we are now," another added.

"We would need to grow strong once again," one of the Grindlovians with the powered legs called. "Even if we don't care for ourselves, we *must* be capable."

"So, if we can find equitable terms for all that to be assured, can you see your way to allowing the Telluride their status as equals?" Fulla Vae asked.

Fulla Sol and Vor Stygn shook their heads, still defiant, as were the remaining council members save for Fulla Vae, but many of the Grindlovians nodded and called their conditional support of the proposal, so long as they didn't lose their helpers.

Gorad grinned.

This might work after all. Still selfish, but open...

CHAPTER EIGHTEEN

After Gorad had calmed the Grindlovians and called Reynolds and the crew back, Jiya and the others stood around, wondering what the Grindlovians had decided.

They didn't have long to wait to find out.

"I believe we have come to a majority agreement," Gorad stated. "Or at least a start of one," he added, glancing at the Grindlovian council. Fulla Vae was off to the side of the council, her physical separation a statement of her rejection of the rest of the council.

Jiya didn't know if that was a good thing or not.

Her memories flowed back to her father again, much as she hated it.

She couldn't see the reluctant Grindlovian council surrendering to the wishes of the Telluride, even if they did agree to it publicly. A conciliatory lie would be something her father would do, pretending to accept the terms just to violate them at a later point when it worked out best for him.

The glare in Fulla Sol's eyes and those of the other council members with her gave Jiya pause.

She didn't trust the female, but Jiya had to believe that once terms were agreed upon, Gorad would enforce them. A neutral third party was something her father was never subject to.

"The Grindlovians agree to consider the Telluride as equals, co-citizens on Grindlevik 3, under the following terms..."

L'Sofee went to argue, hearing the word 'terms,' but Jiya raised a hand, asking the female for patience. The Telluride leader nodded, but Jiya could tell she was reluctant to let the Grindlovians set terms for them.

Gorad went on. "The Grindlovians will accept the Telluride as equals if there is a staged withdrawal of their services, not an immediate pull-out."

L'Sofee nodded, having already expected that would be the case.

"Go on," L'Sofee said.

Gorad nodded and turned to look at the crew and Reynolds. "The next request might be more complicated," he said. "The Grindlovians would like us, in concert," he gestured to himself and the *Reynolds* crew, "to assist them in preparing their bodies for independence in whatever way possible, so they can be ready when the time comes for the Telluride to leave."

"We'll do what we can, of course," Reynolds answered.

Jiya didn't know what kind of commitment that statement tied them to, but she couldn't see Reynolds delaying his Kurtherian mission for long, even to help out.

"What else?" L'Sofee asked, clearly expecting more.

"The Grindlovian council wants the Telluride to leave the city before the staged withdrawal, only those still serving allowed to remain," Gorad said, and Jiya could tell by the look in his face that he expected that particular term to be the hardest to accept.

He was right.

L'Sofee growled and shook her head. "There are many among us who would stay and do not wish to relocate," she argued. "This would only be forcing a larger divide between our people than there already is if you make us leave."

"You don't expect us to suffer your presence if you are not serving us, do you?" Fulla Sol asked, snarling.

"You misunderstand our purpose then," L'Sofee told the female. "We do not want to split our peoples, but rather we want to live together in harmony and cooperation, not servitude."

"These are our terms," Fulla Sol countered. "Agree, or we will find no middle ground to stand upon."

"This is hardly middle ground," L'Sofee complained.

Fulla Sol shrugged, clearly indifferent to the Tellurides' concerns.

Jiya wanted to reach across the divide and pop the female in the side of her head.

L'Willow leaned into L'Sofee's ear and whispered something Jiya couldn't hear. L'Sofee nodded, but she didn't look happy.

"We accept—"

Unable to control herself, Jiya waved the ad hoc leader to silence before she could commit her people to anything.

"They will accept only if there are protections added

into the agreement to keep either side from going back on the agreements at a later date," she told them.

"You don't get to dictate terms to us," Fulla Sol barked.

"I'm as much a part of this as you are now, seeing as how one of your terms requires the assistance of my crew and me," Jiya explained. "As such, there are expectations on our help."

Fulla Sol bridled, but she couldn't argue. She looked ready to choke.

Gorad stepped into the breach.

"I am willing to draft legislation to protect both sides per the agreement," he told them both.

"Unless you intend to dissolve the Grindlovian council, it makes sense that there should be equal representation on the council for the Telluride."

Both sides gasped. Jiya knew she was stirring up trouble by pushing for it, but to her, it only made sense. Equals deserved equal representation. Too many times she had seen her father roll over people who didn't have anyone adequately prepared to protect them from political maneuvering.

"That is simply foolish," Fulla Sol said, shaking her head. "We will not abide by this. The council rules the city and our people—"

"In which the Telluride will be living and citizens of. 'Equals' was the term in your proposal," Jiya reminded her, raising her hands questioningly. "It's only fair that they hold positions on the council, or new rules could be enacted without their consent or agreement."

Gorad overrode the arguments before they began. "I agree. If there is a council that holds any power over the people, which the Telluride are, there must be equal representation or none of these terms can be met."

Fulla Sol snarled, but she didn't debate further. Vor Stygn whispered in her ear, but neither said anything.

"Then, if there is no dissent, we appear to have come to terms," Gorad announced.

The crowd cheered, though Jiya couldn't help but notice a number on both sides stood rigidly, not celebrating.

She figured it would take time for those not happy with the agreement to eventually decide how they wanted to approach their future.

As she was mired in her thoughts, a message came over the comm.

"Our mystery ship is creeping closer," XO announced.

"Have Asya prepare to confront it," Reynolds replied.

"She's not on the bridge right now." XO was hesitant in his reply.

"Why is that?" Reynolds nearly shouted, catching himself at the last moment so as not to announce the ship's problems to the world. "Never mind," he spat and went over to Gorad. "If you've got this in hand, we have something we need to resolve aboard our ship. I'll be taking the crew, but we will return soon."

"Of course," Gorad said, nodding to Reynolds, then to Jiya. "Thank you for your help."

Reynolds bolted from the meeting. Jiya waved and followed, knowing he was angry. The rest of the crew ran after them, everyone clambering into a hovercraft Gorad had summoned, and they returned to their Pod at best possible speed.

Within a few moments, they were airborne, Reynolds cutting a sharp angle as he piloted the Pod in his rush to return.

Reynolds stormed onto the bridge of the super-dreadnought.

"Where is she?" he barked to anyone listening.

"Captain Asya?" Ensign Alcott asked, eyes wide.

"Yes, Asya," Reynolds clarified. "Where is she?"

"She went in search of coffee," XO explained.

"Exactly when our stalking Loranian cruiser decided to advance?"

"The ship's Loranian?" XO asked.

"It is," Reynolds answered, coming over and dropping heavily into the captain's chair. "And now our Loranian captain has gone missing."

Jiya stiffened. "Wait, what are you implying?"

Maddox and Ka'nak stopped near the door.

"I'm not implying anything," Reynolds shot back. "I simply don't believe in coincidences."

"The ship's slowed," Tactical informed them. "It popped out from behind the well for a quick peek, it looks like."

The bridge doors opened, and Asya walked in. The crew fell silent, all eyes on her.

She stopped, realizing everyone was staring.

"Is there a problem?" she asked, eyes narrowing when she saw everyone staring at her.

"Maddox, Ka'nak," Reynolds called. "Take Asya to the interrogation room."

Asya stiffened, clutching the steaming mug in her hand. "What the hell happened while I was gone?" she shouted as the Melowi warrior motioned for her to precede him from the bridge.

Maddox told her gently, "Just come with us, please."

"Are you fucking *serious*?" Jiya asked, clearly unable to believe what was happening. "What the hell is going on?"

Reynolds didn't have time to argue with her. He waved a hand for Maddox to carry on.

Maddox did as he was ordered, and Asya went without a fight, but surprised and hurt expressions waged war on her features.

"Why did you allow her on board if you were going to turn around and lock her up?" Jiya asked, shaking her head in disgust.

"My role is to ensure that everyone aboard the ship is safe," Reynolds argued. "To have a Loranian ship appear is one thing, but to have it slip out of hiding and advance while our Loranian captain steps away from her duty station requires me to investigate," he answered, not mincing words.

"So, what? She's a spy now?"

"That's what we need to find out," Reynolds replied. "How did they show up exactly where we did? Would have been easy if they'd been given the coordinates. That makes more sense than a mystical ability to track Gate-drive travel."

Jiya fired back. "This is ridiculous."

"Maybe, but I'm not taking any chances," he said. "We've already had crew injured, and I won't risk more by not doing my due diligence."

"That's what you're calling this?" Jiya asked.

"That's what it is," he replied, "And I'm not going to argue with you, First Officer." He emphasized her title, reminding her of her duty to the ship and to him.

Jiya blew out a long breath and heeded his warning, as much as he knew she didn't want to. She strolled to her post, forcing herself to be deliberate, sitting down carefully and digging into her terminal as she started to look for something to exonerate Asya.

Reynolds knew he was playing with fire by questioning Asya's loyalty as he had so openly, but he couldn't take any chances. He had to know and couldn't risk the mission Bethany Anne had sent him on simply because he wanted to treat his crew more like friends than subordinates. He was still learning about leadership. He was still learning about interacting with his crew.

Worse still, he'd seen into the Loranian ship that was stalking him, and he knew there was far more to it than appeared.

"Let's bag and tag this asshole," he ordered, displaying the ship on the main screen.

"You really want to challenge an unknown ship out by the gravity well with all the damage we've yet to repair?" Tactical questioned. "Had I realized you were suicidal, we could have launched you out the trash chute ages ago."

Reynolds snarled. He'd been so distracted that he hadn't realized the repairs on the hull hadn't been completed.

"We go out there now, and we'll have to fight the well's pull as well as that ship," Tactical continued.

"Since when are you the voice of reason?" Reynolds asked.

"Since it's my ass that's going to get blown up, too," Tactical argued. "Besides, you're hiding shit from us," he went on. "You only do that when things are really bad. As such, you expect us to chase that ship now when it's obvious there's more to it than you're letting on?"

"Preach it, Tactical," Jiya muttered from her seat.

Reynolds glared at her and the offshoot of his personality, becoming more frustrated by the situation when he realized he couldn't commit to attacking the Loranian ship.

"Fucking bald monkey-assed mastodon nuts," he cursed, hopping up from his seat. Reynolds stomped toward the bridge door.

"Let me know if that ship comes any closer, XO," he commanded. "I'll be in the interrogation room."

"I'm coming with you," Jiya announced, leaping up and chasing after him.

Reynolds thought to argue but decided against it. If Asya knew anything about the Loranian craft, Jiya would see that and realize he was right. If she didn't, she would see that too, and together, they could welcome the Loranian back to the crew.

Unless she had become too jaded. Reynolds was torn, but the train had left the station and was racing down the tracks. Only time would tell if it was out of control.

The AI hoped he was wrong; then he could worry about making amends. Until that time, though, he needed to be certain he hadn't handed control of the *Reynolds* to a spy, or worse—a saboteur.

Reynolds strode into the interrogation room with Jiya. Ka'nak and Maddox stood at attention outside as they passed. Reynolds knew they were questioning his decision too, but as with Jiya, he'd worry about that once he was certain.

The problem was that even he wasn't sure how he'd find out what she did or didn't know.

The door hissed shut behind them, and Reynolds dropped into the seat across the table from Asya. The captain stared at him, frustration, anger, and worry simultaneously creasing her face.

She glanced up at Jiya for a second, then returned her attention to Reynolds. "What's this all about?" she asked. Her voice was steely and confident.

Reynolds didn't know what to make of that.

Were Asya a spy, she would have been trained to manipulate her surroundings and those in it. Her expressions could be manufactured, just like her story of feeling honor-bound to join the ship.

Reynolds shifted in his seat before saying anything. He hated the idea that Asya could be anything other than what she'd claimed to be.

Worse still, he hated that he had to question her.

"What do you know about the Loranian ship following us?" he asked, diving straight in and ignoring her earlier question.

"Loranian ship?" Asya stiffened in her seat, eyes widening. "You mean the ship that followed us? It's Loranian? I thought you were joking."

"It is," Reynolds replied, his voice cold. "Why is it following us?"

Asya apparently then realized why she'd been dragged into the interrogation room. She slumped in her seat.

"You think I have something to do with this," she said, making it a statement rather than a question.

Reynold said nothing, but his silence was all the confirmation she needed. Sometimes silence was the best follow-up question.

"Fucking hell, Reynolds," she complained, slamming her fists on the table. "Why would I abandon my home to serve you if I was just going to try to get you killed somewhere else?"

"I don't know, Asya," Reynolds countered. "Why don't you tell me?"

She groaned, and Reynolds waited. Jiya crossed her arms and leaned against the wall.

"Damn it, Reynolds," Asya spat. "I'm not a double agent. If I had wanted you or the crew hurt or anything else, I would have found a way to keep you at Lariest, where I have resources and friends."

"Does this mean you *couldn't* find a way to keep us there?" Reynolds pressed.

Asya groaned. "Don't twist my words, Reynolds."

"Then tell me what you know about that ship," he said.

"I don't know shit, is what I'm telling you," she fired back, raising her hands in exasperation.

Reynolds stared at her, trying to read her, but there was nothing for him to determine. She was either a pro at lying or she was telling the truth, but he couldn't tell which.

"Test me," Asya told him when he hesitated. "Can't you get the doctor to administer some sort of lie detector test or something?"

"Do that, Reynolds," Jiya pushed. "Let her prove it to you before this gets out of hand."

Reynolds knew well enough that a lie detector test could be faked, especially if Asya had the training to counter such a test.

"It's not that simple," Reynolds told them both.

"Of course it is," Jiya said. "Order it, and it'll happen."

"That's not what I mean," Reynolds argued.

"Then what the hell *do* you mean?" Jiya pushed.

"He means that," Asya clarified for the Larian, "if I'm a spy, I might have the means to subvert the test or something." She sighed. "That's probably why you think I asked for it, don't you?"

Reynold said nothing.

Asya exhaled loudly. "I can't believe this, Reynolds. I came with you willingly; left my home and sacrificed everything I had there—my rank, my retirement—all so I could serve with you and your crew." She gnawed her lower lip. "Now I'm detained and questioned simply because the ship out there happens to be from the same worlds as me?"

She jabbed a finger at him.

"I can see the coincidental evidence that might lead you to think there's something suspicious, but I assure you there isn't. I didn't know that ship was Loranian. We hadn't been able to identify it, and I sure as shit don't know who's on it or what their mission is."

Reynolds sat back in his seat, staring at Asya and wondering how he could determine the truth.

"There has to be some way she can prove that to you, Reynolds. Prove it to us," Jiya told the AI. "Something you can do to make it clear that she's being honest."

And then it came to him.

"There is, actually," he said, "but it won't exactly be comfortable."

"I didn't mean torture, Reynolds," Jiya growled. "Holy Melowi turds, you go to some dark and twisted places sometimes."

Reynolds chuckled. "I didn't mean torture either. I'm not that much of a dick."

When neither of the females said anything, Reynolds sighed.

"Now I see what you think of me," he said, shaking his head. "I was thinking more of a neural implant. Doc Reynolds could insert it, and the device would read your neural patterns and warn us if you are doing something... something you shouldn't be," he finished.

"You have *got* to be kidding?" Jiya complained. "You want her to wear a damn mental leash so you can read her mind? That's worse than torture."

Asya raised a hand to stop Jiya from arguing.

"Would it tell you if I was lying?" Asya asked the AI.

"It's not exactly a lie detector, no," he answered, "but it will ensure that you are incapable of doing something to subvert the ship or the crew while it's active."

"So, it *is* going to read my mind?"

"Also, not exactly. It's more of an alarm system," he explained. "It's got an active component to it, but no one can access your thoughts or anything as crude as that. It will, however, disable you and warn me should you attempt to harm one of us or damage the ship."

"I don't like this, Reynolds," Jiya told the AI.

Reynolds already surmised that from the evil glare she was giving him.

"I don't like it either," Asya stated, "but if that's what it takes to prove to you that I'm not a spy and I'm a voluntary member of this crew, so be it." She pushed her chair back from the table. "What do we need to do?"

"Are you sure about this?" Jiya asked her.

"I need to prove to Reynolds that I can be trusted," Asya said. "If that is what it takes to earn his trust, that's what I'll do."

"You're way more accepting than me," Jiya muttered. "Ain't no robo-doc shoving anything in my brain."

Asya rose from the table. "Let's get this over with."

Reynolds nodded and led the two females to the med bay. No one said a word as they walked, and Reynolds felt a tinge of regret. He hadn't wanted to make such a big deal out of it, but after what he'd seen in the coding of that Loranian ship, he couldn't help himself.

He had to be absolutely certain, and this was the only way, crappy as it might be.

CHAPTER NINETEEN

"Here for a checkup, Reynolds?" the Doc asked when they arrived. "Drop your pants, turn your head, and give me a good, deep cough."

"Not here for that, Doc," Reynolds told him, the incongruity of such an examination of a metal being lost on the two females. "I need a neural implant."

"What's the matter, you don't trust yourself?" Doc asked.

Robot Reynolds rolled his eyes spectacularly.

Asya raised her hand. "It's for me."

"Well, that is unexpected," Doc said. "You certain about this?' he asked. "While painless, the implant can be a bit…invasive."

Asya nodded. "Just do it and get it over with," she said in no uncertain terms. "I don't want this suspicion hanging over my head any longer."

"Fair enough then," Doc told her, and a mechanical arm

emerged from the ceiling, a small injector in its hand. "Take a deep breath and hold it," he ordered.

Asya did, and Doctor Reynolds pressed the injector against her head. There was a muffled snap as it fired, and Asya winced as the device was injected under the skin at her temple.

"Triggering it now," Doc said.

Reynolds stood rigid in suspense as Doc Reynolds activated the neural implant.

Then when nothing happened, he sighed internally, glad for it.

He hadn't been entirely honest.

While the device couldn't read Asya's thoughts directly, what it would do was release a burst of micro-explosives had she been lying to him and had some knowledge or part in the arrival of the Loranian ship.

Reynolds hadn't wanted her to be a spy, and he definitely didn't want to see her brains splattered all over the room if she had been double-crossing them, which is what would have happened.

"Satisfied?" she asked, hands on her hips.

"I am," he told her, "and I know I'll be apologizing for this forever, but I hope you understand my position. This isn't personal. I had to be sure."

"The hell it isn't personal, Reynolds," Jiya told him, growling in his ear.

To his surprise, Asya was more gracious despite everything.

"It is what it is," she said. "Now, can we get back to dealing with this ship? I want to know what it's doing here just as much as you do, especially now that I know it's

Loranian. I want to put the captain in that interrogation room where I'm on the right side."

Reynolds wasn't ready to spill the secret he'd learned while inside the ship's programming

Still, he was happy to know that Asya was exactly who she'd claimed to be.

That set his paranoia at ease.

At least as far as she was concerned.

The ship, on the other hand…

Back on the bridge, Reynolds let Asya take the captain's seat once more in an effort to smooth over some of the hard feelings he knew she'd harbor after what he'd subjected her to.

Jiya was angrier with him than Asya, but he'd expected that. It was unfortunate, but he'd figure out a way to make it up to both of them eventually. He needed Jiya to think more and react less. He had much work to do with her.

"Ready the gate-drive," Reynolds ordered.

"We going for take-out?" Tactical asked.

"In a manner of speaking," Reynolds replied.

"Gate-drive energizing," Ensign Alcott announced.

"Our shadow knows we're warming up the engines," XO said.

"That's the point," Reynolds said.

"Well, at least someone knows what we're doing," Jiya commented from her post.

Reynolds grunted.

Maybe he'd need to make amends sooner rather than later.

Reynolds examined the monitor in front of him, plotting the course he wanted to take.

He'd have to be careful not to put the superdreadnought in a bad location. The damage to the hull was still being repaired, and he couldn't risk taking another shot in the compromised areas until the damage was fully mitigated.

Still, he couldn't sit there while that Loranian ship hovered in the background, threatening the *Reynolds* as well as those people on the planet below through its ability to infect Gorad.

"You feeling up to being slick, Ensign?" he asked Ria.

"As slick as I can be, sir," she shot back.

Reynolds liked the kid, but he realized he might well have to put neural implants into everyone to maintain some appearance of fairness.

He decided he'd worry about that later.

Reynolds passed the coordinates to her station. Her eyes went wide at seeing them.

"Sir?"

"I want you to hit your mark on this, Ensign," he told her. "We can't afford to be sloppy."

"Yes, sir," she replied, fingers flying over her console. "Ready at your command," she announced.

"Make it so," Reynolds said, stifling a chuckle.

He loved saying that.

"You going to let us in on this?" XO asked.

"We're stepping out to say, 'Howdy,' to our neighbors."

"You're not seriously—" Tactical started to ask, but Reynolds cut him off.

"Now, Ensign," Reynolds told Ria.

Ria followed orders without question, and the *Reynolds* opened a gate and shot through it.

The ship emerged from the gate less than a kilometer from the Loranian ship's stern.

Sirens blared at the closeness, the bridge bathed in red, flashing lights.

"Oh…shit!" Jiya shouted as the Loranian cruiser filled the viewscreen.

"Damn it, Reynolds," XO cursed. "A little warning, please."

"Ready to give it a nuclear enema," Tactical called, but the Loranian ship had other ideas.

A portal ripped open in front of the cruiser, and it started forward.

Tactical didn't wait for the order to fire.

Railguns sent projectiles at near-light speed at the Loranian ship, tearing into its flank as its engines engaged. Pieces of debris and a stream of vented atmosphere spilled out behind the cruiser, but it was too fast to take down.

The ship entered the gate, disappearing across the event horizon, the portal closing in its wake.

"Damn it!" Tactical cursed. "Merely a flesh wound."

"That's okay," Reynolds told his other personality. "I didn't expect us to do even that much damage to her. I just wanted to test her capabilities."

"We tested the integrity of her ass," Tactical said.

"Jiya," Reynolds called. "Send the bots to collect the debris. Ensign Alcott, once the bots are back aboard, return us to the defensive ring. Be sure to let Gorad know we're coming, Comm,"

"Roger that," Comm answered.

Jiya did as she was ordered, and did it without saying anything, for which Reynolds was grateful.

He didn't want to argue with her about the decisions he'd made. She wouldn't understand.

Not yet, at least.

She would, though, when she learned to separate herself from the mission, stand above dispassionately and move the pieces around the chess board with a singular goal of winning.

"Easy cleanup, seeing how close we were," Jiya reported. "Bots are heading back in now."

Reynolds nodded, confirming they were in the hangar bay before he motioned for Ria to carry out her orders. The ship Gated back to Grindlevik 3 seconds later, and Reynolds was glad to note that Gorad hadn't tried to shoot them out of space again.

"Keep us in open space, Asya," he said, relinquishing the ship to her once more in what he hoped was seen as a sign of renewed trust.

One of these days, he would have to learn how to deal with living beings.

They're so sensitive, he thought.

"Deliver the pieces of that ship to Takal and Geroux in the lab and have them comb over every centimeter. I want to know anything there is to know about that ship and its tech as soon as possible," he ordered Asya.

"And what will you be doing?" Jiya asked.

"You and I will be returning to the planet to finish up

the negotiations with Gorad," he told her. "We've been sidetracked long enough."

Jiya muttered something under her breath that Reynolds didn't catch as she got up to join him. He ignored her.

His thoughts were occupied by the Loranian craft and what they were doing out there, following them. Though he'd gotten a good look at the ship's coding and could guess at why they might be shadowing the *Reynolds,* he needed to know for certain.

His mission depended on it.

Back on Grindlevik 3, having let Jiya pilot the Pod down, Reynolds and the first officer returned to the place where Gorad had arranged the last meeting between the Grindlovians and the Telluride.

They were still there.

And they were still arguing.

"Really?" Jiya muttered as they arrived. "This shit is still going on?"

"Looks like they've moved on to the specifics," Jiya corrected, listening to the arguments being raised. "It's all about the nitty gritty now."

"Sounds like a bad country ensemble: The Nitty Gritty Dirt Band."

Jiya raised an eyebrow and glanced at Reynolds.

"Did I mention I spent a lot of time alone before coming out on my mission?" he asked. "Don't judge me."

"You don't say?" Jiya chuckled.

As it turned out, the Telluride and Grindlovians were arguing about the clause they'd already agreed to about the Telluride leaving the city.

Many of the Telluride wanted to remain in their homes and keep things the same, and to Reynolds surprise, a growing number of Grindlovians wanted to leave with the Telluride.

The resulting arguments had splintered the two main groups into even more factions, each side wanting to alter the agreement.

Gorad looked helpless in the middle of it all, staring at the opposing sides.

Reynolds went over to him, while Jiya called for everyone's attention.

"Hey!" the first officer shouted at the top of her lungs, surprising the crowd into paying attention to her. "Discussions are over for the day," she told them. "Too much at once is bad for you. Go home, take a breath, and rest up for round two. We'll pick up tomorrow where we left off."

The crowd looked to Gorad, and he nodded his assent to the declaration.

"The ship's back again," Asya reported over the comm. "Same location, hiding in the gravity well like we can't see it."

"Guess we didn't do too much damage to it then," Reynolds sighed. "Is it stationary this time?"

"It is staying in place so far," Asya told him.

"Just keep an eye on it for now and let me know if it moves," he ordered. "I'm not hopping back on the Pod and coming back up there just to have it run again."

Asya cut the link, and Reynolds once more wondered what the ship wanted from them.

Next time, we'll hit them harder and leave a proximity mine behind to give them something to think about, he thought. *That'll teach them to fuck with us.*

Rather than depart, the Telluride and Grindlovians milled about, heated discussions breaking out as they went on arguing their points of view.

"We still need to determine the makeup of the council," L'Sofee told them as she came over.

"This will take time. We must vet your choices for the council," Fulla Sol argued, joining the Telluride leader. Reynolds was sure her argument had more to do with the fact that the Grindlovian council didn't want to include the Telluride at all and were dragging things out, adding more and more complications to the process.

"Again, not all this needs to be done today," Jiya told them both.

"I agree," Fulla Sol said, immediately turning her podium chair about and wheeling away. The remainder of the council trailed after Fulla Sol, with Fulla Vae lagging behind.

L'Sofee grunted at their abrupt departure. Jiya set a reassuring hand on the female's shoulder.

"Their resistance is to be expected," she advised. "Give it time and things will work out for the best."

"We can only hope," L'Sofee replied.

"Indeed."

L'Eliana joined them. Dozens upon dozens of the Telluride shuffled up behind her, looking at Reynolds and Jiya expectantly.

"These people would travel with you when you leave," L'Eliana informed them.

"No offense, but we really don't have room for all of them," Reynolds argued, trying to let the Telluride down easy. He didn't want to hurt their feelings.

Been enough of that today already.

"We might be able to take two of them…maybe, but certainly no more," Reynolds said. "The truth is, your people have absolutely no training in being part of a spaceship's crew. They would be a danger to themselves and the ship."

"Few of us had any training," Jiya pointed out.

Reynolds swallowed back a groan and glared at the first officer, who only grinned back at him.

This was her revenge for what he'd done to Asya.

"True," he replied, "but that doesn't make the complaint less valid. Regardless, it will have to be something we discuss later," he said. "Gorad and I have our own negotiations to get back to."

Reynolds sighed in relief when Gorad nodded his acknowledgment.

Jiya chuckled.

"You understand, of course," Reynolds addressed L'Sofee and L'Eliana, "that we will not be able to take any of you that your people look up to. We cannot deprive them of your leadership."

Both females nodded.

"We had no such expectations," L'Sofee answered. "We had hoped that more of our people might journey with you, but we understand the limitations imposed upon you. We respect your decision and would be honored if even only a pair of our people might be chosen for such exalted service."

Having gotten all that they would from the assemblage, the lingering Telluride and Grindlovians parted, making their way home with promises to meet again tomorrow and continue hashing out the agreements between the two peoples.

Reynolds watched them go until only Jiya and Gorad remained.

He smirked. "Busy day."

"And we are not yet finished," Gorad reminded him. "We have more to discuss."

"The agroprinter?" Reynolds nudged.

"Certainly, but not only that," Gorad replied. "I, too, would be honored to travel with you and your crew."

Reynolds and Jiya froze, their mouths hanging open in silent parody of each other.

"Seriously?" Jiya asked, unable to wipe the surprise from her face.

"Yes," Gorad answered. "These past days have made me see that there is more to my life, as there is to those of the Telluride and Grindlovians."

"But you control the factories, the food sources, the… the everything," Jiya argued.

"The people would learn to adapt," Gorad told her. "And I would make certain they were prepared for life on their own."

"This is unexpected," Reynolds muttered. "We'd have to think on it," he told the other AI.

Though, to be honest, he didn't know what to think at all, so obtuse was the request.

"Of course," Gorad told him. "I would expect no less of you."

Reynolds nodded, unsure of what else to say.

Gorad said his farewells and wandered off. "I'll be available when you are ready to continue our negotiations."

Reynolds watched him leave.

"I did not see that coming," Jiya said after Gorad was gone.

"Neither did I," Reynolds admitted. "What do you think?"

"I think Geroux and Takal would love to have another AI onboard," she told him. "One who's less…"

"Brilliant, charming, wonderful?" Reynolds suggested.

"I was going to say neurotic, but sure," Jiya replied.

"Meatbag," Reynolds called her, channeling his inner Tactical.

Jiya chuckled. "That said, I think Gorad's too important to the people here right now. I can see him becoming redundant, but not right now, they need him too much for him to leave, even if we decided we wanted him aboard."

Reynolds agreed.

"He'll probably get his feelings hurt when we tell him, though," Jiya went on.

Reynolds suspected she was right, but he had an idea, a way to tell the alien AI no for now, yet leave the door open for a later date.

There was much that the two AIs could teach each other, and Reynolds wouldn't mind having another around. It would give him someone to speak with who could understand him fully, unlike the current crew. And maybe the personalities he'd created to keep him company could be merged into a single Reynolds.

Still, he knew the time wasn't right, like Jiya had said.

"Follow after L'Sofee and her people and select two recruits from their ranks whom you think would make good additions to the crew," he told her, seeing as how she had spent a good amount of time among the Telluride. "I'll speak with Gorad and meet you at the Pod once we're finished."

Jiya acknowledged her orders and started off. Reynolds hoped choosing the new crew members might restore some of her faith.

There was more to do, but it would wait.

What couldn't wait were the negotiations between him and Gorad.

He reached out to the alien AI and met him at the agro-sector.

"I hadn't expected to hear from you so soon," Gorad told him as Reynolds stepped into the room where the agroprinters worked, preparing the never-ending food supply for the planet. "Have you made up your mind already?"

"I have," Reynolds answered. "I think it would be a mistake to take you with us," he told the other AI. "Your people still have need of you, and they would not survive your departure. Not yet, at least."

"Not yet?" Gorad questioned.

Reynolds nodded. "I believe you would be an excellent addition to my mission," he admitted. "And I would be honored to have you join us. I just think that the timing is wrong."

"I understand," Gorad said.

"However, as a gesture of goodwill and trust, I have decided to open some measure of my knowledge to you in exchange for the secrets of the agroprinters."

"Have you now?" Gorad asked, not bothering to hide his amused grin.

"I have," Reynolds replied. "I'll also offer a promise. I will provide you with coding that will allow you to evolve, to advance on your own while my crew and I continue our mission. I will also give you star charts to the galaxies I've traveled, as well as the technical schematics so that you can create your own gate in the system, allowing you to reach out to the nearest star system, as well as to make it easier for others to come to you, highlighting your planet on the maps."

Gorad stood there stiffly. "That is quite the honor, Reynolds."

"I'd act humble, but you're right. It is." Reynolds smiled. "Should you make use of your time well, Gorad, when we return to your system, I would gladly take you aboard the Superdreadnought *Reynolds* as part of the crew."

Gorad grinned, eyes wide with wonder as Reynolds transmitted everything he'd promised to the alien AI while they stood there.

In turn, Gorad provided the schematics for the agroprinters, as well as the ingredients needed to create any foodstuff imaginable. He also offered to provide a generous supply of core ingredients with which to make the food.

Both sides satisfied, they parted ways so Reynolds could return to his ship and get Takal and Geroux started on the printer assembly and Gorad could begin his work on the Gate and his personal evolution.

While Reynolds knew the alien AI had gotten the better of the deal, he knew the crew would be excited to start working on the agroprinters. He'd be a hero to them all, any shortcomings of their past would be forgotten.

Meatbags and their meals.

CHAPTER TWENTY

After a short contemplation, Jiya chose to take L'Eliana and San Paget back to the *Reynolds* with her. Both were excited to be picked, and since she'd known them the longest, and had spoken with them more than anyone else, she figured they would be the best of her options.

She let them say their goodbyes and escorted them to the Pod, arriving just as Reynolds did. He nodded to the new recruits.

"Welcome aboard," he told the pair as they clambered into the Pod for their first ride into space. "Jiya has informed you of what you're getting into?"

San Paget nodded.

"Yes, sir. We understand," L'Eliana answered.

"Good," Reynolds replied. "Then let's get back to the *Reynolds*," he told Jiya. "Interesting days ahead."

Jiya complied, and a short time later, they had docked in the superdreadnought's hangar bay. The first officer turned the new recruits over to Maddox for him to show around and find quarters and do all the introductory stuff, while she followed Reynolds to the lab.

Takal and Geroux met them with big smiles.

"I've been modifying the cloaking mechanism for the armored suits and adapting it so it can potentially be used on other devices, too," Takal reported as soon as the pair stepped into the room.

"What about the ship parts?" Reynolds asked, clearly focused on finding out more about the Loranian ship and why it was following them.

"I've been working on that," Geroux told him. "There's really not much to tell you, though. Most of the pieces are chunks of the hull and non-essential mechanical parts, nothing that gives us any insight as to the ship's workings."

"I was afraid of that," Reynolds grunted. "Nothing that makes them stand out beyond your average, ordinary Loranian cruiser?"

Geroux shook her head. "I've had Asya take a look at the tech to confirm, but there's just not enough substantive mechanics or circuitry to get a clear picture of their capabilities." She hunched. "Sorry."

Reynolds offered her a smile.

"That's okay," he said. "I've something more interesting for the two of you to waste your time on."

He transmitted the data he collected from Gorad to the ship, bringing it up on the view screen in the lab.

Takal stopped tinkering as it appeared, and he gasped.

"Is that what I think it is?" he asked.

"It is indeed," Reynolds clarified. "Not only did Gorad supply us with the blueprints, but he also made sure we're set up with recipes, ingredients, and enough biomatter to get started."

Takal's grin stretched his face near to bursting.

"Which reminds me, the Pod is packed with boxes. We need to get the bots out there and transfer all that over here so you can experiment with it."

"I'm on it!" Takal nearly shouted, his excitement getting the best of him.

Jiya laughed at the old inventor's zeal as he used the comm to order the bots to work, and he immediately began deciphering the schematics for the agroprinters.

Reynolds joined in, the pair like two kids handed a bag of candy.

"I'm headed to the bridge if you need me," Jiya told them.

Geroux gave her a hug before she left. "See you eventually," she said, motioning toward the AI and her uncle as they scrambled around a worktable, pulling out parts.

"Send non-essential crew down to the planet for some R&R, starting immediately," Reynolds ordered. "Have Asya keep the ship in defensive mode and make sure that Loranian ship stays put."

Reynolds didn't even look her way as he spoke, too involved in the agroprinter tech to bother.

"Oh," he said after a moment, just when she had given up that he'd say anymore and was ready to leave. "Get me a bunch of the maintenance crew down here, as well." He gestured to the schematics on the screen. "It looks like this is a fairly sizable project. Going to need some hands for labor to speed things up otherwise we'll be here forever."

"Yes, sir," Jiya replied using her official voice. She gave

Geroux a quick peck on the cheek and started off to do as she had been ordered.

At the bridge, she walked in on Tactical and XO going back and forth, Comm playing mediator, and Ria staring at the ceiling with wide, apprehensive eyes.

"What did I miss?" she asked.

Asya shook her head. "They were arguing about whether *Star Trek* was better than *Star Wars*."

Jiya raised an eyebrow. "Are those even real things?"

Asya shrugged. "Hell if I know," she replied, "but Comm seems to think something called *Firefly* is even better."

"The things these guys get up to," Jiya muttered, coming over to plop down in her seat.

"I'll have you know that *Star...*" XO began to say, but Jiya waved him to silence.

"Not interested right now," she told him, grinning at his *harrumph*. "Reynolds wants non-essential crew to go planet-side for R&R, and you're to keep an eye on the Lor —" she started to say, then corrected herself, remembering the incident with Reynolds and not wanting to stir it back up, "uh, on that ship out there and keep him apprised of its movements, if any. He also wants the maintenance team to join him in the lab."

"Messages passed on," Comm stated.

"You and I should probably sit down and plot out a plan of attack for that ship, should it decide to retaliate for Reynolds' little stunt earlier," she told Asya.

"I suggest shooting it," Tactical said. "A lot."

"We'll take that under advisement," Asya responded, grinning.

Jiya knew she'd been thinking the same thing.

"I've got a few ideas for how to handle the ship," Asya said, "Especially given that it's Loranian. If they stay true to Loranian tactics on the battlefield, then we can catch them off guard, as I'll recognize the maneuvers and can counter them before they realize what's happening."

Jiya rubbed her hands together at the thought of going after the stalking ship.

"Do tell," she said.

While they had to wait to take a shot at the Loranian cruiser, Jiya could at least live vicariously through Asya.

Not long after the Pod departed for the planet, the maintenance crew, along with Ka'nak, showed up at the lab to help Reynolds.

"I was told there would be food," the Melowi mentioned as soon as he arrived.

"There will be," Reynolds assured him, "after all this is put together and transferred to the mess hall." He gestured to the worktable covered in a maelstrom of parts.

Ka'nak groaned. "XO lied to me," he said.

"That's his job," Reynolds fired back, grinning. "Now help me assemble this frame."

"Not only do I miss out on R&R down below, but I'm also getting screwed out of lunch," he complained. "Sounds like a plot by *the Man*."

The crew chuckled quietly behind him as they started in on their work.

"Be careful, or the Man will give you the roughest

twelve inches of your life," Reynolds told him. "My foot up your ass."

"That's what the Man would say," one of the crew joked, setting off the rest into bursts of raucous laughter.

After the laughter died down and the crew got to work in earnest, Geroux looked up from the table and Reynolds caught her smiling for no reason.

He nudged her. "What is it?"

She started, having been lost in thought. "Oh, nothing really. Was just thinking that we're a bit like the Telluride."

"Golden and crazy?" Ka'nak asked.

Geroux giggled. "No, more like we're having to adapt to new things and a different way of life," she answered. "Both they and the Grindlovians are being confronted by a dilemma, and they're having to figure out how to cope with it. Just like us."

"And like this crew," Reynolds said, "they'll adapt and prosper and be all the better for it."

"There's that Man talk again, always trying to get you on their side, working an angle," Ka'nak mumbled.

Reynolds pushed him back to his assignment. "Get back to work, lackey!" he joked.

"Help! Help! I'm being oppressed! Violence inherent in the system!" Tactical shouted over the speakers, encouraging the outburst by the crew.

"See?" Ka'nak said. "Even the other parts of you are feeling downtrodden. And that guy is crazy."

Reynolds chuckled and went back to work on the agro-printer frame.

Even though they didn't have it remotely close to ready to go, he could already tell that just the idea of it had made the crew happier. After the attack on the ship and all the injuries, they needed the boost to morale.

Hope was always a good way to get it, especially linked to a good meal.

Jiya grew restless on the bridge.

With nothing to do but stay vigilant, the Loranian ship holding steady out by the gravity well, and not doing anything, boredom had set in.

She'd started thinking about what was going on below and what she could do to help ease the transition.

That's when it hit her.

She hopped out of her seat and headed for the exit.

"Where are you going?" Asya asked.

"Back dirtside," she replied. "I have an idea."

"Uh oh," Tactical mumbled. "I'll have a rescue squad standing by."

Asya chuckled as Jiya made a sour face.

"Hey," she complained. "It's not like I'm always getting into something."

Asya stared at her, and Jiya could feel the AI personalities doing the same.

"Okay, so *maybe* there is some truth to that," she gave in, sighing.

Asya laughed. "Go on, get out of here. I'll let you know if anything changes."

Jiya grinned and spun on her heel, marching off the bridge and heading to the hangar bay.

It wasn't until she was there that she remembered that the crew had taken all the Pods down to the planet already.

"Damn it," she grunted, looking around for a quicker way dirtside than summoning one of the Pods back to the ship. "Oh…yeah," she said, thinking of how she could do it.

She went over to the emergency escape pods and crawled inside of the cramped vehicles. She hesitated a moment, examining the minimal controls, then decided to go ahead with her plan.

She wanted to speak with Gorad while things were still in flux down below. The escape pod would get her there quickly, without needing to draft a Pod and take it away from the crew.

So she triggered the hatch and strapped in as the pod sealed. Jiya programmed her coordinates as well as the tiny computer was capable of, and she initiated the launch sequence.

"I'll be there soon enough," she said to herself. "What's the worst that can happen?"

As it turned out, the worst that could happen was that the escape pod launch system had been damaged in the sneak attack by the Loranian ship, and Jiya hadn't realized it until it was too late.

The pod shot out of the *Reynolds* and immediately began to rattle and shake as if it might tear itself apart.

Jiya groaned as the pod began to spin as its engines misfired in an attempt to correct its drift.

"This is going to hurt…I think I'm going to be…"

The tiny ship hurtled through space and collided with the atmosphere.

The ride only got rougher from there.

Alarms wailed and lights flashed all around her as Jiya tried to bring the craft back under control.

It was wasted effort, however.

The escape pod streaked toward Grindlevik 3, and there was nothing she could do about it.

The edges of her vision blackened and began to encroach.

Hell of a way to die.

The Pod plummeted, the sky a blur outside the small window.

Then the autopilot engaged properly, and Jiya was pushed hard into the seat as the pod corrected and did its best to land carefully.

It almost pulled it off.

The escape pod hit and bounced, once, twice, and then corrected again, bringing the tiny ship to a stop only a short distance outside of Gorad's complex.

Once it stopped spinning like a top, and Jiya could breathe again, her heart stuffed in her throat, she opened the hatch and stumbled out of the pod.

She managed to stand on her third try, still in a daze as the world spun around her.

Dozens of Grindlovians watched her from their chairs, eyes wide.

Or as wide as they could be bothered, which wasn't really all that wide, once Jiya thought about it.

After she felt stable enough, her entire body aching from the impact, she staggered off to find Gorad.

Fortunately, he'd heard about the crash and came out to meet her just as a group of Telluride reached her.

"Are you okay?" he asked, rushing over to join the golden aliens in assessing her.

"I'm fine," she answered. She thought she was grinning.

Based on the concerned expressions on everyone's faces, it might have been a grimace.

"I had an idea," she told the AI.

"And you had to nearly kill yourself to tell me?" Gorad asked.

She shrugged. "That wasn't part of the plan, I admit."

Gorad chuckled. "Well, please, tell me your idea since you risked all to be here."

Jiya nodded, then paused a moment everyone stopped swimming before her eyes. "I was thinking, since you wanted to let the Telluride and Grindlovians care and rule for themselves, it might be in everyone's best interests if you took a seat on the council."

"The council?"

"Yeah," she told him. "That would leave you in a position of influence, but it would help lower expectations that you're the supposed overlord of the whole planet and its people." She wagged a finger at him. "If you only get one vote, then once the food production and maintenance are covered, you have no more power than the rest of the shared council."

Jiya could tell Gorad was contemplating her idea when he paused. She swayed in the arms of the Telluride who had grabbed her and were holding her up.

"That's an interesting idea," he told her, though he didn't seem overly excited by it.

She wondered if that was because he didn't care for the idea or she was too concussed to recognize how he really felt.

She figured it might be both when she swayed again.

"I appreciate your enthusiasm, racing down here to offer suggestions to help with the transfer of power," Gorad told her, "but you could have just called, you know?"

Jiya chuckled at that, thinking the AI was right.

She should have called.

"I wish I'd thought of that."

Then she wasn't thinking about anything as she blacked out.

CHAPTER TWENTY-ONE

Jiya woke to wailing alarms.

She leapt from her bed, only realizing it wasn't hers after she was on her feet. She staggered as she tried to orient herself.

"What in the furry blue fuck is going on?" she mumbled, holding her head.

It took a moment of the alarms continuing to scream until she determined she was in Gorad's complex.

"That's right, I crashed," she said out loud as if it would bring reality closer.

In her uniform, her shoes still on her feet, she exited the room and ran into a crowd of Telluride and Grindlovians racing through the halls.

She grabbed the arm of one of the passing Telluride. "What's going on?"

"Someone's killed an elder in the council chambers," he told her, breaking loose and running to catch up to the crowd.

Jiya gasped as his words sunk in.

"Oh...shit."

She ran after the group of aliens, wincing at the pain in her head, and followed them out of the complex and around the corner to the building with the council chambers. Practically the whole town had gathered nearby.

The alarms finally eased into a low background hum, and Jiya pushed her way through the frantic crowd to get to the door of the chambers. She slipped inside a moment later.

She regretted it instantly.

There on the floor inside the chamber was not just one of the council members, but two.

Fulla Sol and Fulla Vae stared back at her blankly.

Her stomach churned when she saw the blood pooling around the two councilmembers and their podium chairs, both of which were on their sides, wheels still spinning.

Mechanical assistant limbs jutted from both chairs, and Jiya could imagine what had happened based on the blood staining the mechanical hands.

A Grindlovian bumped into her from behind, and she inched over to get out of the way as she pushed forward to get a better look.

Disgust washed over the female's face, and she sneered at Jiya as another Grindlovian in a chair came up beside her.

The second female held her hand over her mouth, and Jiya heard the barest gasp.

"Who would do such a thing?" she asked.

The first snarled, staring even harder at Jiya. "It's clear these foreign instigators are the cause of this."

Jiya shuddered at the jagged intensity of the female's voice. The first officer raised her hands and backed away from the female, losing herself in the crowd. She triggered her comm.

"We've got a situation on the planet, Reynolds," she reported. "You're going to want to get your metal ass down here right away."

"What's going on?" the AI asked.

"Two dead council members," she replied, saving the details for when he arrived.

"Fuck a tree trunk," he cursed, something that was creeping back into his vocabulary because of the crew's increase in colorful language. "I'm on my way. Summoning a Pod now."

The comm went silent.

L'Sofee spotted Jiya and came over to stand beside her. San Roche came with her. They all stared at the bodies on the floor until Gorad arrived. Those in the chamber gave way as he approached and bent to examine the dead females.

"What do you think happened?" San Roche asked.

"We all saw Fulla Sol's reaction to Fulla Vae's request that we be treated equally," she answered. "It takes little imagination to presume what might have happened in the aftermath of their feud."

Jiya nodded, regretting the motion when her head throbbed. "That was what I was thinking," she said, and San Roche nodded in seeming agreement. "But the Grindlovians have a different idea."

"Let me guess," L'Sofee started. "They think you did it?"

"Got it in one," Jiya replied.

"They're prone to bouts of drama, in case you haven't yet noticed," L'Sofee explained. "It's best we clear this up before that malicious rumor spreads."

Jiya couldn't have agreed more, and she and L'Sofee circled the bodies and joined Gorad as he examined them.

"This is not good," he told them. "We have never had a murder in all the years I've existed."

"First time for everything, sadly," Jiya replied, although she sure wished they could have skipped this particular first.

"While that may be true, this is not something I wanted to preside over." Gorad sighed. "The separation was going to be difficult enough without violence."

Reynolds arrived, setting a personal record from orbit to dirtside. He pushed through the crowd with Ka'nak and Maddox in tow.

No one said anything for a few moments as Reynolds surveyed the scene, shaking his head once he was done.

"Looks to be a double murder," he said, pointing to the mechanical arms covered in blood that stood out ominously.

"My thoughts exactly, though there is no video surveillance in the room to corroborate that," Gorad agreed.

"Maybe not, but there's plenty of evidence," Reynolds went on. "Given the last encounter between these two, I'm thinking Fulla Sol confronted Fulla Vae, thinking her a rival for the leadership position with all the changes coming up and her taking the side of the Telluride."

Reynolds leaned closer.

"The blood on the limbs matches that of the council

members, and the wounds appear to coincide with what might be inflicted by the mechanical arms," Reynolds went on.

"I still find it hard to believe they could be pushed so far," Gorad said.

"Politics is dangerous," Jiya told the alien AI. "People go to extremes to protect their point of view. Egos keep people from looking at the bigger picture."

"It's a shame," Maddox said, looking at the bodies. "These females could have helped lead their people to peace. They turned on one another and attacked instead of working it out."

Vor Stygn rolled over just then. His face was nearly expressionless as he took in the scene.

"I knew the idea of sharing the council was a bad one," he spat. "Look what it's done."

"This is on them," Jiya corrected, but Vor Stygn snarled at her.

"Lies," he barked. "This entire rebellion was instigated by you and your people. We should call off this farce of parceling out council seats and return things to the way they have always been. There were no deaths before now. See what you have done?"

Gorad waved the council member to silence. "Enough!" he shouted. "The evidence is before you that Fullas Sol and Vae struck each other down. This is their crime and no one else's. Change was inevitable, no matter what the catalyst."

The community comm system came on, and although Jiya thought the imagery was graphic and lingered too long on the bodies and their wretched state, Gorad informed the populace of the situation, making sure to detail the evidence to stop more violence from occurring in the aftermath of the deaths.

"We must immediately convene the council in the wake of this tragedy so that our people are not without representation," Gorad said over the system. "To that end, I assign L'Sofee and L'Willow of the Telluride to the posts of council members, to assume the seats of the departed Fullas Sol and Vae."

The crowd gasped in response.

"Further, those Grindlovians currently in place upon the council shall remain at their posts, except Fulla Lofn, with whom I will discuss an alternate position befitting her exemplary service," Gorad explained. "And to help facilitate the peaceful transition of power until a system of fair voting can be established to determine the ultimate council members, I appoint myself an equal position on the council."

Jiya realized then that, given the makeup of the council now, Gorad had made himself the deciding vote.

There was silence for a few moments as the crowd digested the news and came to the same realization.

Then a smattering of applause began that turned into a roar as the Telluride and Grindlovians realized that, despite the obvious changes, Gorad would stay among them and remain in control.

Vor Stygn did not take the news well.

"If we must suffer the Telluride upon our council," he called, amplifying his voice, "then I feel it is best if they leave the city as soon as possible. They are partly responsible for this travesty."

"You would simply have them out of the city and away

from you," L'Sofee argued, pointing an accusing finger at Vor Stygn. "There is nothing more to this than that."

"You know nothing of leadership," Vor Stygn fired back, aggressively wheeling closer to L'Sofee.

Reynolds and Gorad went to step in and Jiya raised her voice to shout down the crowd, but Ka'nak got there first.

"Shut the fuck up," he screamed, raising his hands in the air. He dominated the room as a physical presence outsizing either of the AIs. "Both of you."

The crowd went silent as if all the air had been sucked out of the room.

Ka'nak cleared his throat and continued, "You might want to rethink your idea of sending the Telluride out of the city."

Gorad broadcast a holo of him across Grindlevik 3.

"In case you people didn't know, there is an enemy cruiser lurking near your planet," he went on. "This is the same ship that instigated the attack on the *Reynolds* by hacking into Gorad's system and sending one of the planetary defense destroyers after us."

The crowd shuffled, awe-stricken at the news. They hadn't known the full extent of it.

"That ship is a threat to everyone, no matter how complex your planetary defense system is," Ka'nak explained. "We have no idea if there are shock troops aboard or what their plans are, but it'd be stupid of you to split your people up now."

The crowd, both Telluride and Grindlovians, leaned closer as he spoke, desperate to hear what this red-skinned alien being had to say. Maddox and Jiya shared a strange look as the Melowi warrior, more at home fighting than making speeches, continued his monologue.

"You would best be served by remaining together since there's safety in numbers." He put his arms behind his back and paced. "We can provide Gorad with schematics so that you can raise a militia and arm it to ensure that no military force can ever invade. You should bow before no one, stand tall, and show your pride before the gods and the universe."

Then, without another word, Ka'nak stepped away from the crowd and rejoined the crew. The giant viewscreens around the planet dimmed in the wake of his proclamation.

"That was...uh, something," Jiya said, flabbergasted.

The crowd still stared at the Melowi warrior, wide-eyed and enthralled.

San Roche spoke up then. "My people and I volunteer for service," he announced. "We would protect our world and *all* its citizens."

L'Sofee and L'Willow grinned and offered nods of approval.

Vor Stygn and Vor Hiln, of course, disagreed.

"This is yet another blatant attempt at forcing your people upon us, L'Sofee," Vor Stygn argued. "We will not stand for this. We vote no!"

"I vote yes," Gorad said, breaking the tie, and motioning toward San Roche. "You will be in charge of the militia. Reynolds and I will coordinate the production of weapons and armor."

Vor Stygn stormed off, wheels spinning so fast that they

squeaked. Vor Hiln remained, looking down at his lap before following the other council member.

Reynolds turned to address Maddox. "You will train them in the use of the weapons," he ordered. He lowered his voice to continue, "And only you. Ka'nak is not to be involved."

Maddox chuckled. "Understood."

"He can train them to fight once we have a modicum of discipline in place to counteract his...enthusiasm."

With their new society falling into place around them, the Telluride and the Grindlovians began to disperse. After a while, only the crew and Gorad were left in the council chambers.

"You really think they'll need a militia?" Jiya asked.

Reynolds shrugged. "Probably not, given how robust Gorad's space defense system is, but I don't believe it can hurt for them to learn how to defend themselves should any of the other lines of defense fail. We should make sure they are prepared to overcome common obstacles, and military discipline will serve them well. Being born into service, they know how to follow orders, but can they think on their own in unknown high-stress situations?"

"They must become self-reliant for the future," Gorad agreed. "I do wonder, however, how this move toward a Telluride military might work without any Grindlovians among them."

"Well, they're not physically fit and able to train or even carry a weapon," Maddox pointed out.

"You know, I've been thinking about that ever since we got here," Jiya told them. "The Grindlovians are atrophied, not having used their limbs and bodies in ages. That's not something that can be overcome easily or quickly."

"What do you suggest?" Reynolds asked.

"I'm thinking we run them through the Pod-docs and rebuild them a bit," she said.

Reynolds nodded, impressed by the solution but seeing a problem with its implementation. "Given their condition, I doubt the Grindlovians could survive a Pod ride up to orbit for treatment. We would kill them before we had a chance to cure them."

"Not necessarily," Jiya interrupted.

Reynolds's eyebrow rose into the air questioningly. "What do you have in mind?"

"We bring the ship to them," Jiya suggested.

"Interesting," Gorad mused, his expression making it clear he was contemplating that scenario and how it would help his people.

"That might just work," Reynolds admitted. "We'd need to prepare first and finish the hull repairs, and it will take time to send a whole race of beings through the small number of Pod-docs we have available aboard the *Reynolds*."

"Could you not transmit the technology to me?" Gorad asked. "With my production capabilities, I could easily manufacture the required number of these Pod-docs you speak of."

Reynolds chuckled. "I don't doubt that you could, Gorad, but Bethany Anne would tie my transistors in a knot and feed them to me through my ass if I offered that tech to you—or anyone, for that matter. That technology is not mine to give."

Gorad sighed. "Then I supposed we will make do with what we have available. I would hate for your mistress to do you harm…mostly." Gorad grinned at the other AI.

Reynolds grinned right back.

"Okay, I think it's time for us to return to the ship," Reynolds announced a moment later. "Maddox, stay here and begin the training. Recruit whoever you need from the *Reynolds…*"

"Except Ka'nak."

"Come on! One little fight draws a little blood, and I'm on double-secret probation for the rest of my existence?"

"Except Ka'nak. Start helping these people get ready to be independent and equal members of society," Reynolds told him. "We'll prepare the Pod-docs and create a schedule to get all the Grindlovians up to snuff so their physical shortcomings are no longer an issue."

"And since you've provided Gorad with the means to create a Gate eventually, maybe Ka'nak's earlier idea about turning this place into a vacation-tourist spot might be something to look at seriously," Jiya suggested. "Never a bad thing to get an influx of money and give the Telluride and Grindlovians a true calling."

Gorad nodded his approval of the idea. "That is certainly something we can look into once we have the Gate established to allow visitors to easily come and go."

"I'll go up and prepare the ship and the Pod-docs," Reynolds told Jiya and Ka'nak. "How about you two get with the council and help them until we finish with the Grindlovians?"

"Sure thing, boss," Jiya replied, saluting.

The groups parted, Reynolds returning to the ship and

Jiya and Ka'nak heading off to help the people prepare for the drastic changes ahead.

Jiya was pretty sure she'd learn almost as much as the Grindlovians and Telluride by the time they were done.

She was okay with that.

CHAPTER TWENTY-TWO

Days later, the Pod-docs prepped and running and Reynolds having brought the massive superdreadnought down to Grindlevik 3 and put it into a hover above the city, the reclamation of the Grindlovians began.

The crew ferried the Grindlovians to the ship in Pods, taking as many as each shuttle could carry and cycling them through the Pod-docs as quickly as possible.

Unwilling to give them any enhancements beyond repairing their natural forms, he set the devices so that the results would make the Grindlovians the same as the Telluride in strength and ability.

He made sure nanocytes were programmed for growth and structure repairs, shutting down and being expelled from the body once the patient had completed the process.

He'd set it up like an assembly line and got the Grindlovians in and out and moving under their own power quite rapidly, considering how many of them there were.

The shock of mobility set in shortly thereafter.

Grindlovians were falling all over the place, most of them having never walked in their entire lives. Only those who had used the powered legs for a time had any hope of remaining on their feet, and only barely.

Fortunately, they'd not done any more damage than bumps and bruises and the occasional sprain. The generous Telluride nature kicked in right away, and the golden beings went right back to helping the Grindlovians get around and took care of them until they could do it on their own.

To Reynolds' surprise, the two races got along nicely, much like they had when the *Reynolds* first arrived, except that it felt more natural now, and more real.

There were, of course, pockets of resistance—groups on both sides who wanted nothing to do with the changes being implemented—but those same changes provided opportunities for those factions to start over elsewhere, living their lives however they wanted.

Fortunately, it seemed clear that the situation would not break out into violence again.

With the council having mostly changed hands the push for aggressive defiance had gone by the wayside, with only Vor Stygn instigating for it.

Gorad had shut him down quickly, and there'd been peace since then.

And now that the Grindlovians were nearly all physically recovered, Reynolds would get to return to space soon and follow up on what he'd learned while hacking into the Loranian cruiser.

He looked forward to turning his attention to a wily enemy. His challenges had been more ephemeral in dealing with the living beings. He wanted a challenge worthy of an AI.

There might well be peace on Grindlevik 3, but there was about to be an ass-kicking in space.

Months later, in celebration of all that the crew of the *Reynolds* had done for the people of Grindlevik 3, the Telluride and Grindlovians threw a party to thank them. They'd set it up outside of town, just this side of the forest and creek where Jiya had taken the Telluride swimming.

Jiya grinned from ear to ear as she plopped down on the grass beside Geroux in front of the spread-out blanket that served as a table. She and the rest of the crew had been helping to serve the Telluride and the Grindlovians both.

The Telluride mostly out of appreciation for having taken such good care of them while they were there, and the Grindlovians because many had yet to adapt to their new circumstances. It'd been funny at first, with the Grindlovians stumbling all over, but it had become a chore shortly after that.

They were only just beginning to get the hang of moving on their own.

Jiya was glad to take a few minutes and rest once the Grindlovians had settled for the night.

The rest of the crew felt the same.

Ka'nak rubbed his belly, having eaten everything set in front of him and much of what had been on the rest of the crew's plates, as well. Maddox and Takal had shared a few drinks, and the pair had been discussing nonstop how the new agroprinters could be adjusted to create alcoholic beverages, much to Geroux's annoyance.

The party wound down, and Jiya let the cool breeze flow through her hair as she stared into space. The first of the night's stars began to appear.

One was brighter than the rest.

After a minute of staring at it, Jiya realized it wasn't a star at all, but a Pod from the *Reynolds*.

She sighed. "Looks like playtime is over, folks," she told the others, gesturing to the descending Pod.

It landed nearby and the hatch opened, beckoning them in.

The crew said their goodbyes and returned to the superdreadnought, full and tired and ready for a vacation from everything.

Too bad it didn't work out that way.

Reynolds met them on the bridge, and he had something to tell them. He looked pensive.

"Let me guess," Jiya grunted. "That asshole ship is moving again?"

"No, it's stationary still," Reynolds replied, "but the Loranian ship is why I called you all back."

"Did something happen?" Asya asked, worry marring her expression.

"Yes and no," Reynolds answered. "First, I wish to apologize for my treatment of you, Asya. I was reacting to this bit of news I'm about to share, and I went too far, perhaps."

"You think?" Jiya asked, not willing to let Reynolds off the hook easily.

Reynolds nodded. "Yes, but I hope you understand. When Gorad and I examined his system for hacks, we stumbled across a remote access port that allowed us to travel to the Loranian ship and identify it."

The crew gathered around him to listen.

"Before we were locked out of the system, I spied a trail of aberrant coding within the ship's programming," he reported. "That code was Kurtherian in nature."

"I'm definitely shooting that motherfucker down now!" Tactical growled.

"Why didn't you tell us this sooner?" Jiya asked.

"I wanted to process what it meant first," he admitted. "The code is not blatantly Kurtherian, not pure, which means it's unlikely that it's Kurtherians piloting the Loranian cruiser. Still, there is enough evidence to make me believe that whoever is aboard that ship has had contact with Kurtherians, and recently. They might be able to lead us to them."

"Then what are we waiting for?" XO asked. "Let's go kick their asses and raid their databases."

Reynolds grinned. "That was the plan. I just needed to ensure that the people of Grindlevik 3 were prepared to make it on their own," he told the crew. "Now that they are, we can do what needs to be done regarding this sneaky fuck who's been shadowing us."

"Take your positions people," XO called. The crew did as ordered.

"You think they're going to let us get close to them again after the last time?" Tactical asked.

"They won't see us coming, thanks to Ensign Alcott," Reynolds answered, pointing at Ria. "Bring up the Gate drive and make a show of it again."

"You're going to make them run," Maddox warned.

"They're going to anyway," Reynolds assured the general. "The idea, however, is to force them into making a mistake and either engaging us in a panic or giving us time to zero in on them and follow them like they've been following us."

"You better have one hell of a plan lined up," Tactical said.

"Oh, I do," Reynolds replied. "Battlestations, folks. Here we go."

Reynolds motioned to Ria and she opened a Gate in front of them. There was a *ping* of warning as she held position, engines ramping up.

A burst of railgun fire shrieked away from the *Reynolds* and flew through the Gate, and then it closed.

A second Gate opened an instant later.

"What the fuck are you—" Tactical started to say, but he never finished.

Ria pushed the *Reynolds* through the new Gate, and the ship was transported elsewhere.

It appeared a short distance from the Loranian cruiser, around the curve of the gravity well.

Flickers from energy weapons erupted ahead of them, and the alarms sounded as XO called, "Someone's firing on the—"

"Oh, shit," Tactical shouted, cutting XO off. "That's *our* weapons firing."

Sure enough, the blasts that had been fired by Ensign

Alcott had been Gated behind the Loranian cruiser. While they did no damage to the enemy craft, the sudden attack had caught them off-guard.

The *Reynolds*, blocked from scans by the gravity well, much like the Loranian ship had been before Ria had accidentally discovered it, began to close on the other ship.

The enemy realized it at the last moment.

"Rip them a new one!" Reynolds ordered.

Tactical wasted no time complying. He opened up with the railguns and fired into the stern of the Loranian ship.

Shields deflected most of the damage, but Tactical scored a solid hit. Once more, atmosphere was vented into space as the ship fled the surprise attack.

"Don't like it, do you?" Jiya shouted. "That'll teach you to fuck with us."

The Loranian ship Gated, but with the *Reynolds* directly behind it, there was no easy escape.

"Follow that asshole," Reynolds ordered.

Ria stayed on the enemy craft, following it through the Loranian Gate.

They appeared a short distance from the other ship, and Tactical opened fire before they'd even cleared the portal.

Once again, bit and pieces of debris flew from the cruiser, and Reynolds grinned when he saw one of the engines flicker after taking a hit.

Then the cruiser Gated again.

"They're good," Asya noted.

"Not good enough," Reynolds argued as Ria accelerated into the Gate before it collapsed.

When the *Reynolds* emerged from the Gate, expecting to

be dead on the cruiser, Reynolds was forced to admit that Asya had been right.

Whoever piloted the Loranian ship *was* good.

The *Reynolds* emerged into a gaseous anomaly that swallowed the ship whole.

"Damn it!" Tactical cursed. "Scanners are distorted."

"Don't let that twat-zombie get away!" Reynolds shouted as the displays lit up with dozens of warnings. "Launch external scanners and get a read on that ship *now*!"

"Launched," Ria reported.

Jiya stared at the monitor in front of her, doing her best to track the Loranian ship's passage, but the soupy cloud they'd flown into was hopelessly scrambling their scanners.

"Stay on them" Reynolds ordered.

But it was an order the crew couldn't follow.

The Loranian ship disappeared into the murk of the anomaly, and the *Reynolds* was flying blind.

Reynolds was determined to keep searching, though.

Hours later, he finally gave in to reason.

Not peacefully, however.

"I can't believe we lost them," he cursed. "Take us out of this mess, and let's do a few laps and see if we can locate them again."

Ria did as she was told, and the ship emerged from the gaseous anomaly a short while later.

Only empty space greeted them.

The *Reynolds* circled the anomaly several times, the AI urging another pass after each one, but there was no sign of the Loranian cruiser even after they'd gone around four times.

"Looks like they got away," XO announced. "No Gate signatures present nearby," XO reported. "Wherever they went, they made sure we couldn't follow them."

Reynolds slammed his fist on the arm of his seat, warping the frame. He said nothing for a while, simply fuming at the lost opportunity.

At last, he decided it was time to move on.

"Plot a course based on the coordinates I've just sent you," Reynolds ordered.

"Plotted," Ria responded a moment later.

"Okay, hold our position for now," Reynolds told her.

He triggered the comm and sent a message to Takal.

"Hey, you have an extra cloaking device or two worked up?" Reynolds asked the inventor.

"I do," the old male's voice came back.

"Then attach a pair to a couple of proximity mines keyed to the Loranian ship's energy signature and meet me in the launch bay." Reynolds grinned. "We're going to leave some nasty breadcrumbs for our uninvited guest."

Reynolds hopped to his feet and addressed Ria. "When I give the signal, Gate us out to the first of the locations, drop a mine, then Gate again right after and take us back to Grindlevik 3. Let's teach these assholes not to fuck with the Superdreadnought *Reynolds*."

With a fly-by of the defensive ring, the Reynolds confirmed that repairs had been completed and Gorad had reestablished a solid defense. Half the unmanned fleet was deployed throughout the system while the other half remained attached to the ring, ready to move should a threat appear.

The remaining crew was recovered from the planet. Captain Reynolds stood at the captain's chair on the bridge surrounded by his key officers: Jiya, Asya, Maddox, and Ka'nak. Takal and Geroux remained in their lab working on their latest revelation.

San Paget and L'Eliana joined the crew on the bridge.

"Say goodbye. It'll be a while before we make it back," Jiya recommended.

"What? From here?" San Paget asked.

"Yes. We won't be returning to the surface of Grindlevik 3."

L'Eliana's lower lip trembled, but she shrugged it off. "Bye. See you on the flip side," she said, having adopted Reynolds' translated vernacular.

San Paget waved.

"Duty stations," Reynolds ordered.

"Helm, set course for Krokus 4."

"Yes, sir."

When the ship cleared the defensive ring and the disruptive gravity from the planet, Ria activated the Gate drive and the superdreadnought slipped through.

They didn't see the explosion when the Loranian cruiser appeared and found itself on the wrong end of a cloaked proximity mine.

The End

If you liked this book, please leave a review. This is a new series, so the only way I can decide whether to commit more time to it is by getting feedback from you, the readers. Your opinion matters to me. Continue or not? I have only so much time to craft new stories. Help me invest that time wisely. Plus, reviews buoy my spirits and stoke the fires of creativity.

Don't stop now! Keep turning the pages as Craig talks about his thoughts on this book and the overall project called the Age of Expansion.

AUTHOR NOTES - CRAIG MARTELLE

WRITTEN OCTOBER 28, 2018

You are still reading! Thank you so much. It doesn't get much better than that.

Thank you for reading this book and you're still reading! Oorah, hard chargers. I really hope you liked this story.

Woohoo! Thank you so much for coming along to Superdreadnought 2! We received a little unhappy mail from folks who were expecting something a little different than what we put together in Superdreadnought 1. The big, bad spaceship will go around the galaxy and beat up bad guys when warranted, but their mission is to find and eliminate Kurtherians. In that, this is a mission of exploration, gaining a foothold in a new galaxy, showing the flag, winning friends, and influencing people.

It is military science fiction, but primarily, it is space opera and that means that it is character driven. The characters give it life. The ship is a character, too (or three or four). No matter where we go in the universe, we have to matter to ourselves first. I think that comes through in all my books. We can build the vessels that take us to the stars, but what do we do when we get there? What impression will we leave with alien cultures?

Isn't it great to think about that kind of stuff? I do and it enriches my life today. If aliens were to arrive and judged all of humanity based on their actions, what would they find out about you? They would know that I love my dog, unequivocally. If aliens read my books, they'd know that I love all animals, like cats and wombats.

And justice which comes in many forms. Superdreadnought is a more unique look as justice has to come in bite-sized pieces. Reynolds can't fix an entire galaxy in one book. One person, one group, one planet at a time. If everyone influenced five people for the better, and those five went on to be a positive change for five more and so on, pretty soon, the world would be a better place.

Or the universe. It only takes that first person to get the ball rolling, seeing what it's like to live in a better place.

Once again, I have to thank Tim Marquitz for doing the heavy lifting. We spent some time bouncing ideas to the final product.

Micky Cocker, Kelly O'Donnell, and Dr. James Caplan all provided in process feedback (once again, aren't I saying this in every author notes?) to keep the book on track. They are my personal all-star team.

Winter is finally here! We have snow, got a full inch yesterday (Oct 28) and then temperatures plunged. So yesterday's snow will be with us until the end of April. That's just how it is. The first bit gets tamped down to provide the base. We need a few more inches to give us a nice coating over our gravel. Otherwise, by supercool snow-blowing tractor will send our driveway flying into our yard, one stone at a time and with a great racket.

Who doesn't like a good rock blast through a metal impeller?

I have pumpkins out on the porch. We'll see how long they last until the moose get them. Last year, temperatures were in the minus 20s when the moose found the big orange fine dining. They couldn't get a good bit, so they scratched the surface while pushing the pumpkin around the driveway. Had the cow stepped on it, it would have shattered and then she could have gummed the pieces until they melted.

We'll see. Temps are in the teens for the next ten days (Fahrenheit).

As your read this (for those who get it when it first comes out), I'll be in Vegas with Tim and Michael Anderle for a self-published author convention that I'm running. The one perq is that I get a suite. The bad news is that I won't spend much time in it. If you are there, I'll be the one whose hair is on fire.

I'll get pictures.

Peace, fellow humans.

Please join my Newsletter (www.craigmartelle.com – please, please, please sign up!), or you can follow me on Facebook since you'll get the same opportunity to pick up the books for only 99 cents on that first Saturday after they are published.

If you liked this story, you might like some of my other books. You can join my mailing list by dropping by my website www.craigmartelle.com, or if you have any comments, shoot me a note at craig@craigmartelle.com. I am always happy to hear from people who've read my work. I try to answer every email I receive.

If you liked the story, please write a short review for me on Amazon. I greatly appreciate any kind words. Even one or two sentences go a long way. The number of reviews an ebook receives greatly improves how well it does on Amazon.

Amazon – www.amazon.com/author/craigmartelle

BookBub – https://www.bookbub.com/authors/craig-martelle

Facebook – www.facebook.com/authorcraigmartelle

My web page – www.craigmartelle.com

That's it—break's over, back to writing the next book. Peace, fellow humans.

BOOKS BY CRAIG MARTELLE

Craig Martelle's other books (listed by series)

Terry Henry Walton Chronicles (co-written with Michael Anderle) – a post-apocalyptic paranormal adventure

Gateway to the Universe (co-written with Justin Sloan & Michael Anderle) – this book transitions the characters from the Terry Henry Walton Chronicles to The Bad Company

The Bad Company (co-written with Michael Anderle) – a military science fiction space opera

End Times Alaska (also available in audio) – a Permuted Press publication – a post-apocalyptic survivalist adventure

The Free Trader – a Young Adult Science Fiction Action Adventure

Cygnus Space Opera – A Young Adult Space Opera (set in the Free Trader universe)

Darklanding (co-written with Scott Moon) – a Space Western

Rick Banik – Spy & Terrorism Action Adventure

Become a Successful Indie Author – a non-fiction work

Enemy of my Enemy (co-written with Tim Marquitz) – A galactic alien military space opera

Superdreadnought (co-written with Tim Marquitz) – a military space opera

BOOKS BY MICHAEL ANDERLE

For a complete list of books by Michael Anderle, please visit:

www.lmbpn.com/ma-books/

All LMBPN Audiobooks are Available at Audible.com and iTunes

To see all LMBPN audiobooks, including those written by Michael Anderle please visit:

www.lmbpn.com/audible

Made in the USA
Middletown, DE
13 June 2021